BECOMING INSPECTOR CHEN

Also by Qiu Xiaolong

The Inspector Chen mysteries

* available from Severn House

BECOMING INSPECTOR CHEN

Qiu Xiaolong

**SEVERN
HOUSE**

This first world edition published 2020
in Great Britain and 2021 in the USA by
SEVERN HOUSE PUBLISHERS LTD of
Eardley House, 4 Uxbridge Street, London W8 7SY.
Trade paperback edition first published
in Great Britain and the USA 2021 by
Severn House, an imprint of Canongate Books Ltd,
14 High Street, Edinburgh EH1 1TE.

British Library Cataloguing in Publication Data
A CIP catalogue record for this title is available from the British Library.

ISBN-13: 978-0-7278-9044-3 (cased)
ISBN-13: 978-1-78029-753-8 (trade paper)
ISBN-13: 978-1-4483-0491-2 (e-book)

Typeset by Palimpsest Book Production Ltd.,
Falkirk, Stirlingshire, Scotland.

To Guangming and Peiqin, whose friendship has sustained me through all these years.

ACKNOWLEDGMENTS

I want to thank my editor Carl Smith, who helped to shape this book.

'This process of coming to see other human beings as "one of us" rather than as "them" is a matter of detailed description of what unfamiliar people are like and of redescription of what we ourselves are like.'
— Richard Rorty, *Contingency, Irony, and Solidarity*

'When the true is false, the false is true: / where is nothing, there is everything.'
— Cao Xueqin, *Dream of the Red Chamber*

'It is a long night that there are so many dreams.'
— An old Chinese saying

ONE

Chen Cao woke with a start in the night.
In the dream scene fast fading into the surrounding darkness, he appears to be fastening a bronze name plaque to the door of a large office in the Shanghai Police Bureau. He studies the impressive title under his name on the plaque, whistling with a touch of satisfaction, when a headless figure creeps up from behind with a long iron chain trailing, rattling along the corridor—

'Chief Inspector Chen,' he murmured to himself, shaking his head before letting his glance sweep around the dark, dilapidated attic, and adding in self-satire, 'of the Shanghai Police Bureau.'

Still dream-disoriented, he had no idea of the time. He must have left his watch on the wooden dining table downstairs. It was still early – it was pitch black outside the crouching-tiger-shaped window. He decided not to climb down the squeaky ladder. The last thing he wanted was to wake his mother, sleeping beneath the attic.

He had been sleeping badly of late. Because of too many things on his mind? The dream fragments about the new office seemed not to be totally irrelevant.

After so many years, he found himself back in the retrofitted attic. It seemed so strange, distant, as if from another life. Sighing, he stared up at the low, depressing ceiling.

The nightmare had most likely originated from the whispered speculations in the police bureau that he, once a well-known, well-connected Party-member chief inspector, had fallen out of favor – irrecoverably? – with the Party authorities in Beijing. It was because of the conclusion he had pushed for regarding a recent serial murder case linked to China's disastrous air pollution. In the official newspapers, the conclusion of the bizarre case was at first commended as another coup for the legendary inspector, but it did not take long for top Party leaders to find reasons to be upset with the way Chief Inspector Chen had brought about a 'successful' end to the investigation. 'It's not in the interests of the Party, not at all, considering its political ramifications,' they maintained in the Forbidden City. So they were said to be more than ready to remove him from the position.

It was not the first time he had gotten into trouble for walking a thin, treacherous line in his investigations, but this time it came with an astonishing price tag.

'In accordance with the new governmental regulation, I'm sorry to say, Chief Inspector Chen, that your medical insurance policy can no longer cover the nursing home expense for your mother,' Party Secretary Li Guohua, the number one Party boss of the police bureau, had informed him in the corridor outside his office while stroking his chin thoughtfully.

It was little wonder. The governmental regulation concerning the insurance policy was made according to people's position in the Party system. And as they both knew only too well, it was about to be announced that Chen would soon be deprived of his position as chief inspector, not to mention the possibility of a more severe punishment being in store for him.

The soaring nursing home expense was more than he could afford. So he'd had to talk to his mother about moving her to his apartment, but she'd insisted on moving back to her old home instead, which had just one small *shikumen* room under the attic.

'In the nursing home, I have dreamed of it so much. Shortly after your father and I came back from the US, we moved into this tiny yet cozy room, you know. Indeed, so many memories of these years have accumulated here. Don't worry about me. I can still take good care of myself. If anything, I'll call you with the cellphone you bought for me. It's proper and right for me to spend my remaining days in the old home.'

That sounded ominous to him. He suspected her decision was made more out of her unwillingness to be too much of a burden to him at his apartment, where she said he should have peace and quiet for his important work. In a matter of days, however, that so-called important work would be taken away from him. He had chosen not to tell her anything about his trouble, though.

Consequently, he had to make frequent visits to her. Late last night, after getting a bagful of the take-out specials from Peiqin's restaurant, he had come over to her place.

She looked so fragile in the trembling ring of the dim, yellowish lamplight – like a piece of Ming dynasty china in a museum. Consumed with guilt, he stayed on until after she finished the meal and washed the dishes for her. It then started raining outside. She wanted him to stay overnight.

'You sleep in the attic. Just like in the old days.'

To his confusion, the once-familiar attic had an immediate inexplicable effect on him. Looking around, he felt utterly bewildered, with the fragments of the past and the present juxtaposed for him in the dark. He could not help getting sentimental, reminiscing under the surreal spell of the old room. In a corner near the foot of the mattress, a lone cobweb stretched out of the dust. Amidst it the half-forgotten details started resurfacing in the ripples of the night . . .

How long ago was the night that he had lain in the attic thinking about the imminent prospect of chief inspectorship in the police bureau?

And that long-ago night had seemed so much like this night, he recollected: waking from a dream, wondering how he had come all this way, to the eve of becoming an inspector, and what he could possibly do with himself at the start of his new career.

A new Party policy in the mid-eighties had urged the promotion of young Party-member intellectuals to higher cadre positions in the system. 'You are the youngest in the police bureau history,' Party Secretary Li had said to him at the time.

In addition to the new policy, the promotion had material-ized on account of the successful conclusion of a case involving the murder of an old gourmet that he had helped with in Red Dust Lane. It was nonetheless an unexpected advancement, considering his lack of proper training in the police field, what with his major in English literature and his aspiration to be a poet.

Ironic as it might have seemed, it was from another unexpected, though well-meant, interference by an overseas Chinese 'uncle' during the process of the state-job assignment for college graduates that had landed him a job at the Shanghai Police Bureau in the first place. And then, with another twist in the changing political discourse of China's reform under Comrade Deng Xiaoping, Chen had stood out as a most promising candidate for the chief inspectorship in light of the new cadre promotion policy, as few young people were credited with higher education in the police force at that time.

Party Secretary Li had rushed him through the application to the CCP membership; failing that, Li insisted, a chief inspector position would never have been imaginable for a young man like Chen.

In retrospect, how many other unbelievable changes had since taken place in China? Just like the Tang dynasty poem by Du Fu about the shifting clouds in the blue sky, one moment looking like a white shirt, and the next changing into a black dog.

And these changes had changed Chen too.

Now he had come full circle. From the eve of his becoming a chief inspector, to a night that witnessed him drawing nearer to the end of his career. And in the same old attic, he whistled lightly, managing to pull his train of thought back to the present.

Earlier in the day, Party Secretary Li had mentioned a case to him, though it was not one meant for him, they both knew.

'It really takes a poet / inspector to figure out a case of poetry interpretation, right?'

The sarcasm in Li's comment seemed so subtle, but nonetheless palpable. Chen's removal from his position had not been announced yet, but there was no helping him. Internal Security had started investigating the case in question, which had been turned over from the Webcops. It was said to involve an anti-Party poem posted on WeTalk, one of the most popular social media networks with more than a billion users in China. It was out of the question for a politically unreliable man like Chen to deal with such a case at this critical moment.

Still, could there be something else in Li's choosing to bring up the case with him?

Detective Yu, his friend and long-time partner, chose to share that question.

'I'll take a look into the case, Chief. Internal Security needs help from us, so I should be able to find something out. I don't think Party Secretary Li would have mentioned the case to you for nothing. People may say all kinds of things about your position in the bureau. It's not over until it's officially announced, as we all know.'

Chen doubted it, making no response to Detective Yu's assertion. It seemed to be a foregone conclusion to him, whatever he might try to do for himself.

A couple of lines from a Song dynasty poem flashed through his mind:

> Long, long I lament about the lacking
> of a true self for me to claim.
> When can I ever forget
> about all the cares of the world?
> The night deep, the wind still, no ripple on the river.

Shu Shi had written the poem in exile, after waking from a drunken stupor.

Whatever had happened to Chen over the years, the soon-to-be-ex-chief inspector did not think he could really complain. But how could he have gone from a 'black puppy' to a chief inspector, only to now be fired from the position?

It was a journey such as he had never visualized for himself in his middle school or college days. And he remained astonished, exhausted even, at the thought of it. Life is like a poorly written mystery, but even more absurd, bizarre and suspenseful.

That all accounted for his dreaming of his long-ago promotion in the police bureau. But what about the headless monster pulling an iron chain? Possibly something from his deep-rooted, though well-covered, insecurity. From his early childhood, he had found himself lacking in self-confidence, suffering a sort of inferiority complex owing to his black family background in the light of Mao's class struggle theory.

Unbelievable as it might have appeared, the first time for him to gain confidence in anything actually occurred in a hospital at the beginning of the Cultural Revolution in 1966.

But he immediately started to doubt himself, tossing and turning on the mattress as he tried to recapture the details. Could it have been somewhere else? Or was there more than one hospital? Still, what his mother had said to him that long-ago afternoon seemed not to be totally unrelated.

He was getting increasingly confused. He stared at the stains on the attic ceiling, as if they could somehow provide meaningful clues to the mystery of those bygone days. Then more torn fragments of the past began to emerge out of the dark and, even more to his befuddlement, to converge into a sequence with a pattern unrecognized before.

The shapes of the stains shifting in nightly shadows reminded him of something he had seen long ago: a piece of blood-speckled gauze, and a gray lizard with a strange name he failed to recollect . . .

Confidence First Gained

I n the early days of the Cultural Revolution that broke out in 1966, a common scene in China was the 'revolutionary mass criticism' staged against 'class enemies'.

There was no official definition of the nationwide movement. To begin with, it had little to do with 'criticism' in the proper sense of the word. It came closer, if anything, to public denunciation and humiliation of the target in question. Among the accepted rationales for the new trend, one of them was to rally the proletariat and to demoralize the 'class enemies', which also gave rise to a variety of interpretations. In the light of Mao's class theory, the struggle between socialism and capitalism will exist throughout a long, long period of history until the final realization of communism for the whole of mankind. For the proletariat, the class enemies in China include landlords, rich farmers, counter-revolutionaries, bad elements and rightists in the late 1950s, and then for the expanded category during the Cultural Revolution, capitalists, unreformed bourgeois intellectuals, historical counter-revolutionaries and capitalist-roaders, the last being a newly coined term in reference to 'the Party officials pushing along the capitalist road against Chairman Mao'.

As a rule, the format of the revolutionary mass criticism involved the class enemies being marched onto a temporary stage, or into a cordoned-off open space, under a large portrait of Mao, with their heads bent low in repentance, weighed down by blackboards hung around their necks sporting their names written and crossed out – and for a possible variation, further demonized with tall white paper hats on their heads, symbolic of evils from the netherworld. Red Guard organizations made indignant denouncements on the stage, with the audience shouting slogans in thunderous response and raising their fists high in the air. A much-talked-about example might well illustrate it. Liu Shaoqi, the Chairman of the People's Republic of China, seen at the time as the arch rival to Mao Zedong, the Chairman of the Chinese Communist Party, had to face the revolutionary mass criticism, along with his wife, Wang Guangmei, groveling beside him wearing a badly torn, bosom-revealing mandarin dress and a necklace made of ping pong balls – the dress and necklace being emblematic of bourgeois decadency. In the heat of the revolutionary mass criticism, some of the class enemies were savagely beaten, and quite a number of them beaten to death.

For a teenager like Chen Cao, a lot of things appeared to be baffling. Before 1949, his father had studied and taught at an American college, hence was an 'unreformed bourgeois intellectual' in the eyes of Mao's class system, even though he had come back to China and started teaching in a Chinese university. At the beginning of the Cultural Revolution he was seen as a 'black monster with problems in the past and the present' because of his international fame as a Neo-Confucian scholar. As a result, he was deprived of the right to teach. He had to undergo the 'reformation through hard labor' and work like a janitor. What's worse, he had to go through one revolutionary mass criticism after another.

At first, Chen Cao had hardly any knowledge of his father's ordeal, except that neighbors started to call him Old Black Monster Chen, instead of the Mr Chen they had respectfully used before, even though his hair turned white overnight in 1966. In Shanghai, people would often address middle-aged or elderly people by their family names preceded with the character *lao*, meaning 'old', and young people by their family names preceded with the character *xiao*, meaning 'little'. In their case, the neighbors simply called the old one Old Black Chen, and Chen, still so young, Little Black Chen. Some took pity on the kid, however, so more often than not it was simply shortened to Little Chen.

All the while things were becoming more and more heated in China. In Qufu, Shandong Province, the Confucian temple was demolished overnight. The bodies of Confucius's great-grandchildren were dug out of the graves in angry denouncement. The Red Guards in charge there thought about fetching Old Black Chen over to the temple as a live target for the revolutionary mass criticism, but a rival group of Red Guards broke out in an armed power struggle with the first group and the plan was scrapped.

Still, the revolutionary mass criticism went on as before in the college where Old Black Chen had taught. One evening, Little Chen saw him lurching back home with a sudden limp and, on another evening, almost falling to the floor with his face covered in undisguisable large bruises like a rotten persimmon. And with his family gone to bed, the old man still had to work and rework something called a 'guilty plea' under the broken lamp late into the night three or four evenings a week.

The ritual of guilty plea writing came as a new development in the mass criticism against the class enemies, who then had to confess and repent their sins and crimes, which in Old Black Chen's case focused on his advocating the Confucian doctrine that Chairman Mao had vehemently denounced. That would have been difficult, Little Chen imagined, since Old Black Chen was known as a brilliant scholar in the field, and those Confucianist ideas must have been so familiar to him. According to the *People's Daily*, Confucian was a monstrous 'counter-revolutionary' in feudalistic China about two thousand years earlier, looking to the past in a vain bid for the salvation of the decaying Zhou dynasty. And that was that.

But Old Black Chen would have been seen as too bookish, and instead of letting him off the hook easily, the Red Guards demanded him to denounce the 'atrocious crimes' from the bottom of his black heart and soul again and again until their proletarian satisfaction. Little Chen, often called 'Black Puppy Chen' in elementary school, was too overwhelmed by the waves of humiliation and discrimination against him to worry about what might have been happening to his father.

In the second year of the Cultural Revolution, Old Black Chen suffered acute retinal detachment, so the college revolutionary committee told him not to come to work any more. A broken man, he left not without a touch of relief. At least there would be no more revolutionary mass criticism.

But that gave rise to another problem. Under the proletarian dictatorship, sick leave benefit was possible only for the proletariat, not for an 'unreformed bourgeois intellectual'. In other words, neither pay nor medical insurance for Old Black Chen. Because of his class status, the pay for his wife's job at the middle school was drastically reduced too, and far from enough to support the whole family. Back home, he came to the realization that he had to have the eye surgery as soon as possible . . . and then return to work as a janitor at the college.

He managed to check into the Shanghai ENT Hospital, accompanied by Little Chen. Presumably it would take just one or two days for the surgery, and then about a week or two for recovery at home.

Things at the hospital turned out to be very different, however. With a considerable number of experienced doctors and nurses condemned as 'black monsters' and disqualified for work, and with those remaining too busy struggling for survival, the patients had to go through an unexpectedly long waiting period for operations.

On the third day, Little Chen was shocked by a message that came home through the neighborhood phone service: 'A family member of Bed Seventeen has to hurry over to the hospital for revolutionary mass criticism.'

'Bed Seventeen' referred to Old Black Chen, his bed being so numbered in the hospital ward. The message came from a Red Guard organization called 'Fierce Wind and Thunder', its name derived from a Mao poem. That threw the Chen family into a panic.

How could Old Black Chen have gotten into trouble in the hospital? And for that matter, why should his family member go there as well? All seemed totally inexplicable and ominous to Little Chen.

His mother had just suffered a nervous breakdown, so the job was up to him. The realization hit home with a splitting headache. Having heard stories about family members being mass criticized together with the targets, he shuddered at the prospect. As a 'black puppy' he had given up any dream of becoming a Red Guard, going to college, or getting a decent job in socialist China, but those were worries for the future, unlike the revolutionary mass criticism of the present.

His mother served him a bowl of mint-flavored green bean soup, his favorite snack in summer, but it helped little with the headache. He rose to leave for the hospital with a reluctance bordering on resentment.

Along the way, Little Chen tried to figure out the possible cause of his father's trouble. The Red Guards at the college were unaware of the surgery, so they could not have reported anything to those at the hospital. And the old man should have known better than to reveal anything to the people there.

Little Chen cudgeled his brains out thinking, without success, as he sweated in a bus packed like a bamboo steamer of tiny soup buns. At the hospital stop, he stumbled down, drained like one of the broken buns.

Instead of heading to the ward, he decided to pay a visit first to the office of the hospital revolutionary committee.

As it turned out, the Fierce Wind and Thunder organization consisted of patients rather than hospital staff members, who were hardly capable of protecting themselves, and were like 'the clay statues in a temple drifting across the river' in an old Chinese proverb. The organization had popped up in response to Chairman Mao's call for the proletarian dictatorship to be enforced in every corner of Chinese society. The head of Fierce Wind and Thunder, who gave orders in the name of the Cultural Revolution, was a patient surnamed Huang on Bed Thirty-Five in the next ward. It was said that Commander Huang suffered from esophageal cancer at an advanced stage. He was a man in his mid-forties, wearing a red armband on his T-shirt sleeve and a white gauze pad around his throat.

'It's our Party's policy to be humanistic even toward the sick class enemies, but not for an unremorseful one,' Commander Huang began, his voice hissing with a sudden metal sharpness. 'Until he truly repents his crimes to the full, he deserves no medical treatment in the hospital here. Don't ever think he could get away so easily.'

'You're absolutely right,' Little Chen said in a respectful hurry. Under normal circumstances, it might not be too big a deal for Old Black Chen to write and rewrite the guilty plea a couple more times, but if Commander Huang refused to approve the plea, it meant that no doctor would be allowed to perform the surgery on the old man. That would mean he had to stay here for weeks, or even months. As it was, they could hardly make ends meet at home, not to mention the hospital expenses.

Little Chen kept nodding like a wound-up robot. It was an inhuman role to play, pretending he had no feelings of his own.

Once again, those Confucian maxims his father had taught him proved to be totally irrelevant. *There are things a man should do, and things a man should not do.* But what the hell were the *things* in question? For another, *A gentleman is worried not, but a low class man nervous all the time.* But being a young boy, he had been constantly nervous of late.

As for the crime Commander Huang was accusing his father of, he still had no clue. In an English book on Neo-Confucianism written years earlier by Black Chen, an old family friend had recently discovered several paragraphs praising Wang Yangming, a Neo-Confucianist scholar of the Ming dynasty, so he told them in haste to hide the book away. With the ideas of Wang Yangming being advocated by Chiang Kai-shek in Taiwan, those paragraphs could have been considered as evidence and condemned as a serious political crime during the Cultural Revolution. But how could Commander Huang have come to know anything about them? No, Chen decided, that wasn't the reason for the trouble.

'Instead of repenting the bourgeois lifestyle of his in the United States,' Commander Huang continued huskily, as if whistling through a broken steel pipe, 'he actually has the nerve to brag and boast about it in the hospital. He has to write a new guilty plea.'

'Yes, I will definitely help him write a soul-searching, guilty-pleading statement,' Little Chen said. 'Please give me some specific details, Commander Huang, so I can make him dig deeper into his black heart and come to terms with the very root of the evil.'

'Well, he talks as if he alone knew how to make a

milk-powder drink,' Commander Huang said, 'thanks to the bourgeois extravagance he enjoyed in the United States before 1949. Who the hell is he to look down on the Chinese working class people?'

Sirens pierced the back of Little Chen's mind. At home, his father had said little about his life in the US, for fear of 'advocating the American bourgeois lifestyle'. And the grudge he bore against his father for bringing him into the black class family background made it more difficult for the father to open up to the son. More often than not, Old Black Chen wrapped himself in a cocoon of silence. During the so-called three years of natural disasters in the early 1960s – when more than thirty million Chinese people died of starvation because of the Big Leap Forward movement launched by Chairman Mao – his father must have been starved into a delirious recollection of a special campus canteen experience he had enjoyed in the early 1940s. As a work-and-study student with a part-time job at the American college canteen, he could have as much milk as he liked, seven days a week. It was not necessarily fresh milk; occasionally, he caught glimpses of a blonde waitress making a milk-powder drink behind the counter. But that part of the story appeared even more exotic to the son, who listened to it like a fairytale, mouth watering all the time. After all, the family did not have a single bottle of milk for years.

But could the old man have been so stupid as to talk about it in the hospital?

By the side of Bed Seventeen, however, he could not bring himself to complain at the sight of his much-changed father: unshaven, blindfolded, unable to find a pen with his fumbling hand.

So that was one of the reasons Commander Huang wanted a family member at the hospital. To help, Little Chen realized, noticing a jar of milk powder on the bedside table for the patient at the next bed.

He drew in a deep breath, trying to gather the details of the incident that had landed his father in trouble. Those days, milk powder was a rarity, and Bed Eighteen was lucky enough to have a jar, but he did not know how to properly mix it, resulting in an inedible mess. So Bed Seventeen shared with Bed

Eighteen the knack of stirring the milk powder first with a little cold water before pouring in hot water, mentioning his experience in the American college canteen by way of explanation. Sure enough, the little trick made all the difference. Bed Eighteen talked to others about the secret recipe with such great gusto that it soon spread out of the ward. The same evening Commander Huang made enquiries into it, and detected the problem with his ever-present alertness for anything new in the class struggle.

For Little Chen, whatever the possible cause of the problem, the far more pressing issue was how to rewrite the plea, which had to be acceptable to Commander Huang. It would not do to just add apologies, however truthfully contrite, for the bourgeois decadence of a cup of milk-powder drink. He re-examined his father's ejected piece, which began, rather bookishly, about how he had dreamed of a college education in the States but couldn't afford the tuition. So it was just with a stroke of luck that his application for a work-and-study program got through, and he managed by working at the school canteen in a part-time job with acceptable pay and free milk.

That part of his experience as a work-and-study student at the American college had never been shared at home. The pen trembling in his hand, Little Chen came to see the problem with the plea in the eyes of Commander Huang. The attempt to portray himself as a hard-working student who happened to learn through fortuitous circumstances the trick of making a milk-powder drink was unacceptable.

As his father, the 'unreformed, unrepentant bourgeois intellectual', started dictating the new piece, Little Chen decided not to follow his words too closely. Such a piece was bound to be rejected again. In his elementary school, in a big-character guilty plea posted on the front wall, one of his 'black monster teachers' had condemned himself so eloquently, Little Chen recalled, like a Sichuan chef generously throwing handfuls of peppers into the wok.

'*I am totally rotten, black from heart to toe. For my crime, I should be trodden underfoot, unable to turn over for hundreds of years. For fattening myself on the poor people, I deserve to be cut thousands of times . . .*'

As it goes in a proverb, a dead pig does not have to worry about the scalding water, which cannot make it any more dead. So why worry about piling up those revolutionary, or counter-revolutionary, clichés?

He included the milk powder part, of course, as the early but unmistakable sign of his father's decadent indulgence in the West. So his eventual turning into a counter-revolutionary Confucianist scholar was anything but accidental.

About forty-five minutes later, Little Chen finally plodded to the conclusion, jotting down an exclamation mark and nodding to himself, when he heard an announcement coming through a loud speaker in the ward: 'Bed Seventeen and his family member come out to the hospital reception hall.'

There, the first thing Little Chen saw was a long red banner stretched across the half-deserted hall: *The Hospital Revolutionary Mass Criticism.*

Apparently, Huang had seized upon his availability to have the event arranged in addition to the guilty plea, for the blindfolded target was unable to go through the ritual without somebody taking him by the hand. Little Chen turned over the plea to Huang, who stuffed it into his pant pocket without taking a look, and gestured him to take his position beside his father, whose neck was presently weighed down with a heavy blackboard showing his name crossed out in colored chalk. There were two other patients standing aligned with him, each sporting a similar blackboard.

'Lower your heads and plead guilty to our great leader Chairman Mao!' Commander Huang hissed out the command.

Standing aside, Little Chen found his head hung low in spite of himself, though without a blackboard around the neck – the only difference between father and son. The humiliation overwhelming, the former soon became too weak to stand still, putting a hand on the latter's shoulder for support.

Little Chen tried imagining himself into a human crutch, stiff, motionless, unbreakable, without thoughts or feelings. But he was not that successful.

It was perhaps because of his throat problem that Commander Huang did not say anything else, stepping off to return with a chair and sitting like a bamboo pole throughout the ritual.

At the end of the longest hour imaginable, he stood up to wave the people away.

Little Chen decided to stay on by his father's side, believing there could be more rewriting for him to do in the hospital. He felt utterly exhausted. There was no point going home and then hurrying back.

But by the time he finally left the hospital around seven thirty that evening, he still had not heard anything from Commander Huang.

No message the following morning either. Around noon, he double-checked with the neighborhood phone service. Inexplicably, still no message whatsoever from the hospital.

On the third day, a phone message came through: his father was being sent into the operation room and would be released home the next day.

So Commander Huang must have given his approval to the guilty plea; failing that, the doctor would not have moved ahead with the surgery.

It was then surely to the credit of Little Chen. The new guilty plea, with all the creative words and phrases thrown in without his father's knowledge, had worked.

But then some other possible scenarios came up. Commander Huang might have relented at the sight of a child trembling beside his father during the mass criticism; alternatively, he could have suffered an unexpected turn for the worse in his own condition. Whatever interpretation, with the Cultural Revolution engulfing the whole country, it was after all nothing but a storm in a cup of milk-powder drink.

'Unlike your bookish father, you know how to read people's minds like a sleuth, and what to write. Indeed an impossible mission you have done,' his mother said, subscribing to the scenario that held out the laurel to Little Chen.

'A sleuth?' He repeated the word without knowing its meaning.

It was the first time he gained confidence in himself, in writing of all things, which might enable him to sway those people otherwise above and beyond him.

Fall of a Red Guard

Toward the middle of the second year of the Cultural Revolution, Chen caught a nasty flu at elementary school. His father had been labeled a 'black monster of unreformed intellectual' in early 1967 and thrown into 'isolated investigation' at the college, where no family members could visit. That meant, ironically, that Chen did not have to worry about writing guilty pleas for the old man any more. His mother, overwhelmed in the black shadow of it, along with all the extra work pushed onto her as punishment at the middle school, was unable to take him to the neighborhood hospital on the corner of Jinling and Songxia Roads. Recovering from a recent nervous breakdown, she nonetheless insisted that he had to see Doctor Zhang, one of the most experienced doctors there.

According to the hospital regulations, the patients could tell the nurse in the second-floor waiting room about their choice of doctors. Doctor Zhang was popular, having studied in Europe, and wore a pair of gold-rimmed glasses and smoked an indispensable cigar. Usually there was a long waiting period for him, and Chen balked at the thought of it. But it was worth it, his mother declared, as his cough seemed to be much better the night after his first visit to Doctor Zhang.

For the follow-up visit, however, Chen was surprised to witness a group of red-armbanded strangers occupying Doctor Zhang's office, smashing the framed awards and gilded prizes on the desk. They turned out to be members of a Red Guard organization that had taken over the power at the hospital in response to Chairman Mao's highest and latest instruction: 'It is right and justified to make revolution and come up in rebellion.' As a result, intellectuals like the doctors there, having immersed themselves in Western ideologies and knowledge,

were denounced as 'black monsters', to be mercilessly perse-
cuted and punished.

The leader of the Red Guard organization was a high school
graduate surnamed Jia, with no college education or medical
knowledge whatsoever, who had just been assigned to the
hospital as an apprentice to the retiring electrician. That
morning, Jia staged a revolutionary mass criticism with a
group of 'black intellectuals' gathered as the targets underneath
a red-cloth-and-white-paper banner stretched overhead:
'Exposure of the Paper Tigers'. The scene reminded Chen of
his father standing under a similar banner in another hospital
six months earlier.

Doctor Zhang, trembling, with a blackboard hung around
his neck, was given a simple test to take his own temperature,
and he grabbed a thermometer pushed over to him and put it
into his mouth without realizing it as one for anal use. So Jia
gave a dramatic speech there and then:

'Zhang, a so-called authority at the hospital, could not even
tell the difference between the oral and the anal thermometer.
It most eloquently proves Mao's maxim: "*The intellectuals
are the most stupid compared with workers, farmers and
soldiers.*" Shame on those bourgeois intellectuals who are
capable of nothing except engaging themselves in counter-
revolutionary activities and capitalist restoration.'

Chen nodded to the audience before he left the hospital
without seeing Doctor Zhang, who, like other 'black monsters',
was now deprived of the right to treat patients.

Chen coughed harder that night. When his mother heard of
the things happening at the hospital, she said with her brows
knitted, 'Chairman Mao is of course absolutely right, but
temperature-taking is the job of a nurse. For an experienced
doctor like Zhang, what if he failed to tell the difference
between the thermometers? Besides, his head was bent down
by the blackboard, so dizzy . . .'

She did not finish her comment, frowning as she added,
'Observe, but don't speak. If you see anything there you don't
understand, keep it to yourself, Chen. Remember, trouble
comes out of your mouth.'

The last sentence was an echo of an old proverb. It probably popped up in reference to his father as well, who had gotten into trouble because of his speeches and publications long before the Cultural Revolution. He decided to observe it as closely as possible.

What had happened at the hospital was celebrated the next morning in the *Liberation Daily* as a 'revolutionary initiative' of the Red Guards, who were portrayed as utterly justified in humiliating the bourgeois intellectual.

Whatever the interpretation, Chen had to revisit the hospital a few days later, still coughing. There he saw Zhang shuffling out of the restroom in janitor uniform – thus going through an 'ideological transformation through hard labor' – with smudges on his face, his glasses broken and bandage-fixed on his nose. The old doctor carried in his hands a dripping mop, out of which a lizard was seen shooting like a flash of lightning. A slip of a girl seated beside Chen on the bench in the waiting room shrieked at the bizarre sight. Chen reached out to cover her mouth in haste. It could have served as more evidence of Zhang's incompetence even at the janitor job.

With experienced doctors like Zhang gone, the remaining ones were overwhelmed with the large number of patients. A young nurse surnamed Han suggested that Chen take whichever doctor was available there. She was busy filling out the basic information on his record while waving down a thermometer in her left hand. He followed her mischievous glance to Jia sitting at Zhang's desk, wearing a red armband over the hospital uniform.

Jia was said to be pushing the 'revolutionary initiative' to a higher level in the Cultural Revolution. Red Guards were supposed to take power everywhere, and that meant at the hospital too. So Jia took the lead in treating patients as well. It was actually a move in line with Mao's approval of the 'barefoot doctors' – the farmers, while working barefoot in the rice paddy, were also helping their sick class sisters and brothers with traditional Chinese herbs and acupuncture rather than 'Western medicine', and achieved far more miraculous results. That being the case for the farmers in the countryside, then why not for the Red Guards at a hospital in the big city?

Before Chen could say anything in response to Nurse Han,

his medical record was placed beside a copy of *Barefoot Doctor Reader* on the desk in front of Jia. Touching the red armband on the white uniform, Jia checked the record and leafed through the book for a minute or two before dashing off a prescription, similar to the one given by Doctor Zhang, but not forgetting to add a Chinese herb as he declared in a serious manner: 'As our great leader Chairman Mao says, "Chinese medicine is a great treasure." So this will make the real difference.'

For the following weeks, Chen came to find his medical record sent, invariably, to Jia's desk. Maybe the nurse had no choice. It would be too much of a political face loss for a Red Guard 'doctor' to sit there for hours without seeing a patient. Chen was too young to protest against the arrangement.

Then he noticed something. In the office, Jia hardly looked at him across the desk, but stole glances instead toward Nurse Han in the waiting room.

An attractive, well-built girl in her early twenties, she wore her white uniform barelegged and barefoot in crystal-like plastic sandals. What she wore – or didn't – beneath her uniform was easy for Jia to imagine, considering the unbearable summer heat with patients milling around, and with the one and only ancient ceiling fan revolving half-heartedly overhead. She had to fan herself with a manila folder, wiping the sweat from her forehead with the back of her hand, and beating her feet on the floor in a languorous rhythm as if to an inaudible song.

The realization hit home for Chen. That was why Jia wanted to occupy Dr Zhang's desk. An excuse for more contact between the 'doctor' and nurse. Those years, romantic passion was condemned as politically incorrect. The only passion permissible was the passion for Chairman Mao and the Cultural Revolution. How much more so for the head of a Red Guard organization?

As for her, she seemed not to look into the office much. Chen could not help thinking of a proverb: 'An ugly toad's mouth waters in vain at the sight of a beautiful swan.' Han was such a vivacious girl, glowing with youth and energy.

Another proverb, however, declared that persistence may wear an iron rod out into a thin needle. And before too long

Jia was seen touching her hand when taking the medical record across the desk. She did not really push it away, Chen detected.

Then another morning, Chen was surprised to see in the waiting room an elderly nurse temporarily replacing Han, who was said to have an urgent family situation. That same morning, Jia was seen striding out of the office, taking off his white uniform and saying he had to go to a political meeting. The replacement nurse seemed to be rather clumsy, repeatedly misplacing information and records, which added to the work-load of the other doctors there. The patients had to wait even longer outside.

'It's more than two hours,' one of them complained petulantly.

'With Nurse Han gone,' another observed, 'Jia disappears too.'

'Now I see why,' the third one joined in. 'That dirty bastard!'

'Well, it's human to be attracted to a beauty,' an elderly patient said rather bookishly. 'Confucius says, *"Such a slender, sweet girl she is, / a gentleman is eager seeking her hand."*'

It became a heated, though whispered, topic for their discussion and speculation that morning, spreading out like ripples. Chen started working on a more elaborate scenario. Jia could have metamorphosed into the commander of the Red Guard organization because of Han. An electrician apprentice was a nobody at a hospital, definitely not in a position to approach a beauty like Han. Chen was intrigued with the idea of himself turning into something of a private investigator, though he knew better than to discuss the case with others. He had been too traumatized as 'a black puppy'. Still, he had nothing better to do in the waiting room. So he just observed.

As in another old Chinese proverb, weather changes unpre-dictably. Four or five days later, Jia was caught in the act of pinning Han down on the office desk in the late evening, her uniform unbuttoned and her sandals fallen to the floor. It was Zhen, the associate head of the hospital Red Guard organiza-tion, that made the shocking discovery. Zhen showed no mercy to 'a renegade succumbing to the evil influence of bourgeois decadence'. Jia pleaded guilty, shouldering all the

responsibility for himself, with Han sobbing in the emergency
political meeting.

Zhen then became the Red Guard leader, with Jia removed
from his powerful position. There seemed to be different stories
about Zhen's raid. According to one version, he had happened
to gather information from the whispered gossip among the
patients in the waiting room, but according to another, he had
eyed Jia's position for months, watching over him like the
surveillance cameras seen only in Western movies at the time.
Chen observed without offering his scenario.

Whatever the scenario, Jia was demoted to doing odd jobs
at the hospital. Han was transferred to the pharmacy room. In
the meantime, lingering in the waiting room became more
unbearable to Chen, and his bronchitis turned into something
like asthma, wheezing and coughing for hours at night.

During his following visits to the hospital, he caught
occasional glimpses of Han through the pharmacy window,
flitting among the rows of medicine bottles in a yellow summer
dress, like a butterfly blazing in bright light streaming in from
the window.

That was why Jia kept moving back and forth in front of
the pharmacy window, Chen observed, grasping a small
package of pills tight in his hand.

A couple of weeks later, Chen was shocked again. This time
at the scene of Jia working as a janitor, carrying a dripping
mop and a pail of dirty water, the very job once assigned to
Doctor Zhang.

So Chen started canvassing in secret. Waiting in hospital
could be so boring.

As it turned out, Jia did stumble anew because of his obses-
sion with Han. Those days, whenever one of 'the latest and
highest quotes of Chairman Mao' was announced on the radio,
people had to do something in celebration. This time, it
happened to be Mao's reiteration that 'the traditional Chinese
medicine is a great treasure', so for the neighborhood hospital,
the response was supposed to come in the form of propaganda
material on acupuncture for mass education.

Jia was given the job of cutting the stencil overnight. To
illustrate the needle positions, he drew an unclad human body.

Around midnight, he fell asleep, dreaming of Han again. In the first gray light struggling through the curtained window, he woke up with the lingering images of the dream, still so enthrallingly vivid, before he suddenly saw the body on the stencil staring back with neither charm nor curve – as if in accusation of his being so inattentive. He added touches in a hurry, still sleepy-eyed.

The next afternoon, in the middle of his janitor round, he was summoned to the Red Guard office. Zhen pushed the printed material across the desk to him.

'Take a damned good look. The new evidence of your crime against Chairman Mao.'

The print-out showed a female figure with two dots on her bosom, and a line between her thighs, all of which Jia had added as a result of the muddled fantasies of the fleeing night, thus making the naked figure almost as erotically desirable as Han in the dream.

The same afternoon witnessed another revolutionary mass criticism, like the one organized by Jia the first day of the Red Guards taking power at the hospital, except that this time it was presided over by Zhen, with Jia standing under a portrait of Chairman Mao, head low.

'Comrades, the material is meant for the broad masses of people to further understand Chairman Mao's profound teaching about Chinese medicine being a great treasure. But what has this bastard done about it? He presents a nude female body in the text. Consequently, people reading the material could be lost in obscene association. It's a deliberate, diabolic sabotage.'

The accusation was far more serious than before. Nurse Han joined in, making a tearful, indignant denunciation: 'He is so full of dirty thoughts. This rotten egg simply cannot help himself.'

There was no possibility of Jia's remaining in the hospital. It was said he was suspended from work there like a repeatedly defeated cricket thrown out of the cricket-fighting pot.

In the meantime, Doctor Zhang moved back to the office desk, seeing his patients like before. He appeared to be genuinely concerned while examining Chen's medical record. Acute bronchitis should not have lingered on like that, unless it had lapsed into asthma. The old doctor dashed off a new prescription, adding something called *gejie* as an afterthought.

Chen was puzzled by the prescription, part of which he had to fill out at the herbal medicine store outside of the hospital. *Gejie* turned out to be a pair of ghastly-looking dried lizards with long, thick tails. How could they have anything to do with bronchitis? He hurried back with the lizards and the question for Doctor Zhang.

'During the recent political re-education, I studied Chinese medicine in response to our great leader Chairman Mao's teaching,' the doctor said reverently. In spite of his major in Western medicine, that seemed to be the one and only politically correct thing for him to do. He then pulled out a time-yellowed Chinese medicine book from the desk drawer, adjusting the newly fixed gold-rimmed glasses on his nose.

'*Gejie* is a sort of large lizard, proper name being *gekko gecko*. So its name probably comes from the sound it makes, the male-sounding "*ge*" and the female, "*jie*". The lizards always have to move in a pair – male and female. They are inseparable, engaging their indivisible selves in sex with inexhaustible production of hormones, yet with the perfect balance of yin and yang. So the most potent medical element is believed to be in their long tails, which look supersized for the pair in your hand. So it will work out wonderfully for your ailment. Indeed, Chairman Mao's teaching is so profound, we have to study and re-study.'

Chen remained confounded, blinking. Of course Chairman Mao could never be wrong, but the doctor talked in such a bookish way, throwing in all the unnecessary details about the dried lizards.

'Are they so horny?' he finally asked.

'In the traditional Chinese medical theory,' Doctor Zhang said, adjusting his glasses again, 'asthma comes from the lack of yang in the human system, but in some cases, also possibly from the lack of yin. What can help more than the natural, balanced exuberance of yin / yang in a pair of *gejie*?'

It might not hurt to try, Chen thought, leaving and clutching the pair of *gejie* in bewilderment.

When properly brewed at home, the *gejie* tasted like smelly salt fish soup. His mother had to prepare honey water in a hurry to revive his tastebuds afterward. She forgot to ask how Doctor Zhang had got back into the office.

In less than a week Chen began to recover, miraculously, and he could not help wondering whether it was truly because of the dried lizards.

During the follow-up visit to Doctor Zhang, Chen did not see Nurse Han in the pharmacy. There was no prescription for him that day. The old doctor proudly proclaimed that he had been cured.

As he left the hospital, he thought he detected someone sulking stealthily outside. He hurried over, and sure enough it was Jia sneaking glances toward a drop-out window of the pharmacy room, scurrying away at the sight of him like a criminal, and casting a shadow behind like a long tail.

Perhaps like *gejie*, Chen thought, coughing again unexpectedly.

TWO

A gain, Chen woke from a puzzling dream, which seemed to be somehow sequential to the earlier one.

He must have drifted into another disturbed doze while recollecting those traumatic childhood experiences. It was probably for no more than ten or fifteen minutes. The contents of the dream were already becoming elusive, though informed with the same ominous sensation, and with the same iron chain trailing along the corridor, rattling for a second or two, just like earlier.

But the chain is tearing across in a flash to another location, somewhere more somber and sinister. Instead of the headless figure prowling up from behind, it is a bull-headed one squatting on the black marble steps of a magnificent black-painted hall. In accordance with the Chinese folklore, the bull-headed figure is a constable of Hell who is keeping himself busy with disassembling and assembling the colored links of the long chain, as if totally engaged in a game of absurdity. With each of those links marked yin or yang, the proper color pattern of the chain should be alternately white and black, but the bull-headed constable, having had a cup too much, connects the links in random – two black pieces, three white ones, and then just one other black piece before one falls to the ground with a clang.

Chen was having a hard time interpreting the dream. The bull-headed constable is supposed to be in charge of marching the doomed souls from the human world to Hell. But instead of being a constable of real responsibility, he is more of a yamen runner who simply runs around at the Hell King's bidding, incapable of carrying out any investigation on his own.

As for the long chain of colored links, Chen thought he had read about it somewhere, though he was unable to recall the name of the book. It came from a metaphor about the links of yin and yang in the so-called chain of causality, but with the links misplaced, things could turn out to be entirely different. While unnoticed at the time, each of the links in terms of the cause and effect turns out to be unmistakable in retrospect.

'You reap what you sow,' as his mother had frequently said to him. 'Karma.'

Unlike his mother, however, he did not believe in the Buddhist sayings about karma or causality. It appeared too far-fetched to him for things as insignificant as a peck at the grain, a drink of the water, to be preordaining as well as preordained. After all, he merely wanted to do what was expected of him as a cop.

But he was not so sure about what he had done through these years, though he had heard people describe him as one of the few honest cops left in today's China.

His father, too, had quoted to him time and again a Confucius maxim: 'There are things a man should do, and there are things a man should not do.' As far as he was concerned, he might be able to say that he had managed to follow the second part of the Confucian saying, but he was not so confident about the first part, and definitely not all the time.

But he had to pull his thoughts back from the metaphysical speculations. Wherever the misplaced links, he was supposed to do what was expected of him – at least, he was expected to by his partner Detective Yu, for as long as he remained chief inspector. They had worked together closely for years, though at first no one had believed that the two of them, so different from each other, would make such an inseparable team.

Struck by a thought connected with the white and black links assembled at random in the dream, he turned to retrieve his cellphone from under his pillow. Earlier, he had turned the phone to the vibrating mode for fear of waking up his mother sleeping below.

Sure enough, there was a message from Detective Yu.

'The case that Party Secretary Li mentioned to you yesterday is one Internal Security contacted us about for help, and it had been pushed over from the Webcops. From the initial enquiries

I've made, it involves a netizen who placed a *like* emoji next to a poem posted on WeTalk, the most popular social media network nowadays in the socialism of China's characteristics, as you know. Li had said to others that you could have been the very one for a sensitive case concerning poetry interpretation, but Internal Security ruled you out, claiming that you're not trustworthy for a political case like that.

'And coincidentally, the netizen in question happens to be a man that lives in Red Dust Lane.'

It was all the information Detective Yu could have gathered at short notice. That Party Secretary Li and Internal Security did not trust him was not too surprising. Nor was he at all eager to look into a case pushed over by the Webcops. With people complaining, criticizing in the midst of the social, economic and political crises, it was now a top priority for the Party government to maintain political stability through Internet control. Hence a special police force – commonly called Webcops – had come to the fore, in charge of the censorship of people's posts and comments, checking and double-checking them twenty-four hours a day.

It was a hell of a job for them. Anything interpreted as against the interests of the Party had to be immediately blocked or deleted. In a more serious scenario, the netizens concerned had to be ferreted out in one way or another, and deprived of the right to post online. In some of the worst cases, they would be called out for a 'cup of tea', for a stern political reprimand, with possible further punishments. But it was the first time that Chen had learned that an emoji placed by a post could incriminate a netizen.

What astounded him more, however, was the second part of Detective Yu's message, which highlighted Red Dust Lane. He might have told Yu something about his connection to the lane before. But it was beyond him why his well-experienced partner should have gone out of his way to mention it. Did Yu want him to take a closer look?

Arguably it was a sensitive political case. But why should he be worried about it? It was not his case. If anything, getting involved would more likely than not get him deeper into trouble. Unless Detective Yu could see in the case some undisclosed possibility with which Chen could try to turn the tables, or muddy the waters of his demotion, so to speak, through his connection to Red Dust Lane. At least, so it must have appeared to Detective Yu.

Consequently, would the soon-to-be-ex-chief inspector be able to rule out the invisible chain of yin and yang links with absolute certainty?

The way he had ridden against all the bumps on his way to the chief inspectorship, as he reflected in the stillness of the night, appeared to have been informed with such karma in the dark – particularly in regards to his connection to Red Dust Lane.

Red Dust Lane was close, located on Fujian Road, about three or four minutes' walk from his mother's. In the years of the Cultural Revolution, that short distance had truly made a huge difference for him. Most of the people there knew little about his family background, so he could step into the lane without having to worry about recognition or discrimination as a 'black puppy' in those 'red revolutionary years'.

And the evening talks in front of the lane, where the residents would gather to tell stories in the warm or not-so-cold evenings, proved to be a special attraction for him. Those days, with libraries and bookstores closed, and books burned except for the red-covered *Quotations of Chairman Mao*, the different stories narrated under the starry nights literally opened a window unknown to him before.

And through an incident he learned of one evening, his interests expanded further in the days when he was still a middle school student. Paradoxically, he did something like an investigation about it, even though he had never dreamed of becoming a cop. Then, when he first became a cop, it was the background knowledge of the lane that contributed to his cracking some cases related to the neighborhood.

'*Over thirty years has elapsed. / What a surprise to find myself still here!*' Those were the lines from Chen Yuyi, a Song dynasty *ci* poet he liked. He wondered whether it was 'twenty years' in the original poem, but for him it was more than thirty.

In retrospect, even the things that had happened in the lane so long ago, with him staying far away as a college student in Beijing, led, albeit indirectly, to the beginning of his police career.

Now near the end of it, he might as well pay another visit to the lane, as Detective Yu had suggested, whether he would be able to do something about the case or not.

In my beginning is my end, or *in my end is my beginning.* And he caught himself feeling superstitious, all of a sudden, about Red Dust Lane.

Because of Doctor Zhivago I

I t was a summer night in the year of 1969 when a group of special police came out of the blue, rushing into Red Dust Lane to raid Mr Ma's bookstore next to the side entrance of the lane. Two or three hours later, they snatched Mr Ma away in handcuffs, with Mrs Ma running barefoot behind them, weeping, begging, all the way out onto Fujian Road.

It threw the lane into confusion. A Red Guard raid was not uncommon in those days, but a special police raid was a different story.

'Mr Ma can hardly harm a fly. Besides, the bookstore has been closed for a couple of years,' Dehua, a neighbor of the Mas in the same *shikumen* building, whispered in puzzlement. 'Why?'

It turned into a question shared by many in the lane, but there was little they could do about it. In the middle of the Cultural Revolution, it was a matter of course for the Party authorities to whisk someone away without explanation or warrant. That was what the proletarian dictatorship was all about. The Party decided everything – and every case, too. No attorney, no jury, and no court. No questions about it at all.

'We have to believe in the Party authorities. There must be a reason for it. No innocent man would have been wronged under our great leader Chairman Mao. If Mr Ma is to be found not guilty, he will soon be released,' Comrade Jun, the head of the neighborhood committee, said earnestly in a lane meeting.

Such a speech was of course politically correct, but it did not throw any light on the mystery. For a police raid like that, however, the less said the better – that much people knew only too well. So all they did was try to console the inconsolable Mrs Ma, who remained in tears all the time, repeating over

and over that she knew nothing about the cause of her husband's
trouble.

When the news came that Mr Ma would be sentenced as a
current counter-revolutionary, the lane was immediately shut
up like shivering cicadas in the approaching winter. They knew
better than to talk about it openly in the 'evening talk' in front
of the lane, where the lane residents would gather during the
warm or not-cold weather, talking, cracking jokes, gossiping,
telling stories related directly or indirectly to the lane.

Then, along came a middle school student surnamed Chen,
who wasn't a resident of the lane, but was occasionally in the
audience of the evening talk. It was not uncommon for people
to gather there from nearby neighborhoods. He was known to
have once been a regular customer at the bookstore in the days
before the outbreak of the Cultural Revolution. As Mrs Ma
later recalled, Chen must have read all the Chinese translations
of Sherlock Holmes available in the store without buying a
single copy. So he was perhaps eager to find out more about
what had happened to Mr Ma, and to try his hand at gathering
information like a 'private investigator'.

Such an unofficial investigation by a kid could have appealed
to the collective curiosity of the lane. A file about Mr Ma was
soon gathered, not just with contributions from Chen, but from
the neighbors in the lane, too. According to the file:

> Mr Ma had grown up in the lane. In 1948, just one year
> before the Communists took over power, he inherited
> from his father a small bookstore consisting of a front
> room opening onto Fujian Road and a back room leading
> into the lane. With the new class system that came into
> effect in the early fifties, he was classified as a 'small
> business owner', merely one shade less black than a
> 'capitalist' in the classification of the new socialist China.
> It was such a tiny bookstore, however, where he worked
> by himself, incapable of exploiting anyone – not even in
> light of the Marxist surplus value theory.
>
>   He renamed the bookstore 'Mr Ma's', in a subtle
> allusion to a poor, idiosyncratic scholar in *Stories of
> Scholars*, a classical Ming dynasty novel. An equally

poor, idiosyncratic bookseller, Mr Ma kept extra-long business hours, sometimes as late as eleven or twelve at night. He was fond of quoting a proverb: 'It always benefits you to read books.' So he made a point of not driving away those penniless customers who would stand and read for hours, a group that included Chen.

Mr Ma was amiable to his neighbors, despite the fact he did not mix too much with them. To their questions about why he did not try to find a state-run company job, he would simply quote another old saying: 'There's a beauty walking out of books, and there's a gold chamber appearing in books.'

For Mr Ma, at least the first part of the maxim proved to be true, as a beauty came to him, literally, out of books.

One late May evening at the beginning of the 1960s, a young girl fainted in the store, still clutching a book in her hand. As it turned out, with its price unaffordable to her, she had stood there for hours reading the poetry collection. She had recently dropped out of college because of her poor health, and she collapsed there after the long reading hours without taking in any food. He made her a bowl of hot beef noodles on a gasoline stove in the back room, and gave her the copy of the poetry collection for free.

Several months later, to the surprise of the lane, he married her in the same back room – now a wedding room for the two – with space just enough for a double bed, yet with a row of golden-ridged books shining above their headboard.

As the one and only decoration for the occasion, Mr Ma chose to have a long silk scroll of calligraphy hung on the white wall: 'To hang on in a dry rut, two carps try to moisten each other with their saliva.' It was a quote from Zhuangzi, an ancient Chinese philosopher about two thousand years earlier.

The bookstore then developed into a sort of husband-and-wife business. The two eccentric yet contented bookworms enjoyed every minute of their working together, wrapping themselves in a cocoon of bookish imagination. Their neighbors regarded the two with a touch of tolerance, and of superiority too. After all, their small private business was nothing compared to the state-run enterprise that boasted all the benefits of the new socialist system.

Because of their passion, the small bookstore with a well-chosen selection of books began spreading its name out of the neighborhood. Some college professors and newspaper reporters were said to be among the regular customers, including a well-known writer who brought a white-bearded foreigner with him. Mr Ma knew a bit of English and stocked a small number of foreign language books. Mrs Ma was a gracious host, serving a pot of Dragon Well tea for the special customers. The business appeared to be steadily picking up, which added to the visibility of the lane.

As in a Chinese proverb, however, there is no fore-casting a change in the weather – and especially in the political weather. The Cultural Revolution changed every-thing, including in the tiny bookstore, where they could stock only the red-covered Chairman Mao books. They knew nothing except books, but those days few customers came to the store. The red-covered books were more often than not given out by the government for political studies. It was hard for the two of them to keep the wolf from the door. And two or three years into the Cultural Revolution, the bookstore was closed.

Then came the special police force pounding on the door of Mr Ma's bookstore that summer night.

There was something inexplicable about Mr Ma's case, the neighbors mostly agreed, discussing the file in a stealthy way, with possible clues assembled and analyzed in the evening talk in front of the lane.

While confounded like the others, Chen went on conducting his investigation, inspired by all the Sherlock Holmes he had read, collecting bits and pieces here and there. It was not an easy job for him. For a 'current counter-revolutionary' case, Chen could not afford to appear to be too nosy, or he would have gotten himself into big trouble. So he adopted an 'approach of exclusion'.

One possible cause for Mr Ma's catastrophe, Chen speculated, could have been that of business tax evasion. The government authorities had been hard on the private business sector. Even in the days before the Cultural Revolution, a considerable number of private business owners had been targeted and punished. But it was such a tiny neighborhood bookstore, which carried only Mao's books in addition to some political propaganda booklets specially ordered by the government authorities during the first couple of years of the Cultural Revolution. Hardly any profit or tax to talk about, or it would not have been closed. And several neighbors confirmed that Mrs Ma actually had to do laundry for others to support the family.

Another possibility, though quite remote, was that of Mr Ma's 'bourgeois lifestyle'. A happy couple to all appearances, the Mas did not have a child – possibly because of her health problem. According to Confucius, one of the most unfilial things imaginable would be for a man to go without offspring, and for a bookworm like Mr Ma, that could have been a matter of crucial significance. But the neighbors also testified that it would have been out of the question for Mr Ma to carry on behind Mrs Ma's back; the two of them stayed together practically all the time, in the store, or in the tiny room at the back.

Partially because of Chen's unwavering effort, the people in the lane approached Comrade Jun, who refused to give out any straightforward information, simply reiterating that Ma had been arrested as a current counter-revolutionary, with the bookstore serving as 'a secret black center of anti-socialism activity'.

But with the location of the bookstore in the lane, whatever Mr Ma might have been doing there could have easily been seen by the neighbors through the open door at the front, and through the half-open door at the back. So they pressed Comrade Jun for a more detailed explanation, who then felt obliged to deliver a speech at a neighborhood meeting.

'According to Chairman Mao, the principal contradiction in our society is between the proletariat and the capitalist, and throughout China's socialist period the danger of capitalist restoration continues to exist, so awareness of the class struggle should be stressed day by day, month by month, and year by year. In the middle of the Cultural Revolution, it's a matter of course that the bookstore carries nothing but Mao books. But what could those bourgeois intellectuals have been doing in the bookstore before the outbreak of the Cultural Revolution? Mr Ma had customers staying there for hours, talking and discussing. Think about it, comrades. There're a lot of books anti-Party, and anti-socialism too.'

But some lane residents remained unconvinced. It was not uncommon for people to stand browsing in the bookstore for hours. They also detected something suspicious about Comrade Jun, who looked troubled in his effort to answer their questions. What's more, he seemed to be surreptitiously nice to Mrs Ma, who was not without a graceful charm in her early thirties. Considering Comrade Jun's Party cadre position, however, it did not appear likely that he would make a move on her. Still, there was no knowing for sure about one's motive, as in those Sherlock Holmes stories, Chen observed.

As a 'family member of a counter-revolutionary', Mrs Ma had nowhere to turn for help. One of the feasible remedies, as suggested by her neighbors, would be to divorce Mr Ma so she could start from scratch, securing a new class status, if nothing else, for herself. Those years, it was fairly common for a woman like her to denounce and divorce her husband if he was in overwhelming political trouble.

But she swore to wait for his return, despite all the political pressure. The front room – the bookstore – had been taken over by the neighborhood committee as a storage room for its propaganda material. Refusing to send the remaining books to the recycling center, she carried all of them into the back room, which had hardly any space left for her to move around in. Sleepless at night, she would sometimes play a simple tune from a tiny music box, her neighbors heard. Not a revolutionary song, but the music box was said to be a gift from Mr Ma in addition to all the dust-covered books.

'I'll keep the books until his return,' she declared. 'I can feel him in them.'

But she could not live on them. Nor could she find a job with such a current counter-revolutionary husband shadowing her all around. So it was Comrade Jun who came up with a job proposal for her in the neighborhood. To sweep the lane for the minimum pay – no more than seventy cents a day.

'It's necessary for us to carry out the proletarian dictatorship against the class enemy,' he said, 'but it does not mean that their family should starve to death.'

The job, though far from desirable, could have been seen as one created especially for her. Neither too heavy, nor requiring any particular skill. At the evening talk of the lane, some people could not help suspecting an ulterior motive behind the surprisingly 'humane' arrangement.

After urging from Chen as well as those neighbors, Old Root, a respected figure in the lane, also an erstwhile reading customer in the bookstore without buying a single copy, agreed to take a look into it.

Old Root dragged Comrade Jun out to a dumpling eatery on Zhejiang Road. There, after bowls of minced shrimp dumplings, a dish of sliced pig ears, and two bottles of nicely warmed sticky rice wine, Comrade Jun divulged that the trouble for Mr Ma could have come from his own meeting with Commissar Wen about two months earlier. Commissar Wen, a leading cadre in the district government, had held a meeting with a group of neighborhood cadres focusing on the latest trend in the class struggle emphasized by Chair Mao concerning the bourgeois intellectuals. As in the past, the new campaign during the Cultural Revolution had to meet a certain quota of class enemies for punishment. After the meeting, Commissar Wen questioned Comrade Jun about his silence during the discussion, and the latter came up with an excuse: 'Our lane is made mostly of ordinary people. No intellectuals, they're barely interested in anything out of the lane.'

It was a true statement, but not what Commissar Wen would have liked to hear. He sat frowning, his back as stiff as a bamboo pole.

'Not all the people in your lane could be that simple and innocent, Comrade Jun,' Commissar Wen said. 'Red Dust Lane is known for something called the "evening talk". I've heard quite a lot about it.'

'Oh, the evening talk is often for political studies,' Comrade Jun said nervously. 'In the summer, it's too hot for people to stay inside, so they sit outside talking or studying *Chairman Mao's Quotations* for a while before going to bed. As for any intellectuals in the lane, well, there's only one I can think of. Mr Ma, who runs a small bookstore. But not exactly an intellectual. Self-educated. Not even with a college education. Nothing but a bookseller, and a bookworm too. He keeps saying that it always benefits you to read books, but the bookstore was closed a couple of years ago.'

'It always benefits you to read books' was an old proverb. Comrade Jun did not see anything wrong in it.

But he was wrong.

'What books?' Commissar Wen demanded even more sternly. 'There are books and there are *books*, Comrade Jun. Class struggle is everywhere, even in a bookstore.' Commissar Wen added after an emphatic pause, 'As Chairman Mao has said, "It's a new invention to write a novel in conspiracy against the Party."'

'Like other state-run bookstores nowadays, Mr Ma's tiny store had nothing but Chairman Mao books during the days of the Cultural Revolution.'

'But what about the days before the Cultural Revolution? What about those books kept under the counter?'

What Comrade Jun said in response, he could hardly remember. He was too scared. But he kept wondering afterward whether his panic-stricken response had anything to do with the subsequent development at the bookstore, though he clung to the belief that he had not said anything incriminating. Nevertheless, Comrade Jun remained secretly guilty for what had happened to Mr Ma, which accounted for his offer of help to Mrs Ma.

Comrade Jun kept shaking his head at the end of the dumpling meal. Old Root ordered another bottle of rice wine and poured out a small cup for him.

'As long as you have not done anything wrong, Comrade Jun, you don't have to worry about devils knocking at your door at night.'

'I've made enquiries about that raid. The special police found some books Mr Ma had had before the Cultural Revolution. Among them, a foreign language novel particularly incriminated him. According to Chairman Mao's instruction about the class struggle in China, those should be Chinese novels. But the one in question was not a Chinese novel. That really beats me.'

'What novel?'

'A book about a doctor surnamed Qi . . . Qi Wage, not that likely a Chinese name, but then those intellectuals could have made up strange names, you know.'

Neither of them had ever heard of the book before, or of the doctor, either. Anyway, it was said that the higher authorities had ordered Mr Ma to be jailed – a decision in the light of Chairman Mao's class struggle theory.

'No, I don't want to cause trouble for anybody, Comrade Jun,' Old Root said, adding a large pinch of black pepper to the remaining dumpling soup. 'It's just that I too read a book or two for free those days before the Cultural Revolution. Mr Ma never said anything about it. And Mrs Ma is such a pitiable woman.'

'I know,' Comrade Jun said. 'That's why I've tried to help her.'

Days and then weeks passed like the water in the gutter near the lane entrance. At the end of the summer, the mystery remained unsolved. Far, far away in Beijing, Mao repeated his warning about the danger of capitalist restoration through literature and art. As the head of the neighborhood committee, Comrade Jun declared that it would be in everybody's interest not to talk any more about Mr Ma. The political weather had been changing so drastically, no one could be too careful.

Old Root concurred in the evening talk of the lane, unfolding for dramatic effect a white paper fan, which bore a line written by Zheng Banqiao, a Qing dynasty scholar: 'It's not easy to be ignorant.'

'The line is so cynically brilliant. Indeed, an old maxim put it so well: "Once a man starts reading and writing, he gets totally confused."'

'But people have to know,' Chen said, not yet ready to give up.

'For so many things in the world, you may never find the final explanation. Why bother that much?'

Chen's continuous effort was not without any result, though. He learned at least an anecdote about Mr Ma.

Mr Ma had made one request from prison: to have some books brought in for him from the closed bookstore. Another surprise considering the cause of his trouble. The warden granted it on the condition that Mr Ma could have only one book, and not a literary one.

Then, Chen succeeded in learning something else from a schoolmate whose father was a senior officer in the city police bureau. According to the cop, the book in question had been banned in the Soviet Union. A Russian novel about a Russian doctor. *Doctor Zhivago*. Being a foreign language book, it must have somehow escaped the police radar before the Cultural Revolution. Chen wondered how such a novel, not yet translated into Chinese, could have harmed socialist China, but he knew better than to talk to the people about it in the evening talk of Red Dust Lane.

Old Root had commented that Chen was 'like a good detective', but also tipped him off that some people had begun to pay extra attention to him. After all, he was not a resident of the lane, but just a regular to the evening talks of late.

Chen was alarmed. And he decided not to appear again in the audience of the evening talk, at least not for a while. One late December morning, during his last visit to the lane for Mr Ma's case, he happened to see Mrs Ma sweeping through the lane with a rough bamboo-slice broom, which loomed taller than her.

It was a cold afternoon. He shivered. And he thought of those days of his standing and reading in the bookstore for free, taking a cup of hot tea from her. He tried to say something, but without success.

The next moment, she vanished out of sight.

Nothing but a fallen yellow leaf stuck to a wet corner of the lane.

In a Tang dynasty poem, a fallen leaf awash in a rain pool served as a metaphor for a forsaken woman's loneliness, but he failed to recall whether he had read the poem in Mr Ma's bookstore.

THREE

*H*e is spellbound by the sight of a blue-headed fly buzzing around a sticky stain – perhaps merely a suggestion of a stain – on the wooden dining table underneath the attic. Unable to tell what the brownish smudge really is, he keeps gazing at the dramatic scene, holding his breath as if obsessed. Every time a hand is seen raising up above the table, the fly drones away in a hurry, only to return a couple of seconds later, circling like a cliché around the same spot. Finally, it seems to somehow get stuck on the suspicious stain on the table, still insistently humming, when the hand hacks down with a bang that comes with a mysterious red fireball flickering behind a lone curtain flapping against the surrounding darkness—

The dream was shattered by a dog barking violently in the night. Chen failed to remember other details, other than the inscrutable fly buzzing, flitting around the stain and the hand reaching out of nowhere.

But it was strange to hear a dog barking in the neighborhood. For so many years under Mao, the concept of pet-keeping had been condemned as one of the Western bourgeois decadences. Chinese people kept cats at home, not as pets, but for the one and only purpose of catching rats. Comrade Deng Xiaoping had once made a well-known statement: 'Whether it's a black or white cat, it's a good one as long as it catches the rat.' At the beginning of China's reform in the early 1980s, paradoxically, it was a much-quoted metaphor meaning a pragmatist approach, regardless of its being capitalistic or socialistic, in the new market economy advocated by Deng.

But in those earlier days, people did not keep dogs at home – not in a crowded city like Shanghai. Dogs served no practical purpose, not to mention the expense of the dog food. However, things had been changing so fast in China and it now served as an emblem of one's social status to keep pets. So a dog must have found its way into a relatively poor neighborhood like his mother's.

Alternatively, could he have dreamed of a dog barking in the depth of the night?

He checked himself, rubbing his dreamy eyes, before he was hit by another thought: like the fly clinging to the dubious stain, he too could have been stuck in a job for reasons beyond his comprehension.

Propped up against two pillows, he lit a cigarette. It was a bad idea to smoke in the attic, he knew, but he had to concentrate – hoping against hope that the nicotine might prove helpful to his thinking – on what he could do in the event of his making a visit to Red Dust Lane next morning, as Detective Yu had suggested.

Absentmindedly, he pulled the cellphone out from under the pillow again. Sure enough, another short message had come from Detective Yu:

'The Red Dust Lane resident is surnamed Huyan.'

Detective Yu must have been working late into the night. And the message appeared to be unmistakable this time. Huyan would be the one Chen had to approach in the lane.

With Huyan being a rare surname, he tried to recall the lane residents he had met or known during those years. To his dismay, he failed to remember anyone surnamed Huyan.

It would not do for him, however, to tap the neighborhood committee for help, as Internal Security must have already been there. Any move on his part would only serve to alarm his adversaries.

And even if he somehow located Huyan in the lane, the netizen must be under close watch. It would be extremely difficult, if not impossible, for him to approach Huyan on the sly, undetected by the radar of Internal Security.

And what would Huyan be able to tell him? He was probably just an ordinary lane resident who'd happened to read that poem online and place a *like* emoji before the post was blocked, and then detected by Webcops.

Besides, how could a poem have turned out to be such a big deal in an age when few people were interested in poetry?

'There are more things in heaven and earth, Inspector Chen,

/ *Than are dreamed of in your poetry.*' What was behind the case of the anti-Party poem, he had no clue. He had not even read the poem.

So could the stain in the dream have predicted something?

In Chinese folk literature, dreams could sometimes point out the direction for people like Judge Dee or Judge Bao to follow in their investigations. He had read a number of dreams like that in *Gong'an* stories in classical Chinese literature. So was he meant to return to that same spot, Red Dust Lane, without knowing why and how, just like the thoughtless fly against the backdrop of the enigmatic curtain illuminated with a red fireball?

The night was sinking deeper into silence. He tried hard one more time to focus his thoughts on the possibilities waiting for him in Red Dust Lane, to no avail.

For all his efforts, his mind was a total blank.

Perhaps he should make a visit to Bund Park next morning, before heading to the lane. In the early 1970s, the park had witnessed a crucial turning point for him as he started studying English there. According to his friends, the park was an auspicious feng shui place for him. He had since visited and revisited it a considerable number of times. It was not just out of nostalgia, for it helped him to think more clearly during difficult investigations. He would review the details of cases in his mind while walking around the park, breathing in the tangy air characteristic of the river, just like during those days of his English studies.

Those days, had he ever heard a dog barking on the way to the park, he wondered again, suppressing a yawn with his fist.

Bund Park

C hen was the youngest in the audience at the evening talk in front of Red Dust Lane. He knew many of those in the lane did not know much about his black family background, so he did not have to worry about it there.

The contents of the evening talk had to change with the times, of course, particularly so in the middle of the Cultural Revolution in the early 70s. It was out of the question for people to say anything remotely 'feudalist, bourgeois and revisionist'. In fact, the time-honored convention of the lane would have been banned but for the intervention of Old Root, one of the most experienced narrators there, who managed to keep the evening talk alive by tailoring it into a sort of political studies class, waving a Little Red Book of *Quotations of Chairman Mao* in his hand. Being a worker in his class status, Old Root was capable of pulling a trick or two with impunity.

For instance, he made a point of choosing the stories mentioned favorably by Marx, Engels, Lenin, Stalin or Mao as a sort of political endorsement, so the Red Guards in the neighborhood had to think twice about finding fault with it. That evening, after declaring that Marx quoted from Dante's *Divine Comedy* on the front page of *Capital*, he recounted a romantic episode from the masterpiece.

'Marx could read Italian?' Chen asked.

'Of course he could. For *Capital*, Marx had to conduct research in more than ten languages. "Follow your own course and let others talk," that's exactly the quote from Dante. And Marx said on another occasion, "A foreign language is a useful weapon for your battle in life."'

Afterwards, when most of the audience had left, Chen remained sitting on the bamboo stool, looking up to see the

night clouds floating aimlessly across the sky like a scroll of
the traditional Chinese landscape.

He was not such a young boy any more, he told himself.
He came to the evening talk because of the exciting stories
told there, but more because he had no idea about what to do
with himself at the moment.

He had just graduated from Yaojin Middle School. It coincided with the onset of the national movement of 'educated
youths going to the countryside for re-education from the
poor and lower-middle class peasants', a political campaign
launched by Mao to send millions of young people from the
big cities to the poor rural areas, where they were supposed
to reform themselves through hard labor. Still, a certain
number of young people remained in the city because of
health problems – real or not real – including Chen, who
happened to be suffering from bronchitis. They were consequently classified as 'waiting-for-recovery youths', which
meant they still had to leave the city upon recovery for the
far-away, impoverished countryside.

Now, out of school, out of a job, waiting, with no light visible
at the end of the long, long tunnel, he worried himself sick.

Later that evening, he had a talk with Yingchang, a resident
in Red Dust Lane. Two or three years his senior, Yingchang
was not counted as an 'educated youth' and had been assigned
to a job in a state-run factory in Shanghai before the movement began.

Yingchang suggested they go to Bund Park in the morning
to practice tai chi, a popular exercise, and 'politically OK'
too. The park was not far from the lane. Chen jumped at the
suggestion.

As it turned out, several other young people in the lane
were also interested in the idea. The next morning saw Chen
joining them and setting out for the park.

It was a small group. Yingchang was eager to find an outlet
for his young energy, which was being laid to waste in the
dead-water-like factory. Sissy Huang joined simply because
he followed Yingchang everywhere like a tail. Meili, an
attractive woman in her early thirties, having recently divorced
and turned in her immigration application to Hong Kong, had

nothing else to do for the moment in the city of Shanghai, so she also joined them. Weiming, another waiting-for-recovery youth like Chen, who looked like the eldest of the group because of his premature white hair, tagged along as well.

As they were filing out of the lane, Chen heard several cocks crowing in succession. It was against the government policy to raise chickens in the city, but facing the severe food shortages, those capable Shanghai housewives managed to keep chickens out of sight in the secret corners of their *shikumen* houses. After all, there were far more important things for the neighborhood committee cadres to worry about those days.

'Like in an old proverb, we practice sword to the cock's crow,' Chen said, his steps quickening at the recollection of an ancient legend. In the third century, a young hero practiced sword the moment a cock started crowing at dawn.

'Well, people play tai chi sword in the park too,' Yingchang commented.

The park was an attraction in itself. In spite of its small size, the location made it popular to Shanghai people. Its front gate faced the Peace Hotel across Zhongshan Road and its back gate adjoined the Waibaidu Bridge, a name unchanged since its construction in the colonial era, meaning *'foreigners cross the bridge for free'*. At the Bund's northern end, the park opened to a curving promenade above the expanse of water joining the Huangpu and Suzhou Rivers, along with a panoramic view of vessels coming and going against the distant East China Sea.

In the school textbook, Chen had read that at the turn of the century the park had been open only to Western expatriates, with red-turbaned Sikh guards standing at the entrance, and a large sign on the gate saying: *No Chinese or dogs allowed.* True story or not, it was included in the history book for the sake of patriotism education.

But Chen found it difficult to keep himself in high spirits, in spite of the ancient proverbs or the legend of the park.

In a small clearing called 'tai chi square', he soon came to the realization that tai chi did not become him. It emphasized slow rather than fast movements, subduing the hard by being the soft in accordance with the ancient Taoist yin-yang

principle. He was too young, and too restless. While others
made rapid progress, he stumbled, wrecking one pose after
another. With him, 'a white crane spreading its wings' actually
turned into 'a white crane breaking its wings'.

As for his friends from Red Dust Lane, they did not come
to the park just for the sake of tai chi. Meili began to meet
with a married man nicknamed 'horse face', a melancholy-
looking man with a long face, carrying a Japanese camera
with an unmistakable suggestion of being fashionable. She
posed for him with a Hong Kong umbrella twirling in the
sunlight, leaning her upper body precariously over the water,
her cheeks flushing, her smile blossoming into the flashing
camera. Yingchang had his eye on a girl in a different tai chi
group. Without having learned her name, he nicknamed her
'graceful', in reference to her pose in *tuishou*, a push-hand
exercise he practiced with her palms to palms, pushing and
being pushed in a slow, spontaneous flow, their bodies moving
together in a seemingly effortless motion. The moment she
became aware of his ulterior motive, however, she rotated her
left forearm to ward off his advance, and he lost balance,
staggering, falling flat amidst people's laughter.

Chen saw no point in continuing to spend his mornings
like that. Standing by the river, he recalled several lines from
a Song dynasty *ci* poem, scanning the mist-mantled horizon
in the distance: *'East flows the grand river, / the celebrated
names rising and falling / through waves upon waves / for
thousands of years . . .'*

Like another Chinese proverb, there's no story without
coincidence.

To the left of the tai chi square, Chen saw a young girl
sitting quietly on a green-painted bench holding a book in her
hand, her shoulder-length black hair occasionally rumpled by
the breeze from the river. She read in absorption, paying
little attention to the people moving around. Behind her, the
glistening dew drops clung to the verdant foliage, like myriad
bright eyes waking up to the morning light in curiosity.

It was an uncommon scene. A popular political slogan
those days declared that 'It's useless to study', an ideological
notion that underlay the movement of educated youths to the

countryside. Judging by the red plastic book cover, it would most likely be a copy of the *Selected Works of Mao* in her hand. However, she had on the bench a smaller book, which she picked up from time to time.

Usually, she arrived among the earliest regulars in the park around six, where she stayed until eleven. In all probability, she was another waiting-for-recovery youth out of school, out of work, just like Chen.

People could not help casting looks in her direction. Yingchang, too, came to walk around that bench, like a lone crow circling a night tree. According to his close-range observation, the smaller book was an English–Chinese dictionary, and the book in her hand turned out not to be the *Selected Works of Mao*, but an English textbook, for which she used the red plastic cover for camouflage. It was not too difficult to understand such a trick. Red-armbanded park patrollers could storm over at any moment demanding: '*For what purpose are you studying English in the days of Cultural Revolution?*'

That posed no question to Chen, though. For the future, in which she believed, he believed.

The girl appeared to be more than strikingly attractive, wearing a long red jacket, like blossom against the verdant foliage around her, her large, clear eyes looking up from the book, radiating with an inner beauty.

For him, she made the scene of the park.

The morning was enveloped in a light mist. Chen saw the young girl glance up from her books. Their eyes met for a second. She was wearing a pink sweater, silhouetted against the white clouds drifting over the river. Aware of his gaze, she hung her head low with a shy smile, like a lotus flower swaying soft, supple, in a cool breeze. It somehow reminded him of a short poem by Xu Zhimo:

> *Softly, you hang your head low,*
> *like a water lily,*
> *shy, trembling in a cool breeze,*
> *farewell, farewell,*
> *with sweet sadness in your voice*
> *S A Y O U N A R A.*

Then he saw a stout, gray-haired old man shambling over to sit beside her on the bench. It was not uncommon for people to share a bench in the park, but she seemed to start reading with the old man nodding beside, murmuring and pointing at her open book, almost imperceptibly, when no one else was around.

So the old man was giving instruction in her English studies. Those days, English teaching in a public place could have appeared suspicious. Hence the deceptive appearance of the two – like strangers who happened to be sitting on the same park bench.

If she could choose to study English for the future, what about him? He felt so ashamed, all of a sudden, about wasting his time like that.

So he decided that instead of admiring her from a distance, he too was going to consult the old man with questions in his English studies.

But English textbooks were not available in bookstores or libraries those days. He managed to get a set of the College English from his uncle, who had succeeded in transforming himself into an ordinary worker, but who had managed to hide all the college textbooks in a cardboard box under the bed.

Early the next morning, Chen came to the park with a copy of the first-year College English textbook, and chose an unpainted wooden bench not far from the girl's.

The change in the morning routine kept him away from his tai chi friends, who came up with all sorts of interpretations for the abrupt shift on his part. In their eyes, he must have fallen for the girl on the green bench, but instead of openly approaching her, he was making just a pathetic attempt to catch her attention. Yingchang took the initiative on his behalf, which turned out to be unsuccessful. Without giving any details, Yingchang simply dubbed her as 'Ice-and-Frost Cold', a negative nickname suggestive of her unapproachableness.

'That's not what I mean, Yingchang,' Chen protested, 'not at all.'

But that made him even more nervous about approaching her. Whatever the motivation for his shift from tai chi to English, he just hoped that he would be able, one of those mornings, to speak to her in a language understandable only to themselves.

His mother became worried about his longer stays in the park, but his father calculated that it might prove to be propitious for the young man, elaborating on his favorite theory of five elements.

'The character for his name Cao is similar to Zao, which means dryness. Too much soil and fire, no water at all,' his father said feebly, sick in detention. 'But Bund Park, a place in close association with water, could prove to be beneficial.'

In the park, the old man sitting beside the girl on the green bench, surnamed Rong, was a retired English teacher. The outbreak of the Cultural Revolution had cut short his teaching career, and he'd ended up coming to the park, practicing tai chi, and offering help to young people there instead. He readily took Chen as another student.

Mr Rong made a point, however, of talking with only one of his students at a time, wary of being seen as a teacher in the park. There was no chance for the girl and Chen to sit together on the same green bench. But that was fine with Chen. No hurry for that.

The knowledge of her being there in the same park, with the book open on her lap, made it possible for him to progress in leaps and bounds. He kept marveling at the subtle change in her in the morning light. One moment she was a graceful 'bluestocking' nibbling at the top of a black fountain pen, the next she was a vivacious young Shanghai girl wearing a light green jade charm with a thin red string over her bosom, curling her sandaled feet underneath her. Behind the bench, a European-style pavilion with its white verandah stood out in colorful relief.

It took him less than two months to finish the first volume of the College English. Mr Rong was so impressed that he chose to spend more and more time with him. He was catching up with the girl, he thought.

Then one morning at the beginning of early September, to his surprise, she did not come to the green bench as usual.

He did not think too much of it, not initially. Unlike in

school, people did not have to appear in the park each and
every morning.

But a week passed without seeing her stepping light-
footedly across the cobble trail to the green bench. What could
have happened to her? There was hardly any way for him to
find out.

Another week. Still no sight of her. He became worried.

He asked Mr Rong, who did not know anything about her
sudden disappearance. He did not know her address. Perhaps
somewhere close to the park, that was about all the old man
could tell Chen.

Once again, the group from Red Dust Lane were eager to
offer their interpretations about her evaporation into thin air,
as well as about its possible consequence. Waving a cigarette
like a magician's wand, Yingchang predicted that Chen would
now come back to tai chi.

But Chen went on with his English studies as before,
glancing up from the book from time to time at the unoccupied
green bench.

Weeks, then months, passed. Not far from the park bench,
the river flowed on, with white gulls hovering above the waves,
their wings flashing against the gray light, as if soaring out of
a half-forgotten dream. More than once, he did not leave the
park until the dividing line between the Huangpu and Suzhou
Rivers became invisible in the gathering dusk.

One day she would come back, he believed, to find him
still sitting there on the bench close to hers. They would then
speak to each other in English.

The members of the Red Dust group began to drop out, one
by one, like leaves with the arrival of the autumn wind. None
of them turned into a martial arts master.

Chen was the only one left in the park when he started
studying the third volume of the College English. Mr Rong,
too, appeared less and less because of his high blood pressure
in the cold weather, but Chen managed to continue studying
by himself.

One afternoon, he mounted a flight of stone steps to the
bank. To his right, he saw a white-haired man practicing tai
chi, wearing a white silk martial arts costume, loose-sleeved,

red-silk-buttoned, moving in perfect harmony with the *qi* of the universe, striking a series of poses, the names of which Chen still remembered: *grasping a bird's tail, spreading a white crane's wings, strumming the pipa lute, parting a wild horse's mane on both sides* . . .

Would he have turned into such a master had he persisted in practicing tai chi, he wondered, breathing in the familiar tangy air from the waterfront.

Standing there, he opened the book in his hand. It was an English novel titled *Random Harvest* in which there were still a considerable number of words he did not truly understand, although he managed to follow the storyline. It had been made into a movie, he had heard, with a romantic title for the Chinese version: *Reunion of Mandarin Ducks*. The water birds were symbolic of lovers in classical Chinese culture.

This, as well as some other English novels and poems, had opened for him a brave new world that was unknown and unimaginable before.

A fitful wind was tearing at the pages of *Random Harvest*. It was not a good spot for him to read. He closed the book with a sigh. Looking over his shoulder, he suddenly saw her again – still in the pink sweater, sitting on the same bench, the bush behind trembling eerily in the breeze.

Halfway down the steps, he had to acknowledge to himself that it was another young girl, carrying a genuine Little Red Book in her hand.

The morning in the arms of Bund, her hair dew-sparkled . . .

He thought of the ending of the English novel in which Paula ran over the hills toward Smith in England, and prayed that the miracle could prove to be real in Bund Park, too.

Evidence of Youth

D ong Haiming was born with a passion for photography, as people usually said in Red Dust Lane. It came from his father, a *Wenhui* photo journalist killed in a car accident in 1957 while on duty, just one day before his being officially labeled as a 'rightist' for picturing the seamy side of socialist China. Some of his colleagues even suspected that it had been a suicide staged as an accident for the benefit of his young wife Juqing and their little son.

Dong was just turning two at the time. At his father's funeral he was a toddler, dragging his step, tugging at the black-creped sleeve of his mother, who held in front of her bosom a black-framed picture of his father as she walked, sobbing, back into Red Dust Lane.

Following his father's death, his would-be rightist status was rumored to have been kept secret in the governmental archive. And Juqing changed her son's surname to Dong – her maiden name – instead of that of his father. Without getting to the bottom of the reason for her doing so, the neighbors supposed that it was understandable for a young attractive woman like her to think about marrying somebody else and moving out of the lane.

More than a decade later, Juqing remained a widow in the lane, and Dong was state-assigned a job at a seedy tavern near the intersection of Henan and Nanjing Roads. It was in the middle of the Cultural Revolution, with Chairman Mao's revolutionary campaign slogan of 'the educated youths going to the countryside for the re-education from the poor and lower-middle class peasants' resounding all over the city. So Dong had to consider himself lucky getting such a job in Shanghai, ladling out the yellow rice wine, Shao sticky rice wine, double rice wine and Maiden Red wine from those ancient earthen urns stacked against the discolored, mildew-covered wall.

When he returned from his first day at work at the tavern with despondence written on his face, Juqing presented to him an old, leather-cased 'Seagull' camera, the only thing of value left behind by his father.

The Seagull flashed unexpectedly brightly against the drabness of his job. Dong kept the camera a secret from the lane. For one thing, a camera those days was commonly regarded as part and parcel of bourgeois extravagance. And besides, it was something of too great an emotional value for him to share with the neighbors at random. He made a point of carrying it with him concealed in a small black shoulder bag.

But the camera also proved to be more and more of a white elephant for him, with his monthly pay barely enough for a dozen rolls of film, not to mention the expense of picture development and enlargement at the studio. Providentially, he discovered among his father's things a time-yellowed photography booklet, the information from which enabled him to convert the attic into a darkroom whenever he needed.

It turned out to be an easy job of two or three simple steps: pull up the ladder, cover the attic opening with a sliding board and the window with a deep-colored curtain, and change the bulb to a red one when everything was ready. It surely saved a lot of money for him. When it was too late at night, he would simply sleep on the floor of the attic/darkroom without climbing down the squeaky ladder. He did not want to wake his mother. He actually enjoyed a sense of privacy there, though it was not comfortable for him to lie, tossing and turning, on the hard floor.

Like other young people, he started dating in due course, falling hard for a pretty girl named Lanlan from Treasure Garden Lane, which was three or four blocks away on Jinling Road.

Juqing was overjoyed. After the death of her husband, the only meaningful thing for her to do in the world of red dust, she declared to her neighbors in the lane, was to see Dong get married and have his own family. It was by no means easy, though. They had just one single room of twelve square feet. The attic, in which no one could stand up straight without hitting his or her head against the darkened cedar beam, did not count. A pretty young girl would have balked at the prospect of climbing up the shaky ladder and dating him there, with any possible sound audible to the would-be-mother-in-law below. Still, Lanlan proved to be the one that came over a second time, and then a third . . .

There's no knowing what she saw in Dong. According to Dong himself, Lanlan too was really interested in photography, but the neighbors wondered about it.

The topic of marriage still too far in the future, Dong and Lanlan had a more immediate problem on their hands: a private space for their budding affair.

Billing and cooing with Juqing in the room was far from desirable. So they ventured out to parks, all of which turned out to be overcrowded, with at least two pairs of lovers nestling up against each other on one single bench, and with the red-armbanded park patrols prowling in high alert, ready to pounce on any 'suspects' who might get carried away in the passion of the 'bourgeois lifestyle', huddled and hidden in the shady corners. Those days, people displaying pre-nuptial intimacy such as a kiss or a hug could have been charged with criminal behavior. As a last resort, Dong dragged Lanlan up the ladder, precariously, into the attic.

Juqing, a traditional, virtuous woman in the eyes of her neighbors, felt rather uneasy about the two of them staying up there alone. But Dong came up with an excuse, declaring that they were simply developing pictures in the attic. It was true sometimes, but there was also something else he chose to hold back from Juqing.

Lanlan, like some girls of her age, wanted to have her youthful moments captured in pictures, so she posed in the attic – in scanty dresses, in swimming suits, and in a white bath towel too, her slim body stretching out, like supple clouds gently rolling, dissolving into soft rain.

'Evidence of youth,' she whispered, her hair brushing his cheek.

And precious evidence they appeared to be, as a state-run

photography studio could have turned those pictures in to the authorities as 'evidence of decadence'. That made the attic darkroom even more attractive to Lanlan.

As for Dong, shooting and developing pictures there, with her humming tunes beside him, '*Youth is like a bird, / it perches, and flies,*' he found the attic a paradise.

One Saturday afternoon in May, Lanlan called into the Red Dust Public Phone Service, leaving a message through a mobile service woman named Caixiang, who trotted over to a spot underneath Dong's window and shouted loudly with a battery horn, 'I'm coming over this evening. The red curtain as usual. Lanlan.'

Upon getting the message, Dong set out to make the necessary preparations for the evening. He bought used liquid concentrate at a discount from Guanlong Camera on Nanjing Road, having tried the cheap concentrate with acceptable results. On the way, he also purchased a bag of black coffee dregs from Deda Cafe. He had never tried them, but they were said to be still stimulating at a price affordable to him. They might stay up quite late. Coffee could add a romantic touch to the night, breathing aromatics in association with the so-called Western lifestyle.

Lanlan arrived after dinner. They lost no time climbing up into the tiny attic. With the small window covered, the opening boarded, the two of them felt so secure, yet soon, so hot and stuffy up there.

Sweating profusely, Dong ended up donning just a beater and boxers. Lanlan still wore the skirt, but shed the blouse, leaving only a tank top on.

Time really flies on a spring-intoxicated night. Much more so in a secure darkroom, the water rippling in the plastic basin, her bare shoulders gleaming against the shadows on the wall, their hands touching lightly, the red-draped window blushing back at them.

In spite of the promise made to Juqing that they would never cross the boundary, Dong found it hard to contain himself, being constantly aware of her soft hand meeting his under the aura of the red bulb, caressing the images which began appearing gradually in the papers in the water, like the

miracle of their passion. But the spell was shattered all of a
sudden by a commotion breaking out downstairs.

'Open up!'

'The police!'

'The neighborhood security!'

The retractable ladder landed down in haste, and the raiders
rushed up helter-skelter. It did not take long for them to turn
the whole attic upside down, searching around with the two
lovers stunned, huddled up in a corner, he having snatched
back on only his pants, and she having mislaid her blouse.

A highly suspicious scene presented itself there, what with
the two in scanty clothing, with the mattress in disarray
on the floor, and with the plastic basin occupying the only
chair in the semi-darkness.

A neighborhood security activist put his finger into the water
in the basin, questioning its possible purpose. Another activist
nicknamed 'Hunchback Fang' examined the coffee, sniffing
at it like a dog. Finally, an elderly neighborhood cop surnamed
Peng noticed the pictures floating in the basin.

'Damn,' Peng said, glancing at the red bulb, picking up
from the basin a picture of the two kissing each other on the
Bund, and shaking his head with the picture still dripping.
'It's not at all what you thought.'

Whatever the cop's comment could have meant, any move
taken in the name of the proletarian dictatorship had to appear
correct and justified. The fact that the two half-clad young
people were caught alone in the attic appeared to be incriminating enough. In spite of the equipment that supported Dong's
statement about their having picture development tools in the
attic darkroom, Hunchback Fang exploded.

'What were the two of you really doing up here, with the
window covered up, the red light blinking, you in your beater
and she in her top? You two are not married yet, are you?'

The two shuddered at the accusation for which they could
have been put into custody in the neighborhood police
station. To their surprise, Peng signaled Hunchback Fang
and others to leave without any further ado, except that he
turned round to put several still-wet pictures into a plastic
bag. As evidence, presumably.

A bunch of damaged pictures left behind stared back at the two lovers left alone in the attic. Because of their exposure to light, most of them were now totally black – like their imaginable future.

Juqing was heard sobbing inconsolably in the room below.

In the age of Chairman Mao's class struggle, a 'black stain' like that would never be washed away.

For days, weeks and months afterward, what had happened in the attic that May night hung over their heads like a sword capable of falling down at any moment. They suspected that their respective companies, having been notified about it, must be working closely with the police bureau to measure out the punishment.

At the tavern, Dong could barely keep the ladle steady while selling customers the wine. Back at the lane, he felt like a naked rat trying to scurry through the speculations that began enclosing around with barbed wire. Lanlan too fell prey to the continuous trepidation, so nervous that she chose not to step into Red Dust Lane again.

No matter what the people in the lane might be imagining or gossiping, no one could say for sure what the two were really up to in the attic that night. But irreparable damage had been done, particularly to Lanlan as a young girl. In her neighborhood, not too far away, wild stories surfaced like uncontrollable weeds, spreading over from Red Dust Lane, making any prospective young man hesitate about approaching her in Treasure Garden Lane.

About three months later, the two young people gave in to the unbearable pressure of uncertainty. They turned in their marriage application to the district civil bureau. It was not so much a move to make themselves a virtuous couple, but a desperate attempt to bring an end to the suspense. If the application was rejected, it meant serious trouble was still in store for them, but at least they would no longer feel suspended like forsaken balloons in the air.

To their pleasant astonishment, they got the license without any questions at the civil bureau. So the wedding came to be the order of the day for the two of them, a surprise for a lane full of surprises.

The young couple saw no point in having a grand wedding party in the lane. The neighbors would take it as a belated cover-up anyway. Lanlan simply moved in without as much as a five-minute fanfare of firecrackers under the attic window. It happened to be politically correct, ironically, as the government were re-emphasizing the proletarian lifestyle in the newspapers.

Juqing delivered a tiny bag of wedding candy in person to Comrade Jun, the head of the neighborhood committee, who readily accepted it with a broad grin. Another reassuring signal to her. Back home that night, she heaved a long sigh of relief while lying in bed listening to the creaking from the attic overhead, where the newlyweds tossed and turned with a tremulous cadence. Like the roar of pebbles, the sleepless, darksome waves kept flinging out and drawing back anew at return, beginning, ceasing, and then again beginning.

She murmured her late husband's name in the dark. Perhaps their child could carry his surname again in the not too distant future, she prayed.

So grateful for Buddha's blessing, Juqing reverentially lit a bunch of tall incense in front of the clay image, placed a platter of fresh fruit, and kowtowed for more than fifteen minutes before she dug out the picture of her late husband, the same black-framed portrait she had held in front of her bosom when walking back into the lane, taking the hand of her son, still a toddler, about twenty years earlier . . .

Lanlan turned out to be an exceptionally filial daughter-in-law. She was not only willing to stay in the retrofitted attic with Dong on the same old mattress with no bedframe – though with a new sheet – but to also carry down the chamber pot for cleaning early in the morning, to start the fire on a coal briquette stove out in the lane, and to make breakfast for the family like other good young wives there.

Despite the lingering stories about the dubious circumstance of the two coming to tie the knot, it did not take long for them to settle down just like other young couples in Red Dust Lane.

If anything still struck their neighbors as slightly different about the two, it was that their attic window could appear covered with a red curtain once in a while, reminiscent of that eventful night. Thanks to their changed status, however, the neighbors now seemed to consider it quite understandable for the young couple to fancy a bright colored curtain for their shabby attic window.

Time dripped away, drop by drop, barely noticed by the residents of the lane, just like water from the worn-out public faucet under that occasionally red-curtained window, as if in an unwavering effort to wash away any traces of what had so inexplicably happened that May night.

Still, the mystery of the red curtain remained.

'Neighborhood cop Peng has retired,' Old Root concluded in the evening talk of the lane. 'So no one could explain what really happened that night. But why should we worry about it? Indeed, all's well that ends well. Juqing is going to be a grandma soon. And Dong has recently had some pictures of his on display in an exhibition.'

FOUR

Waking up again in the increasingly surreal night, Chen blinked his eyes in the dark, with the remnants of the dream still blurring in a swirl . . .

He is receiving a grand poetry prize on the brightly lit stage of a prestigious library, reading a poem from his newly released collection:

> *Master Zhuang awakes*
> *wondering if it is he who dreamed*
> *of being a butterfly, or if it is*
> *butterfly that dreams of being*
> *Master Zhuang—*

The reading is abruptly disrupted, however, by droves of red-armbanded Rebels and Red Guards, who burst in like crazy, tearing and burning books, beating and kicking at the audience, singing and chanting the thunderous Cultural Revolution songs . . .

The next moment, he finds himself still standing on the stage, but turning into his father, a target of the revolutionary mass criticism during the Cultural Revolution, drowning in the angry waves of the slogans the Red Guards are shouting, his head bent low with a large blackboard hung around his neck declaring: 'Down with the counter-revolutionary poet in the frenzied attacks against the Party government . . .'

For several seconds, he failed to shake off the feeling of the nagging nightmare. It was an uncanny night of repeatedly broken sleep, invaded with one foreboding dream scene after another. Was this the third or fourth time that he had woken up in a startle in the attic?

For some unknown reason, he wanted to grapple with the question implied in the dream.

The poem had probably been inspired by a fable from Master

Zhuang, a celebrated Taoist philosopher in ancient China. The metaphysical reflection about the interchangeable identities of the man waking under the ash tree and the butterfly soaring in the sunlight, as it seemed to Chen, posed a modernist or postmodernist question.

To put it simply, what was one meant to be?

For so many years, that had not even been considered as a question in China. Each and every person is nothing but 'a screw fixed on the socialist state machine', as declared by the Communist role model Comrade Lei Feng.

This was the pervading view, with the possible exception of one short period, perhaps, when some young people questioned the political correctness of being a selfless screw at the disposal of the Party. After the ending of the Cultural Revolution in 1976, the official newspapers started talking about the 'liberation of the mind', though only in a very limited way. It coincided with Chen's enrolment at Beijing Foreign Language University in 1977, through the first college entrance examination restored after the Cultural Revolution. Like other young people at the time, he was so infused with the idealistic enthusiasm for China's reform that he too started dreaming of self-realization, a term newly introduced into the Chinese language. A professor at the Beijing university discussed his future plans after graduation, and encouraged him to pursue a literary career, which he would be able to wholeheartedly embrace, he believed, in the post-Cultural Revolution China.

So Chen started writing and translating poems, and before long he became known for his modernist style in a small circle. But just as in a Song dynasty poem written by Xin Qiji – '*Again, the spring leaves / so soon, unable to sustain / the wind and rain any longer*' – the real splendor of the spring lasts only for a short period of time.

In existentialism, self-realization comes through making one's choices and taking the consequences. In China, however, it was not up to him to make the choices. On the contrary, the choices were pushed onto him.

And what was worse, one's identity or being could always be changed with the changes in China's political discourse.

'Being is an empty fiction,' as Nietzsche put it – like the poet, like the chief inspector . . .

But he hastened to channel his thoughts away from abstract ruminations. Sitting up, he resisted the temptation for another cigarette.

Still, how had he come to the dream of reading the poem on the stage prior to turning into a target for the proletarian denunciation? The first part of the dream was not difficult to interpret. But could the second part have reflected his anxiety about his fall from favor in the Party system? Not a poet, nor a chief inspector, but a target of the 'proletarian dictatorship' like his father in an earlier dream of the night. It was not unimaginable. The slogans of the Cultural Revolution kept echoing in the present-day China. In fact, more and more people were talking about the possibility of a second Cultural Revolution.

And what could he hope to accomplish by going to the lane the next morning? With the persecution and punishment of dissidents – even on the Internet – taken for granted as a part and parcel of the socialism of China's characteristics, there was hardly anything he could do, whether as a cop or as a poet.

After all, he knew so little about the case. About the netizen in Red Dust Lane either. Nothing for him to work on. Like in an old Chinese saying, no matter how capable a chef proves to be, he cannot make a meal without rice.

There came another burst of the dog's barking in the night, hollowly, as if from a dungeon.

Struck by an idea flashing out of nowhere, he stood up under the attic ceiling, which seemed oppressing, crashing down on him like an unanswerable question, and moved over to the pants draped over the back of the chair.

When he had left Peiqin's restaurant earlier that night, she had handed him a new menu, smiling like the gracious proprietor she was, asking him to read it in leisure back home. He'd stuffed the menu in his pocket, thinking he knew all the specials at her place.

Now on the back of the restaurant menu he could see something like a web link written in pencil.

'Thoughtful Peiqin,' he murmured in a rush of gratitude.

Compared to her husband Detective Yu, Peiqin knew much more about how to gather information online. The link must have a bearing to the poem in question or the netizen in Red Dust Lane.

He typed the link into his cellphone, but the screen showed a post already blocked out with a red warning sign: *It violates the governmental regulations. Forbidden access.*

It did not explain which governmental regulations the post violated. For a case that had prompted both Webcops and Internal Security into action, the post must have been instantly blocked, whether it was a poem or not.

Still nothing for him to work on regarding the case, then, without it being assigned to him, and without any clues, either. So was he not meant to be a cop or a poet after all?

'But you are meant to be a poet.' What a dear friend had once said to him came to mind – probably because of the ironic coincidence that, for tonight, he could not even have access to a poem posted online. Still, he remembered so vividly the way she had said those words to him, smiling a shy smile like the water lily in a breeze, with the White Pagoda of the North Sea Park shimmering against the approaching dusk.

The pagoda was still standing there, but those idealistic days in her company had been so short. Before he could even choose to do anything for 'self-realization', he was state-assigned as a college graduate to the Shanghai Police Bureau. Period.

So, with the memories shored against the doom drawing nearer, how could there be any choice except to do what he was expected to do?

In the Imperial Shadow of Beijing Library

I t was an early summer morning at the beginning of the 1980s when Chen parked his bike in the parking lot of the Beijing Library.

He felt exhilarated at the idea of another day in the midst of books. With the Cultural Revolution ending in a whimper, he had passed the restored college entrance examination with the highest score in English – thanks to his studies at Bund Park – and entered the Beijing Foreign Language University. Like other young idealistic people passionate about China's unprecedented reform, he believed he saw his own future in the dramatically changing country.

At the reception hall of the library, he put down the information on his book request slip as always, added the time and date, and slid it across the counter to a young vivacious librarian named Ling, who reached out for it with a smile, her fingers lightly brushing his as if by accident.

'Your reserved books are still here,' she said with an engaging dimple. 'I'll have my colleagues bring up the new ones as quickly as possible.'

It was said that the library would soon develop an open-shelf system, but no one could tell when. As it was, it took a lot of time for the books to be found by the staff members in accordance with the request and sent up from the lower level. Ling really helped speed this process up.

That day she was wearing a pink short-sleeved blouse and a white skirt, holding out the pile of his reserved books in her bare arms. She was like a peach blossom blazing out of a white paper fan – an inexplicably enchanting image he recalled from a Ming dynasty play. He began conceiving some lines in the back of his mind when the noisy arrival of several teenage readers interrupted his reveries.

According to the library rules, it required a special card to check out any foreign language books; otherwise he had to read them in-house. The Cultural Revolution having ended not too long ago, the government authorities still saw English books as informed with subversive Western ideologies, and exercised control as a matter of course.

For the English Department at Beijing Foreign Language University, there was only one library card for staff members, and that with a limit of three books. As a third-year student, he knew better than to approach his teachers for the use of the card, but for his paper on T.S. Eliot, he found in the university only one collection of Eliot criticism, which had been published almost thirty years earlier.

As the one and only solution, he had to visit the Beijing Library as often as possible, to read there as long as possible, and to make bunches of cards with reference notes on them for his thesis. It was the last summer vacation of his college years, and he chose to stay in Beijing. Though homesick, he could hardly succeed in concentrating, he knew, in that steamer-like attic room in Shanghai.

And he believed he was making some progress, thanks to the contributing ambience of the profoundly peaceful, ancient library. Putting down the cards, he caught his thoughts wandering to the origins of the library, of which there were differing accounts. It was most likely a complex of numerous imperial halls attached to the Forbidden City, where the emperors discussed various issues with official scholars. After 1949, it was renamed the Beijing Library, and the *People's Daily* used the change as another opportunity to rave about the new socialist society, in which ordinary people could spend their days reading and studying in the erstwhile imperial complex. Its location was truly excellent, adjacent to North Sea Park with the White Pagoda visible through the vista of green foliage, and across the White Stone Bridge, close to the Central South Sea Complex, the present-day residential complex for the top Party leaders.

It was not ideal, however, as a library. The wooden lattice windows, refitted with tinted glass like in the old days, admitted little natural light. So along the vast desks each reader was equipped with a green-shaded lamp. But he actually liked that, feeling a subtle effect of the once imperial surrounding him. Some of the dust-covered shelves could have been leftovers from the old days too, instilling the tradition as well as the history in an invisible way.

'Another long day in the library?' Ling came back to him, asking the question rhetorically. 'It's a bit later for you this morning.'

'Something wrong with the bike tire. It took quite a while for me to find a repairer around the Xisi area.'

Usually he arrived at opening time and stayed till closing, she knew that. He had to make the best of his time there. Retrieving a butterfly bookmark from a reserved copy, he added half-jokingly, 'Thanks to your help, now I can read while waiting for the arrival of the new books. But it's just like in a classical poem, "A beauty's favor really weighs you down."'

'Come on, Chen Cao. You don't have to put on your poet cap for me.'

Since when had he got used to talking to her like that? Perhaps it was just a pleasant prelude to a long day of reading in peace and quiet – surely not like those scenes in Eliot's 'Prelude', with a lonely horse steaming and stamping in the lighting of the lamp, or an ancient woman gathering twigs in the vacant lots . . .

Three or four weeks earlier, he recalled, sitting alone at the desk, it was to her that he had handed his first request slip in the library. An attractive girl in her early or mid-twenties, she looked up at him with a ray of sunshine suddenly squeezing in through the tinted windows. She asked him a couple of routine questions over the counter, her large, clear eyes reminiscent of the high, cloudless autumn sky over Beijing.

The next day, when he was waiting at the counter, digging out a copy of *Poetry* from his satchel, she said, eyeing his college badge on the breast pocket, 'You're from Beijing Foreign Language University? Not too many books in its library. I know, I studied there too.'

So she had noticed him. Possibly because of the odd mixture

of his reading list: poetry, philosophy and mysteries, the last of which he needed simply to refresh his mind in the midst of the difficult paper.

'Then you know what? There's only one book about T.S. Eliot in the university library, a collection of New Criticist essays, which was published so many years ago.'

'Wow,' she said, her fine features animated with a cute, exaggerated arching of her eyebrows, 'you are writing your paper on T.S. Eliot. On *The Waste Land*?'

He nodded, not without a touch of excitement. It was unusual to have someone talking to him about Eliot. And she was an alumna as well. Presumably a worker-peasant-soldier college student during the years of the Cultural Revolution. Those days, students had been selected in accordance to Mao's class theory. It was beyond his wildest dreams at the time, dogged with the shadow of his black family background.

'Since you practically come here every day,' she said, 'you can leave your books on hold at closing time. They will be kept here overnight. Then you won't have to wait for them again the next morning.'

'That's a great idea!'

That did indeed save him a lot of time. Normally, it took at least half an hour for the books to come up on a small lift from the lower level, a sort of basement, where the royal households allegedly used to keep large ice blocks for summer use, as he had read in a martial art novel.

'But I may not be able to come every day, so the reserved books—'

'Don't worry about that. I'll tell my colleagues about it,' she said, putting a cardboard '*reserved*' label on top of the books. 'No one will touch them for a couple of days. You are special.'

Special's the special way people says it. On a moment of impulse, he produced out of his satchel a newly published magazine, and opened it to the page with his poem printed on it. 'It's a copy I bought on the way to the library. By the way, my name is Chen Cao.'

She read the poem, and then another time, more closely. 'I like it very much. My name is Ling.'

It was perhaps just an exchange of polite words between a helpful librarian and a grateful reader.

That evening, however, he pushed his bike out of the parking lot to see her standing with hers under the ancient arch of the library gate. He pulled out abreast with her, as if by chance.

With her taking the lead, the two of them rode through a maze of quaint *hutong* lanes, past those old *sihe* quadrangle houses with white walls and black tiles. A stray tabby cat, startled by his bike bell spilling into the tranquil corner, jumped out in front of them. The two of them exchanged pleasant words, making turns through the gathering dusk till an intersection at Xisi, where she parked her bike to change for the subway. He stood there, watching her move down the subway stair to a landing, above which a mural showed an Urge girl carrying grapes in her bare arms, walking up with the bangle on her ankle shining, in infinitely light steps, like grateful smile in summer breath.

Now this morning, like other mornings, he was enjoying a moment of reverie before he started reading under a green-shaded lamp. Sitting at a seat not far from the counter, he could look up sideways for the arrival of the requested books – and at her too, occasionally, as it had been too much of a temptation for him.

She had been nice to him, going out of her way to help him, but he knew little about her.

Among the reserved books, one was an annotated collection of Eliot's early poems. It was a difficult period for the poet, who insisted on writing and working hard instead of opting for an easy life with a well-paid job through the connections of his family, or through those of his wife Vivienne.

But what fascinated Chen was the tension between Eliot's impersonal theory and personal writing. Vivienne's neurotic worries about 'Prufrock' being his swan song drove him to a nervous breakdown, which precipitated, paradoxically, his writing *The Waste Land*. The long poem included the frag-mented scenes of her bored monologue, as well as bleak allusions to his sexual frustration. Taking a deep breath, Chen started to make cards for his paper. Those contradictions in the poet might provide him an unexplored perspective.

Soon he lost himself in the lines which stretched on like a tedious investigation, in spite of his effort at sorting through the suspicious clues. At one stage of the earlier drafts of *The Waste Land*, he was surprised to find Eliot had actually played with an alternative working title: 'He Do the Police in Different Voices'.

But he found himself looking up again, feeling slightly disappointed at failing to see her there. He caught himself thinking about a mermaid singing, dancing, coming through the waves in ever-changing colors, white and black, wreathing herself with seaweed . . .

Surely these Eliotic lines made his mind digress again, and he shook himself out of the trance.

In a year, after completing his paper on Eliot at the end of his college studies, where would he possibly find himself?

His mother, all alone in Shanghai, wanted him to go back there after graduation. She needed his support after his father passed away toward the end of the Cultural Revolution, though she had not said so explicitly to him. But it was not up to her, or to him, to choose. Under the policy of state-assignment for college graduates, he had to take a job wherever the government assigned him. If he said no, he would be politically stigmatized, and remain jobless for years.

Perhaps he would have to consider himself lucky for obtaining a job like Ling's, with which he would at least be able to read to his heart's content. But then he hastened to tell himself that he was here because of his paper, not because of anything, or anybody else.

Again, he managed to pull his thoughts back to the books, wondering whether it would be feasible to translate some of Eliot's poems into Chinese as an appendix of his paper.

The next time he put down the poetry collection, it was past twelve. Lunch then presented a problem. Reaching into the satchel, he touched the cold steamed bun that was as hard as a rock, practically unchewable, from the school canteen the day before. It was arguably not too much of a disaster for the summer time, but he did not have any appetite for it.

There were some inexpensive snack eateries he liked in Beijing, but few in the area around the library. Nothing except for a Cool Korean Noodles sporting a long hose of cold water in front to cool the noodles. The chilly noodles did not agree, however, with his stomach. As for the tourist-frequented restaurants nearby, they were way beyond his budget. Fangshan, for instance, was a high-end restaurant which used to serve the Qing royal family exclusively in the North Sea Park.

He walked out to seat himself on the stone steps of the ancient courtyard outside the library, with the Qing dynasty bronze cranes and turtle still staring out along the ancient verandah. Before reaching his hand into the satchel again, he gazed up at the tilted eaves decked with yellow dragon tiles, woven with constantly changing white clouds.

All of a sudden, he was aware of Ling standing behind him, holding in her hands two enamel bowls.

'Lunch time,' she said.

'Oh, I almost forgot. But there's nothing really good nearby, you know.'

'I know, but we have a staff canteen here. It serves deep-fried croaker today.'

'That's fantastic.' It sounded incredible to him. Croaker was served only during the national holidays at the college canteen.

'Then you just follow me.'

'How?'

'We're allowed to take in our visiting relatives.'

She appeared to be in earnest, raising the two enamel bowls in her hands. It was an offer too good for him to decline.

He followed her to the back of the courtyard, moving across another winding ancient corridor to the staff canteen, in front of which an apple tree was blossoming like a transparent dream.

Immediately, he became aware of people's curious glances at the two of them. Some of her colleagues knew the man walking beside her was nothing but a reader.

She ordered a portion of deep-fried croaker for him, and of Shanghai-style pork ribs for herself. The fish tasted more delicious than he remembered. With his portion gone in less than three or four minutes, he felt embarrassed as she put pieces of the sweet and sour ribs into his bowl.

'I cannot have too much meat,' she said by way of explanation before she rose to fetch a bowl of tomato and egg drop soup for him.

It might not be true. She had an athletic figure with long and shapely legs. A colleague of hers sidled up to their table in the corner, as if anxious to discuss with her some library issues, but ended up saying only two or three irrelevant words, studying him across the table most of the time. He kept eating in silence, his head hung low over the bowl.

At the end of the lunch, Ling, walking out by his side, said, 'You want to take a short lunch break?'

In Beijing, people were used to taking naps in the middle of the day. In the library, he too took an occasional nap with his head resting on the desk. For the moment, after a generous portion of the deep-fried fish plus the ribs, he didn't feel like going back so quickly to Eliot's poems.

'That would be nice. But—'

'You may take a break at my office.'

So she had an office for herself. Apparently she was not just an ordinary librarian working at the counter. That accounted for her not being there all the time. But a short break in her office?

'Beijing Library has some exchanges with other libraries in the world,' she said, seeing the question in his eyes. 'Still, with not too much work in the foreign liaison office, I do not have to stay in it all the time.'

This job of hers was even better than he had imagined. She came to the counter merely to help.

'Alternatively, how about a visit to the rare book section?' she said, aware of his hesitation.

He had heard of the rare book section, which was said to be open only for 'distinguished visitors', which he was not.

'Don't worry about it. I'll take you there.' She seemed so confident of her capability or privilege, leading him to the office at the end of a long corridor. 'But I have to stay with you in the room. It's the library rule.'

So they arrived at a large room at the end of the corridor.

In spite of a note on the door saying that it was closed for restoration, she took out a key and opened the door to the spacious room with glass cabinets lined along the walls, containing books in exquisite blue cloth cases. Almost like a special museum exhibition from the Ming and Qing dynasties, except that he could take the books into his own hands for a closer look, as she explained to him. A thin layer of fine dust under those cabinets seemed to speak about the long, forgotten history.

'Sorry, I have to write a fax,' she said, seating herself in a folding chair in the corner, 'to an Australian library. You can look around for yourself.'

Instead of those valuable thread-bound books in blue cloth boxes, he found himself drawn toward a silk scroll unfolded under a glass counter. The time-yellowed paper of the scroll testified to its age. The scroll presented a tiny figure pushing out the bamboo hut door to the high mountains, and to a large blank space covering about half the size of the painting. He tried to make out the elusive meaning of those lines in the cursory style above the mountains, but with limited success.

Taking out his pen and card, he started scribbling the characters, stroke by stroke, as if lost in the vision that the mountains alone might be able to understand against the surrounding blankness.

The moment the painting / of a man opening the door / in the mountains, and of the door / opening the man into the painting . . .

How long he lost himself studying the scroll, he didn't know. When he looked up, she must have been done with the fax sheets quite a while ago.

The room seemed to be suddenly hot. She had kicked off her sandals and put on her earphones, listening to a Walkman on her lap, looking relaxed. He felt a violent wonder at her bare feet beating a Bolero on the ancient floor. She looked up, smiling, as if taking his intensity over the scroll like the silver fish escaping the sleepy eyes from the inscrutable lines, before she said she was going to send out the fax from her own office.

It was time for them to leave, he understood.

Afterward, she did not reappear behind the counter in the reading room. It might be just as well. A beauty's favor, he reflected with a touch of self-irony, might not be that easy to pay back. Already more than enough favor for him in one single day.

But like in a proverb, it takes coincidences to make a story. Later that afternoon, the electricity suddenly went out in the library, and the readers had to return the books and leave in a rush. Ling hurried over to the counter to help.

He carried the pile of books back to her and said, 'If only I could carry them back to the campus.'

'I understand. But what if there's also an electricity outage on the campus? It's citywide, I've just heard.'

'Well . . .' In that case, he might not be able to do anything back at school. 'You're leaving at five or five thirty?'

'Five. Why?'

'If you have no other plans for the day, how about taking a walk in the North Sea Park?'

'Today?' she said with hesitancy in her voice.

He decided not to push. It was a suggestion made on the spur of the moment. And he was already beginning to wonder whether it was appropriate, feeling almost like the diffident Prufrock.

'But I have to go home around eight. A relative from . . .' She glanced at her watch without finishing the sentence. 'I'll make a phone call first. How about us meeting at the Jing Mountain Park?'

That he thought he understood. After the lunch, she might not want to be seen again in his company by her colleagues. The North Sea Park was too close to the library.

'The Jing Mountain Park will be nice.'

'Then I'll see you at the back entrance around five thirty.'

At five twenty, he arrived at the back entrance to the park. Outside, it appeared quite deserted, except for an old man selling colorful paper wheels stuck along a straw-wrapped bamboo pole, and a peddler hawking sugar-covered haws from a large cloth bag strung across his shoulder. Chen stepped over to an engraving on the wall about the history of the park.

The Jing Mountain Park, like the North Sea Park, used to be part of the imperial outer compound during the Ming and Qing dynasties. After 1949 it became a public park, close to the Central South Sea, where the top Party leaders might look out the window to the verdant hills in the park.

After reading through the park introduction, he took out a bunch of the note cards he had made in the library. According to several critics, Vivienne did not make an ideal wife for Eliot. What particularly puzzled him was a story that Vivienne, while still on honeymoon with the young poet, went away with the philosopher Bertrand Russell for a vacation.

But before he succeeded in finding any clues about the romantic mystery, he saw Ling moving light-footedly down a bamboo bridge partially visible through the gate, hurrying toward him.

'I have the monthly pass for the parks in the city. So I stepped into it from a side entrance and took a short cut to the back gate here. Sorry about that, Chen.'

'Nothing for you to say sorry about. I'm just reading the history of the park.' He stuffed the cards back into his pocket in haste. 'Really interesting.'

'The park is known for the man-made hills. The "Mountain" part of its name is an exaggeration, just like the "Sea" in the name of the other park. The imperial hyperbole.'

He started to stroll along with her. The park was large, but with not too many visitors for the time of the day. After making several turns, he came to a green hillside. It was not high, nor steep, so they climbed up to a secluded spot.

There he seated himself beside her on a long slab of rock under an old tree, in view of the evening spreading out against the glazed eaves of the splendid palace. Beneath the hills, waves of buses were flowing along the gray road, of which he was trying to recall the name, but without success.

'It's possibly part of a moat hundreds of years ago,' she said, looking at him. 'What are you thinking?'

'*You are looking at the view from the hillside, / and the view-seekers are looking at you . . .*' he improvised in a half-teasing way. It was an imitation after the fashion of Bian Zhilin's *Fragment*, which was commonly taken as a love poem written for his girlfriend, paying tribute to her beauty in a characteristically roundabout way. Chen only changed the view-taking location in the two lines.

'I like the poem too,' she said, with a suggestion of blushing, 'especially the next two lines. *"The moon adorns your window, / and you adorn another's dream."'*

'I have tried to translate the poem into English, but the deceptively simple lines can be the most difficult to come out in another language.'

'Yes, it's difficult. Not just a love poem, but also one about the relativity of things and people at the same time.'

She knew the poem well. The two of them began speaking some words in Chinese, then in English. That was another advantage of being in her company. It might be so hard to say something in one language, but surprisingly easy in another.

By a dragon-shaped rock several steps behind them, a bronze stork seemed to be reaching out from a turn up the hill, harking to the talk between the two of them. It could have once watched the Ming Emperors, and then the Qing Dowager, and was still staring ahead at this moment, infinitely, across time.

'Last night I dreamed of becoming the gargoyles gurgling at *Yangxing* imperial in the Forbidden City,' she said quietly, 'babbling all night long in words comprehensible only to us.'

He was more than intrigued with the plural 'gargoyles' used in her sentence. Grammatically incorrect, he detected. But he chose to say nothing about it in the mist of silence that ensued peacefully around them.

With the hill now enveloped in the dusk, they started to slowly descend. Turning at the foot of the hill, he came to an unexpected view of a withered tree hung with a small white board saying, 'It's here that Emperor Chongzhen of Ming dynasty hanged himself.'

He slowed to a stop, wondering whether it was the same tree, or just another one planted hundreds of years later at the very spot. In 1644, Chongzhen, the last emperor of the Ming dynasty, had committed suicide on the hill as the then capital was falling to the peasant rebels led by Li Zicheng. In the

official history textbooks, the rebels were invariably represented as the positive, revolutionary force in the light of Mao's
class struggle theory. Hence the lone, ignominious board at
the foot of the hill.

All of a sudden, he started to shiver at the sign's weird
resemblance to the blackboard hung around his father's neck
in the Cultural Revolution. The unmistakable sign of humiliation and denunciation in the revolutionary mass criticism held
by Red Guards.

'There's something I need to tell you,' she said abruptly,
without noting his mood change. 'I have an opportunity to go
to Australia for one year. For an exchange program between
the Beijing and Canberra Library.'

'What! Congratulations, Ling. That's fantastic.'

'Thanks, Chen. But what about you? You're graduating the
next year.'

What was implied in her question?

It soon began to dawn on him, the white pagoda still shimmering in the failing light.

What about him in relation to her?

It was hardly a 'date' for the two of them, nothing but an
evening out in the park, an accidental meeting prompted by
the loss of electricity in the library.

'Yes, the next year,' he echoed meaninglessly, like a hollow
man filled with straw from Eliot's poem.

She looked at her watch again.

How could she make it back home for eight? It was already
seven forty. She lived quite a distance from the library, he knew.

'Oh, here is something for you, I almost forgot,' she said,
leading the way to the front exit of the park.

It was something like a blue plastic-covered notebook. He
read the words printed in gold on the cover, 'Beijing Library
Card'; it looked quite different from the one he had seen at
the college.

'You may use it when you need to check books out for your
paper, but I certainly look forward to seeing you here.'

It was not her library card. The first page showed a picture
of a middle-aged, serious-looking man in a Mao jacket, with
a fine line underneath saying that the card holder was entitled

to check out ten books at one time – in either Chinese or foreign languages. That was unbelievable.

'That's my father's card,' she said in a low voice.

Then he recognized the card holder in the picture on the first page, other pictures of whom he had actually seen in the Party newspapers. A Politburo member who was still rising, possibly on the way to the very top. So the maximum of ten books for him made perfect sense.

'He is too busy to read much, so you may use it for a good reason. By the way, people here won't question you about the card.'

Because of her, and to be more exact, because of her Politburo-member father.

What had struck him as mysterious about her was becoming transparent. Her position in the library, the privilege of taking him to the staff canteen, the key for the rare book section – and now the opportunity for her to go to Australia in an exchange program.

How could all these things have been possible for an ordinary librarian? He should have suspected, detected from the very beginning.

Whatever you are, you don't have the making of a cop. That's probably why Eliot had conceived the original title 'He Do the Police in Different Voices' for the long poem which was eventually changed to *The Waste Land*.

Chen was not unaware of her being so nice to him, and of the possibility of her going on like that upon her return from Australia as well. With her walking beside him, he would have access to a lot of things otherwise inaccessible to him. Much more than what she had already made possible for him. To say the least, he wouldn't have to worry about getting books out of the library. And about having a good job assigned to him after graduation. It was more than likely he might also have opportunities like hers, for an all-expenses-paid trip to the United States, perhaps even to the city of Saint Louis, where the poet Eliot was born.

But all this would come to him not because of his own efforts, but because of her – of his being with her, or his becoming someone else because of her.

'Thank you so much for your help.' He uttered the words abruptly, realizing he had not yet said so, clutching the library card tight in his hand.

They walked on in another spell of silence, like the scroll of traditional Chinese painting he had just seen in the rare book section, in which the blank seemed to contain more than what was presented.

There is always a loss of meaning / in what we say or do not say, / but also a meaning / in the loss of the meaning. He had thought of the lines too while gazing at the scroll of the ancient painting in the rare book section.

At the end of a somber park trail, he turned round with her, following a sign pointing to an exit of the park. She slowed down, her steps hesitant at the sight of a luxurious black limousine waiting outside for her.

'It's my father's car,' she said with a suggestion of embarrassment. 'I have to hurry back for dinner at home, a visitor from—'

'I understand, Ling.'

After all, it was because she had not wanted to say no to his invitation to the park that she now had to hurry back to the family dinner.

'Perhaps your family is moving soon.' He made a comment out of nowhere.

'What makes you say so?' she looked up, catching the hint of sarcasm in his voice.

'It will then be really close to the library.' He refrained from going on, but she must have guessed something, a fleeting frown across her forehead. He was referring to the Central South Sea, the Forbidden City in today's China, where her father would soon move as one of the top Party leaders, and from where she could walk to the library.

Parting outside the park, she reached out her hand to him. The moonlight through the pale sky fell chilly on her bare arm.

'"*I'm only afraid it can be too cold / in the jade and crystal palace so high.*"'

'What do you mean, Chen?'

'Oh, nothing. I'm just thinking of some lines in Su Shi's poem—'

A uniformed chauffeur hurried out of the limousine to pull open the door respectfully for her.

He did not think the chauffeur would open the door for him, and wondered if anyone would ever choose to do so.

FIVE

A gain, he woke with a sudden jerk of his head. This time, perhaps no more than five to ten minutes after he had closed his eyes. Another horror-filled dream that drenched his body in clammy sweat.

A headless corpse is swimming against the turgid currents in a large river, his nipples looking daggers, his navel sucking in air desperately, his right hand still grasping a cleaver shimmering against the night, and all around him, dead fishes drifting with their ghastly pale bellies reflecting in the sallow moonlight. Something about the corpse strikes him as oddly familiar – something so stubbornly determined to fight on despite its being beheaded.

It was not because of Georges Simenon's *Maigret and the Headless Corpse*, which he had recently reread, he observed in confusion. More likely it was Xingtian, a Chinese giant who remains defiant after being beaten and beheaded by the Yellow Emperor in the classic mythology collection *The Classic of Mountains and Seas—*

He felt the phone vibrating again under the pillow, like a fallen leaf trembling in the autumn wind.

It was from Peiqin. This time, the phone screen showed another web link, its contents saved in a PDF file. With sensitive posts deleted or blocked in no time under the twenty-four-hour governmental Internet control, experienced netizens had to save them in different files so they could read them later if needed. He clicked it open to see a poem titled *Reading Animal Farm*.

Notwithstanding the title that looked like a book review, it was a sonnet, though not strictly following the metric pattern. The poet had a WeTalk name, 'Dragon Brother', which did not immediately ring a bell for him. But it was a common practice for seasoned netizens to have a number of pen-names. With a post under one name blocked, another could have popped up and enabled the resurfacing of the post for another short while, and then possibly still another name for one more round.

In your dirty pigsty, stop the squeaking!
Fed, more than full, you pigs mill around,
then dream your big dream – sty-bound –
of a moment of freedom, peeking

around the stall. Refrain from any comment
criticizing the Party for any reason.
Bathing in the light of his Majesty Napoleon,
you may wallow to your heart's content.

What – a swine pandemic with fever high?
Even the possible has to be spun
into the impossible. Search the sty,
seal and sear the squeaking tongue.
Who cares about the blood flood drowning the sky
afterward? I'm the Emperor, the only one.

It was so cleverly done. Revolving around the contents of *Animal Farm* by George Orwell, it would have appeared as nothing too suspicious to readers knowledgable about the novel. In the name of a book review, however, it made a scathing satire against the current totalitarian regime – particularly against the new number one Party leader in the Forbidden City. For something like that in contemporary China, a netizen/poet had to write in a very cautious way – though from time to time, they were still detectable under the radar of the Webcops.

After all, the name of George Orwell could itself have triggered the alarm for the Webcops. And what the poem was driving at, Chen contemplated, appeared to be quite obvious once the alarm started going off. China was suffering from a widespread swine flu. In spite of the government effort at a cover-up, people were complaining about eating the bad meat with the soaring price. Coincidentally, the new number one Party boss was nicknamed 'Pig Head' by some netizens in

reference to his stubborn stupidity, and the nickname immediately became a more highly sensitive word, with 'pigs' in
intertextual association as well. But more than anything else,
it was the word 'Emperor' in the poem. Shortly after the 'Pig
Head' came to power, he changed the part of the constitution
specifying the term limit of the presidency, so he could rule
on as long as he pleased – like an emperor. As a result, the
word 'emperor' had become an extremely sensitive word in
the eyes of the Webcops.

That was why Internal Security wanted the police bureau
to join forces for the case of the 'anti-Party poem'. It was
such a serious 'thoughtcrime' that they were really anxious to
get hold of the netizen under the pen-name of Dragon Brother.

But that did not add up. Chen frowned. In China, people
had to register with their ID cards for access to a social network
website like WeTalk. So the Webcops should have had no
problem tracing the identity of the netizen.

A couple of years earlier, he had been involved in an investigation in which a netizen had succeeded in covering up the
IP address for a comment posted online by using a fake ID
in an Internet café. Nowadays, with such places closely moni-
tored by plainclothes cops and numerous surveillance cameras,
it was a mission impossible for someone to post online there
without being caught – fake ID or not. As it was whispered,
the number of surveillance cameras was catching up with
China's population, and with the increasingly bigger Big Data,
the government was boasting of a 'Heavenly Net' – that
anytime, anywhere, the Governmental Net could catch people
in violation of its regulations. Chen was well aware of that
because he knew he himself had been closely watched of late,
and he had made a point of moving around with extra caution.

And what could have brought the man named Huyan in Red
Dust Lane into the picture? If he had been connected with
Dragon Brother, the Webcops could have easily made Huyan
spill out everything he knew about the poet. It would have
taken a much higher stake for the Webcops to contact Internal
Security, and then the police bureau, for help.

If the case had been assigned to him, he could have tried
to interpret the poem as nothing but a book review. Some

sensitive words, that's true, but they all came from the novel. After all, the pig emperor is the very protagonist, and the description of Napoleon is not too far off the mark. In short, nothing really to raise the alarm about.

But it would be a totally different story as to whether Internal Security would accept his interpretation. On the contrary, they could interpret his reading as a cover-up of the true intention of the anti-Party poem.

So why should the soon-to-be-ex-inspector try to put his finger into such a messy pie?

Confucius says, 'At fifty, one knows about his destiny as determined from the above.' There was no point his bumping around like a headless fly any longer. Indeed, 'Why should the aged eagle stretch its wings?'

The dire complications of the case aside, could it have been a devious trap set up by the government? As Party Secretary Li knew only too well, the bookish chief inspector might not be able to resist the temptation of a case involving poetry interpretation, as well as someone in Red Dust Lane—

Sitting up again, he leaned over to look out the attic window. In the unfamiliar distance, a red gleam flickered like the wild burning eye against the night woods before fading into the surrounding darkness.

He had no choice. It was a decision he had to make in the dark.

Decision in the Dark

Minmin, a long-time neighbor and friend of the Chen family, was heading back underneath the dark cover of the night, shivering in the chilly wind laden with a wet message against her face.

All along the way, yellow leaves appeared to be continuously falling in fitful rustles, portentously, like drops of bamboo divination slips falling to the ruined floor of an ancient temple.

Mr Kong, the overseas Chinese staying at Jing River Hotel, could have easily arranged a taxi for her, but he chose not to. He merely mumbled polite yet meaningless words at the parting, his shrunken face like a frost-bitten persimmon in the light of the guarded hotel exit. For a business-like deal, a shrewd businessman like him did not have to go out of the way for her before signing the contract. She had not yet made up her mind, which he knew only too well.

But for his first trip to Shanghai in the early 1980s, Mr Kong, white-haired like a legendary wise owl flying out of a different world, might have had no idea that after cups of coffee, after the 'inside' kung fu movie unavailable to ordinary Shanghainese, after the room service of the dainty, delicious dim sum, she had missed the last trolley bus back home to Red Dust Lane. It was extremely difficult for her to find a taxi at this late hour, nor could she have afforded one, which would have been inconceivable to an overseas Chinese visitor after having stayed abroad for more than forty years.

It was a long walk for her. After the rain, Huaihai Road became so slippery, she had to make careful steps, maneuvering around the tiny rain pools, but her thoughts kept wandering away.

Minmin did not think she was exactly disappointed with the date with Mr Kong in the hotel. It had been suggested by

Mrs Chen, not at all like something conveniently arranged by such a notorious matchmaker as Auntie Yang in the neighborhood. Mrs Chen had made a sincere effort, Minmin believed, in return for her 'favor' at the beginning of the Cultural Revolution when she had helped the Chens hide away some precious books. So Mrs Chen had gone out of her way to provide Minmin with details of Mr Kong's background, which she had not told others, she said, not even her only son, for some of these things could have caused them trouble.

In the early 1950s, Mr Chen had decided to take his family back to China from the United States, where he had already secured a tenured university position, bought a large house, and hired Kong for occasional yard work. An internationally known neo-Confucian scholar, Mr Chen got into trouble upon his return to China, and passed away a broken man in the early 1970s. And about four decades later, Mr Kong came back to Shanghai as a successful overseas Chinese with several high-tech companies to his name, but he did not forget to pay a visit to Mrs Chen. She then asked Minmin over and approached her with a proposal that Mr Kong and Minmin should meet.

'What has happened to Mr Kong these years, I know very little,' Mrs Chen added in earnest, hardly able to move around in the tiny room. 'But he chose to see me with a lot of gifts and to kowtow to Mr Chen's tablet here. He told me that my late husband had not only paid him well for the yard work, but also helped him enrol in the university with a scholarship, which I did not know. What's more, he offers to help with my son's job assignment upon his college graduation in Beijing. Mr Kong promises to speak to the government officials who are after his investment in Shanghai, so they may be able to do something about it. It's really like sending a cart of coal in the snow. Such a man is trustworthy, I have to say.'

Mrs Chen was anxious about the job location of her only son, who would be state-assigned to work next year. Whether Mr Kong's promise to help could work out or not, Mrs Chen believed that it spoke volumes about his character. After all, Kong did not have to offer to help a present-day nobody like her, penniless, connectionless. That earned him a sort of endorsement from Mrs Chen.

Minmin's parents lost no time throwing in their approval for the meeting. For them, 'an overseas Chinese' meant someone 'super-rich, capable of buying all the nice and wonderful things in the West, staying in a five-star hotel in Shanghai, and spending money like water for himself as well as for the people related to him, not to mention the prospect of his eventually taking his spouse abroad'. It was little wonder that the materialistic scale of theirs tipped decidedly to Mr Kong, even though he was more than twenty years older than Minmin.

Trying to unravel these tangled thoughts seemed to add to the solitude of her walk back home. The night appeared still young. Near Huangpi Road, a ramshackle bike shot recklessly out of nowhere in the dark, with neither bell nor light, splashing up the dirty rain water around her.

Minmin bent over to take off her shoes, which had cost more than a month's salary for her. The shoe tassels appeared sodden, entangled, possibly damaged beyond repair. Was that another omen from the dark, rainy night? Tramping barefoot on the cold street, she felt inexplicably tired, sick to the stomach. She must have had too much coffee at the hotel, black and bitter. How could Mr Kong really enjoy that stuff, cup after cup in the luxurious hotel room?

Mrs Chen must have seen Mr Kong as a reasonably good match for Minmin, though. Aside from his overseas Chinese status and richness and trustworthiness, what made the matchmaking scale turn more in his favor, however, was another factor Mrs Chen had chosen not to say to Minmin's face. After all, this was possibly the best that could have happened to Minmin, a woman already close to her mid-thirties, fading like yesterday's chrysanthemum.

At the beginning of Ninghai Road, she found herself stepping into view of the street food market, shrouded in darkness except for the few erratic, languid lamps with long intervals between them. Along the cobbled street, the sordid stalls and concrete counters loomed deserted for the moment, sheltered or unsheltered, like crouching monsters in the night woods.

Again, she became depressed at the thought of the possible development of the 'arranged date' at the hotel. She knew better than to describe herself as young or attractive, so she had to be realistic. She had no choice but to give up the dream of marrying someone of her own age, and after her own heart, with the prospect of moving out of the single convenience room in which she had been packed with her parents and brothers like sardines all these years. What's more, with an 'indelible stain' in the political archive about her having been thrown into custody for kissing a young man in Bund Park – a crime of indecent bourgeois lifestyle during the Cultural Revolution – she knew she had little hope left for her future here.

The edge of an upturned stone on the sidewalk stung her bare foot. Back at the hotel, Mr Kong had insisted on her taking off her shoes on the luxurious carpet of the room, saying that it was soft like the lawn in the backyard of his mansion in the US, and studying her shapely feet like a prize.

'*You have no choice.*'

She spun around, trying to locate the voice in a shadowy corner of the market. But she saw nothing there except a long line of baskets – plastic, bamboo, rattan, wood, straw, in all shapes and sizes, leading up to a concrete counter. Deserted for the moment, the counter stared back at her under a cardboard sign of 'yellow croaker', a not-too-expensive yet delicious fish much in demand in the city of Shanghai, and usually gone in the first fifteen minutes after the sounding of the market bell. People had to stand in a long line for hours beforehand, sometimes overnight, but it was too cold for them at this time of the year. So the baskets left there earlier stood as their representatives, and their owners would then come hurrying over in the first gray of the morning, securing their positions in the line, clutching the food ration coupons in their frost-bitten hands, their eyes still shiny with the dream scene of the happy family at the dinner table.

A trodden bamboo basket creaked unexpectedly, its plastic-wrapped handle reaching out, as if trying to point at an invisible projection of Minmin standing at the very spot in fifteen or twenty years.

Was she relapsing into some nocturnal hallucination? She rubbed her eyes.

She then began wondering if things here could turn out to be like Kong's description of his life in the States.

Behind the high walls of the Forbidden City in Beijing, economic reforms were said to be contemplated by some senior Party leaders, but what would really happen in China, no one could tell.

The chilly wind was sobering her. Time and tide wait for no woman, like in a half-forgotten Tang dynasty poem.

Bang – bang – bang – she looked up to see another line, much shorter, consisting of stones, ropes, bricks, with just a couple of broken baskets in the midst, leading to another counter close to a ramshackle warehouse.

In front of the warehouse, the silhouette of a night-shift worker – faceless with the upturned collar of a cotton-padded overcoat – was cracking a gigantic frozen fish bar forcefully with a heavy hammer, before chopping off the fish heads with a long cleaver.

She stood transfixed, as if under a spell. The sign over that counter said 'Beheaded Carp'.

Shanghainese loved the carp head pot, taking the fish cheeks and lips as the most delicious parts. With the fish heads chopped off for the special pots in restaurants, the bodies were considered less desirable, though edible, for a cheaper price, which accounted for the shorter line in contrast to that for the yellow croaker.

So that's what she was.

She was on offer in another market, with her youth gone, still likable but no longer that delicious, desirable to the palate of a much older man like Mr Kong, who was waiting at the luxurious hotel for her decision.

She shuddered at the realistic realization in the dark.

SIX

U *nder a murderous sky woven with snarling black bats,*
he is trying to cross a muddy river by stepping on
large or small stones scattered in the swift eddies, not
at all sure of the wet, slippery footholds. Most of them appear
to be barely visible above the water's surface. It is a highly
risky attempt, but he keeps telling himself that he has no
choice.

Behind him, a torn red flag flares up into a huge fireball
engulfing the scarlet horizon. Sweating profusely, he feels the
summer heat remaining steady, relentless like an iron grasp
with these bats flipping, shrieking horrors all around him. He
starts lurching, balancing himself precariously, flailing his
arms in panic. Hurrying for another foothold in the water, he
slips and falls face-down—

He woke with the thought that he again found in the
vanishing dream a sort of relevance, albeit symbolically, to
the social realities of the mid-1980s. The period just before
his becoming a chief inspector in the Shanghai Police Bureau.
It was perhaps no coincidence. They were now at another
turning point, not just for him, but for the whole country. No
one could tell, however, in which direction the wind was
blowing in China, like in a poem he had read those days when
he had been first assigned to the police bureau after college
graduation.

At the time, an editorial in the *People's Daily* had made
an intriguing analogy about China's unprecedented reform
in the post-Mao era, comparing it to wading across the
turgid, uncharted water of a river and reaching a point of
no return. Whatever might happen in the course of it, 'We
have to cross the river by stepping on one stone after another
in the water.'

It was so mystifying for the trouble-plagued inspector that
his dreams should keep shifting back to those scenes at the

beginning of his police profession. Was it because of a full circle it had just made, with him now toward the very ending of it?

Or it was because of something else? For one, he had not slept in the old attic for years, and it induced his subconscious mind to repeated digressions into the past, what with the cobwebs of memories clinging there and with the dog barking in the depth of the night.

Or was it because China had drastically regressed in the last five or six years? The case about the 'anti-Party poem' was one such example. After a period of off-and-on 'opening up', during which books like *Animal Farm* and *1984* had been translated into Chinese, it was closing up again. Initially, a lot of people had believed that with the economic growth, political reform would prove to be the order of the day. But that did not happen. The Party government simply claimed the materialistic progress as the legitimacy of its authoritarian rule, and tightened ideological control again, shifting back to the practices characteristic of the Mao time. As officially announced, it was a crime to think or talk about any things said or done by the CCP government, and particularly by the current Party President – the Pig Head.

That might have accounted for the appearance of the dangerous river-crossing scene in his dream. It looked backward to the days when the economic reforms were initially launched by Deng Xiaoping, like the hazardous wading across the uncharted water. Or even worse. Now, with the help of new technology, the omnipresent government surveillance and propaganda were heightened like never before, and a poem like *Reading Animal Farm* inevitably turned into a thoughtcrime to the Webcops – just like the Thought Police in *1984*.

As for the background of the sky woven with those black menacing bats, which were missing in the propaganda in the official newspapers at Deng's time, but it became understandable when juxtaposed with the present-day political landscape of China.

The presence of the bats was not just spooky, but realistic too. In the Chinese language, the bat is pronounced *fu*, like the character meaning wealth and happiness. So the image of a bat was used as a symbol of good fortune in the old days, particularly in the traditional red paper door posters in celebration of the Chinese New Year. Also, the flitting bats were capable of making the sound of *shou* – like the Chinese ideogram for longevity. So they were considered lucky as well. It was said that because of that absurd superstitious belief, the Qing dynasty Empress Dowager Cixi spared no trouble to keep a sky full of bats over the magnificent Summer Palace.

He had even read of Big Bucks in today's China feasting on bats – presumably for the same reason, even though the bats could have carried deadly viruses with them. In fact, China had recently suffered a pandemic because of the bats in the wet market. But some people went on devouring them, which was totally beyond him. In spite of his being called a gastronome by some, he would never touch a bat. For him, bats simply meant something unpleasant, repulsive, unhealthy.

But could the bats have served as a bad omen for what he was going to do in Red Dust Lane? After all, his first case – the murder of the old gourmet – that started his journey to the chief inspectorship had taken place in Red Dust Lane, though he did not think the victim had ever had anything to do with bats. He checked himself. Whatever had happened to him since then, he did not want to dwell on it too much at the moment.

In the present moment, he needed to focus on the possible case waiting for him in Red Dust Lane, ominous as it might have appeared, like the menacing bats in the dream.

Being and Becoming

Once again, Chen Cao looked up from the translation of the US police procedure on his desk, the job he had been working on for a couple of months – and perhaps a couple of months more – in the so-called reading room of the Shanghai Police Bureau.

Already more than halfway through the project, he still had no idea as to who was going to read it in the bureau when it was done. But what choice did he really have? He could do nothing else here, a cop in name only among all the other cops.

How could it have happened?

He stared at the incomplete translation, which stared back at him. He still felt so disoriented with the abrupt change in his life.

Upon graduation from Beijing Foreign Language University in the early eighties, Chen had been state-assigned to work in the police bureau through a conspiracy of circumstances. Perhaps like in a proverb, it takes coincidences to make a story. A straight-A student with his file sent in to the Foreign Ministry, Chen came to view a diplomatic career as acceptable, though not as ideal as one in creative writing, when the unexpected surfacing of a 'Chinese uncle in America' in the political screening messed up his chance. Politically disqualified for a sensitive position at the Foreign Ministry as a result, Chen was pushed over to an unexpected opening in the Shanghai Police Bureau.

As the overseas Chinese uncle, whom he called Mr Kong, used his connections to push for Chen to be assigned to a job in Shanghai, the arrangement seemed not to be so unacceptable. On the contrary, that's what his mother had prayed for.

With the practice of college graduates being state-assigned declared as a benefit of the socialist system, there was no way for young people like Chen to choose for themselves. All job decisions were justified with the rationale that the Party authorities knew better in terms of the economy, despite the problems in the arbitrary state quota system.

In his case, the Shanghai Police Bureau happened to get its annual quota of college students because of the new propaganda wave about the importance of intellectuals in China's reform. As a college graduate, Chen was supposed to infuse new blood into the police system, so he could not say no to the assignment. Otherwise, he would be politically stigmatized, and rendered unemployable for years. No company would come to hire a man who had turned his back on the command of the socialist system.

But a problem faced the bureau too, which had no real need for one with an English major instead of proper police training. In the interpretation of Party Secretary Li, however, there was a reason for everything done in socialist China. So he came up with the idea of having Chen translate a booklet of American police procedure.

'With the great reform launched forth by Comrade Deng Xiaoping, it's necessary for China now to open up to the world. Of course, we don't have to follow the Western models, but it won't hurt to see how other people are working in terms of procedure in their country. So it's an important job for you to translate the materials for the bureau. You're one of the first college graduates on our police force. Welcome, Comrade Chen Cao.'

The translation would mostly likely be shelved, untouched, dust-covered into oblivion, and turned to its own dust, eventually, Chen supposed. With the Party interest placed above everything else, no one really wanted to bother about so-called procedure, which in fact was a word hardly used in China's official discourse. No one here seemed to be interested in the translation. Still, that was what Chen had been doing from day one in the bureau. And for that he was given, instead of an office or a cubicle, a shaky desk in the reading room. With few visitors coming into the reading room, he was alone there most of the time, translating, reading, undisturbed, though more and more aware of his awkward role, like an idle librarian in the name of a cop.

After a cup of lukewarm tea, he resumed the translation mechanically, with only half his mind on the work, and the other half wandering far away.

He thought of a popular political catchphrase: 'We each of us should be just like a screw fastened by the state wherever it chooses to.' But a human being is not a screw. For that matter, what about the screw being a misfit? Useless, it would soon become rusted, unusable.

It was twelve thirty when Chen rose from the desk to move down to the bureau canteen.

The canteen appeared crowded as usual. He spotted Dr Xia sitting in a corner waving a hand at him from afar. Chen stepped over in a hurry so they would share the table with no one else approaching them – two different, lone ducks.

Perhaps the only 'other' like him among the cops, Dr Xia had been assigned to work in Forensics in the early sixties, despite his college major in surgery. Like Chen, he was in no position to complain about the assignment, though he'd hardly had anything to do for years, with most of the cases being predetermined in accordance with political needs. After Deng's reform gained momentum in the early 1980s, things began to improve in China, but Dr Xia had already reached his mid-fifties and was ready to retire soon.

'The pork steak braised in brown sauce looks like an excellent choice, but . . .' Xia said with a chuckle, pointing a black-painted chopstick at Chen's chipped enamel bowl.

'But what?'

'You came too late. Guess what else the canteen served earlier today? Pork brains. I had two portions of it. Well steamed with lots of yellow rice wine and chopped golden ginger and green onion. Sold out in just two minutes.'

That was one more thing the two had in common: neither could resist the temptation of exotic food.

'You surely know the folk belief?' Dr Xia went on.

'According to it, whatever animal part you eat is supposed to be a boost to the corresponding part in your human body.'

That Chen happened to know well. In the early sixties, when his mother had suffered hepatitis, he had had to go to the street food market early in the morning, time and again, for a slice of pork liver, standing in a long line for hours because of the severe food shortages at the time.

'But you don't have to worry about that, Dr Xia. You're the recognized brains of the bureau.'

'Well, the pork brains could be quite harmful because of high cholesterol. I simply cannot resist the texture, so soft yet creamy when it's steamed well. But there's also something inexplicable about that folk belief, you know. Fish roes are actually said to be harmful to the human brain. What's the possible connection between the two? And if that's true, the Western foodies must all be dummies.'

Xia was talking about caviar, Chen guessed, having had it in the Friendship Hotel in the company of a literature professor from Scotland. He could not say he really liked it, but it might be a matter of acquired taste.

'High cholesterol or not, who cares? Not me. A soon-to-be retiree. *"Alas, years gone by with no achievement, / no opportunity until one's gray and old. / Had General Li served under the First Emperor of the Han dynasty,"'* Xia sighed, quoting his favorite lines from the Song dynasty poet Liu Kezhuang. General Li, as mentioned in the poem, was a brilliant one in the Han dynasty, but also an unlucky one, without the due recognition from the untrusting emperor at the time. That was perhaps another reason that the two had struck up the unique canteen companionship in spite of the fact that Dr Xia had a passion for classical Chinese poetry, but no appetite for the modernist poems written by Chen.

'But you may have more opportunities, Chen, in the changed times of ours. You are still young. If you care that much about your T.S. Eliot, how about taking an MA program in Western literature?'

'My mother also wants me to make an MA application at Fudan University, but for that, you have to get the approval of Party Secretary Li first. Even with his approval secured, I may or may not be able to pass the MA entrance test. Then what will other people say about it in the bureau? And what about Party Secretary Li?'

'That's true. In the system of ours, you may have to make do with whatever job you're given for the present moment. After all, there's no telling how long you have to wait for something else to happen to you— Oh, there's another reason I had the pork brains today,' Xia said, changing the subject. 'Guess what? I was just reminded of the latest case of the homicide squad.'

'What are you talking about, Dr Xia?'

'About exotic food, of course. This morning, I had a body sent into the lab from the homicide squad. When I cut it open, the mixed cuisines in his stomach more than astonished me.'

'Mixed cuisines, you mean?'

'Much more than that. So inexplicably mixed indeed,' Xia said emphatically. 'To begin with, a not-too-tiny amount of undigested fish roes, bigger and blacker than you can possibly imagine.'

'Caviar!'

'Exactly. Obscenely expensive, you know. Then something else – like Chinese transparent green bean noodles, but much tastier, I would say, before getting soaked and sodden like a mess of paste in the gastric juice. Guess what it could have possibly been?'

'That surely sounds weird. Now let me take a wild guess – shark fin?'

'Right again. For a young gourmet, Chen, you're fairly well informed.'

'I just happen to know something about it through an embarrassing mistake I made. Last year an overseas Chinese uncle took me to a high-end restaurant in Beijing and treated me to a tiny bowl of soup, which I finished in two or three large spoonfuls without tasting anything that special. Nothing but transparent green bean noodles, I assumed. Not until the end of the meal did I realize that it was the pricy shark fin. But that's truly strange – I mean the mixing of the two in one's stomach. Caviar and shark fin.'

'Exactly. West and East! Now imagine throwing the

drunken shrimp into it. That's typical Ningbo cuisine. Simply unbelievable.'

'That surely beats me. Drunken shrimp! Uncooked but drunken with liquor, the shrimp still twitching on a gourmet's tongue. Anything else you have learned about the dead?'

'No, nothing else, the identity is not established yet.' Xia added, shaking his head, 'Possibly just another cold case in a week or two.'

After lunch, Chen checked the mail that had been delivered to the reading room. There was a package from Shang, his friend and college mate with a French major. It contained a copy of *The Unbearable Lightness of Being* in English, and a letter suggesting the two of them should join forces translating the French novel.

'The novel is so poetic, Chen. It takes a poet like you to do it justice in the Chinese language. You have a lot of time on your hands right now, haven't you?'

A lot of time on his hands, that was true. He did not have to spend every minute translating the police procedures – at least the Party Secretary seemed not to be in any hurry for it. And he too had heard a lot about the novel. It could be a really worthy project. But it should be up to someone well-versed in the French language to do a proper job of the translation. Besides, what if he was caught moonlighting in the reading room?

If the book was professionally related, he might be able to claim he was reading or translating in an effort to familiarize himself with police procedures. In fact, he'd begun reading mysteries in the reading room in earnest, and that with a good conscience. Some of them proved to be quite thought-provoking, especially those with a sociological focus, greatly expanding the whodunit horizon for him.

And it might have been a coincidence that a publisher in Guilin contacted him about the possibility of his translating a mystery at a tempting royalty rate. It appeared to be a work-able idea for him to read it in the bureau first, and then translate it in the attic back home.

Then his train of thought shifted back to the talk with Dr

Xia in the canteen. In spite of his personal interests, Dr Xia was now seen as an acknowledged authority in the forensic field, having done a remarkable job over the last several years. Hence his presence in the police bureau was justified. What about Chen? Why couldn't he try to do something in the line of a cop in addition to the translations assigned to him? Realistically, he'd better make the best of his present job in the police bureau before any other career opportunity presented itself.

He decided to pay a visit to Detective Ding, the head of the homicide squad, with the ready-made excuse of consulting him about those investigation terms for the translation project, which happened to be true.

A veteran cop in his mid-forties with rugged features, Detective Ding let him into the office with a suggestion of not-too-pleasant surprise on his face. After his rehearsed questions about the proper terms in the translation of police procedures, Chen brought up the topic of the body recently examined by Dr Xia.

'Something I've just heard from Dr Xia today in the canteen, I cannot help feeling curious about it.'

Nothing new came from Detective Ding, however, except a note of impatient frustration about what he took as a case of a mugging gone wrong.

'So far nothing reported matches the description in the missing person's file,' Detective Ding said, taking out a close-up of the dead. A bespectacled man in his late sixties or early seventies, with a clean-shaven, deep-lined face. 'We'll have to post it for possible information.'

'Any signs on the body?'

'No signs of a struggle on the body or at the scene. A fatal stab to the heart from behind. Presumably with a sharp kitchen knife. Possibly died instantly.'

'When was it reported?'

'The following morning. According to Dr Xia, death occurred before midnight. Four days now. It does not add up. None of his family members have noticed or reported him missing so far, unless he lived by himself.'

'Where was the body found?'

'North Zhejiang Road, near Tianmu Road.'

'The location is fairly close to the railway station—'

'Well, we've thought about the possibility of his being a traveler who was passing through Shanghai. If that's the case, more days may go by before people will contact us about it,' Ding said, with noticeable irritation, looking Chen in the eye for the first time.

'You're right, Detective Ding.'

Still, Ding seemed not to be taking that possibility seriously. The squad was short-handed. In the case of someone traveling here from another province, it could also prove to be out of the squad's jurisdiction.

'You're truly experienced, Detective Ding,' Chen said, standing up. 'In spite of my college major in English, I'm a cop now, and I think I have to learn the basics of the profession. Particularly from a veteran like you.'

'If you're really that interested,' Ding said, rising and turning back to the desk to pick up a manila folder, 'here's a copy of the crime scene report. Possibly not as interesting as those mysteries in English.'

'Thank you so much,' Chen said, taking the manila folder. Detective Ding must have heard something about his 'work' in the reading room.

That same evening, Chen paid a visit to his middle school buddy Lu, nicknamed 'Overseas Chinese Lu', an even more impossible foodie than Dr Xia. For Dr Xia, it was a matter of eating for living, but for Lu it was the other way around – a matter of living for eating.

Chen and Lu were quite different, but 'birds of the same black feather flocked together' in their middle school years, and they became friends because of their black family backgrounds. Still, while Chen kept his tail humbly tucked in, Lu struck another pose, holding his head high, his hair mousse shining. Lu might have been a 'black puppy' too, but he turned out to be one with the tail wagging in defiance. Far from feeling ashamed, Lu took an obstinate pride in coming from that 'good old family' of his, maintaining that his father

'Ludwig' was the 'white fox fur king' in the pre-1949 era. In contrast, Chen would have never dreamed of bragging and boasting of his father as an internationally known Neo-Confucianist scholar. That accounted for the origin of Lu's nickname. 'Overseas Chinese' was unmistakably a negative term during the days of the Cultural Revolution. Nevertheless, Lu managed to openly cultivate 'the decadent bourgeois taste', coming to school in a jacket made out of a Western-style three-piece suit of his father's, brewing coffee, tossing fruit salad, frying onion rings, and treating Chen to those delicacies at home.

That evening Lu was making a pot of fish soup at home, greeting Chen with the pot lid grasped in his hand, hardly looking up from the steaming soup.

'The mandarin fish was barely dead when I bought it at the food market, its eyes still clear in the late-afternoon light. For the soup, I fried the fish, added boiling water, and threw in a slice of Jinhua ham left over from the Chinese New Year. According to the recipe, it should take two or three hours for the soup to simmer over a small fire. Almost two hours now, you won't regret waiting for just fifteen minutes more with me. You'll relish it like nothing else, I give you my word. The milky white soup will be so delicious, so palatable, so tasty, you'll simply bite off your tongue.'

Lu's impassioned exaggeration was nothing new to Chen, who readily agreed, smiling, taking a seat for himself.

'While we are waiting for the soup, Overseas Chinese Lu, let me tell you something really intriguing about the food in someone's stomach on the autopsy table.'

'Wow, a food mystery! Yes, you're a cop now, little wonder about it. Go ahead, I'm all ears.'

With the soup bubbling on the fire, Chen recounted what Dr Xia had told him in the canteen. For some important parts, he practically repeated Xia's description verbatim with all the details included.

'Now you have come to the right man as your consultant,' Lu said, with unmistakable pride in his voice. 'I too have got a large piece of shark fin from my cousin in Hong Kong. We'll do it together next time, Chen. It has to be immersed in water beforehand for several hours. I've been experimenting with special recipes of the exotic stuff—'

'But that's more than exotic. I mean, what was discovered on Dr Xia's autopsy table,' Chen hastened to shift back to the question he wanted to ask. 'In just one meal with both caviar and shark fin left in his stomach. One typical of the West, and one symbolic of the East. Not to mention the drunken shrimp as well. How could such a combination have been possible? I cannot visualize them together even in my wildest imagination.'

'Well, that's a new trend you know nothing about in this magical city of Shanghai. Now let me ask you this question first. What's the cuisine for Xinya Restaurant on Nanjing Road?'

'Guangdongese. We've been there quite a few times, why?'

'Yes, you love the beef in oyster sauce, I know. So tender, it practically melts on your tongue. Then, what about North Cloud Pavilion?'

'Pekingese, I mean the cuisine.'

'You have not forgotten the Peking duck that nearly finished us there, have you?'

'Of course not.' It had happened toward the end of their middle school years. The two of them had finally saved enough for a 'duck enjoyable in three ways' – duck skin wrapped in a pancake, duck meat slice fried with green bean sprout, and duck soup made of the bones, but at the end of the meal, the restaurant charged them for the pancake, the green onion and the special sauce as well – all extras not listed in the menu. So Lu had had to run back home for three more yuan.

'Those days, one specific cuisine for one restaurant only, no question about it, that's the traditional way in China. But not any more, whether fortunately or unfortunately. Last week in a meal with an old friend, we ordered beef in oyster sauce plus roast Peking duck plus Fujian fish ball soup, all of them exquisitely spread out on the same table. The experience is really not bad, I have to say, just like visiting three restaurants of different cuisines all at once. For the latest fashionable person, it is called fusion, you know.'

'But the fusion of Occidental and Oriental?'

'True, that's a bit weird. Not conceivable even in one of the most fashionable fusion restaurants . . .' Lu said, nodding in deep thought. 'Oh, there's a new restaurant called "Imperial Recipes" that's increasingly popular among the newly rich in China.'

'Imperial recipes?'

'The ancient Chinese emperors believed they were the rulers of the whole world. So the delicacies of every cuisine imaginable would have been served in the palace. Some chefs nowadays claim that their ancestors served in the royal households. No one could tell whether it was true or not. Anyway, the trick is to put the expensive or exotic dishes of various cuisines on the one and only imperial table. The drunken shrimp, for instance, may appear to be too homely for a high-end restaurant, but there's a tale about the Qianlong emperor of the Qing dynasty falling for the sensation of the shrimp jumping and kicking on his tongue with a young, half-naked boat girl kneeling beside, sucking him. So a present-day customer enjoys not just a simple dish of live liquor-drunken shrimp, but all the imagination of enjoying a sensationally sensual delicacy that the Qing emperor fell for. And you may also know the story about Songjiang river perch—'

'Yes, I know, I've read a poem about it,' Chen said in a hurry, having to prevent Lu from digressing into a prolonged epicurean discourse. 'Zhang Jiying, a high-ranking official of the Jin dynasty, missed the fish so much that he resigned the highest official position under the emperor for the live fish available only in his home town—'

'Oh, the fish soup,' Lu said, jumping up in haste. 'It's time to throw in a pinch of fresh ground black pepper.'

With the bowl of soup placed on the table, the talk was lost in an unbroken string of Lu's exclamations, his spoon delving in and out of the soup, clinking in a quick succession. He would not talk about anything else, and the steaming hot, milky white fish soup truly exceeded Chen's expectations.

When they finished the last spoonful of the fish soup, it was almost ten.

'The location of the crime scene is close to the railway

station, right?' Lu asked abruptly, picking his teeth with a bamboo toothpick in satisfaction.

'How do you know?'

'Because of the inspiration of the fish soup. Don't worry, Inspector Chen. I'll let you know as early as possible.'

At noon the next day, as Chen was about to go down to the bureau canteen, he got a phone call from Lu.

'Yes, it's such an "imperial recipe" restaurant, known only in a limited circle. Obscenely expensive. And it's not far from the railway station.'

'You're so effective, Lu.'

'The chef/owner is said to be from a family that used to cook for the Qing royal family. Just one room with enough space for a round table. No printed menu. The chef chooses from whatever he sees as the freshest in the food market for the day. It's so popular in the city that customers have to make reservations weeks beforehand. Because of the exorbitant expense, customers may choose to share the table with others, and the courses are served the Western way, with a separate spoon for each dish, and a small plate in front of each customer. Each of the customers just needs to pay for his or her portion—'

'That's intriguing,' Chen said, having to cut short Lu's passionate report again. 'Give me the name and address. I'm going there right now.'

He left the bureau without getting lunch in the canteen.

About half an hour later, he found himself arriving at an old *shikumen* house tucked in a winding narrow lane on North Zhejiang Road. There was a small sign barely noticeable on the doorframe: *Aixin's Imperial Recipes*. From the half-open door, he looked into a littered courtyard, which served as a sort of open kitchen, with large basins containing fish and shrimp and vegetable and some other indescribable stuff. Across the courtyard, he had a partial view of a front room sporting a round table already covered with a white tablecloth, and a lacquer screen behind that partially obscured an old ladder leading precariously to a retrofitted attic, which probably served as the bedroom for the family.

A middle-aged man was preparing for the dinner in a corner of the courtyard. Wearing a purple Qing-style vest plus a gray apron instead of a white uniform, he was busy scaling a live fish on a bamboo cutting board.

'*The swallows, once the visitors to the noble families, / are now flying into the ordinary homes . . .*'

Chen thought of the Tang dynasty lines as he approached the chef in the supposedly imperial Qing costume, and introduced himself as a writer working on an article about the restaurant, taking out his Writers Association membership card in support of his statement.

'This is a restaurant carrying on the glorious Chinese culinary tradition for thousands of years. I appreciate what you are doing here. And I will do my best for the article.'

The man in the purple vest turned out to be none other than the chef/owner and was surnamed Aixin, who apparently had no aversion to publicity.

It was not a difficult role for Chen to play, truly being a member of that association, and a self-styled gourmet too. After spending ten minutes on rehearsed questions about the restaurant and the supposedly imperial recipes, he said, 'For the purpose of the article, I've interviewed several gourmets in the city. One of them surnamed Lu has heard a lot about your restaurant, especially from an old friend of his.'

Chen produced a notebook showing the picture of the dead man placed between the pages.

'Oh, Mr Fu.'

'Yes, that's him,' Chen said vaguely, registering the name *Fu* in his mind. 'He's one quite well known both in and out of the gourmet circle.'

'I do not know about that, but he seems to be a modest, old-fashioned gentleman, never boasting and bragging about himself like some other customers here.'

Judging by the present tense, Aixin had no knowledge that Fu – the man in the picture – had been killed at a location not far from the restaurant.

'Well, tell me something about Mr Fu for the benefit of the article, particularly from your advantageous point of view. It'll be a plus for the publicity of your restaurant.'

'Mr Fu is a regular customer of ours. About five days ago. Hold on . . .' Aixin said, turning to dig out a notebook from under a pile of old newspapers. 'Yes, five days ago, he came over for dinner, sharing the round table with nine others, each with a small plate in front—'

'Yes, that's very practical, I mean the table-sharing arrangement. Anything else special about him?'

'A really nice old gentleman, but he books only for himself, never bringing in any company with him. Quite well to do, apparently, though he's never dressed like a Big Buck. He keeps pretty much to himself. So we know little about him.'

'He called in for reservations here?'

'Yes, we sometimes call him too. Because he wants us to keep him informed of anything new or exciting in our imperial recipes, and about the table-sharing opportunity, too. It's not always available, you know.'

'Do you have his phone number?'

'The number of his neighborhood public phone station,' Aixin said, taking out the address book. 'He lives in a lane called Red Dust, on the corner of Jinling and Fujian Roads, in the former French Concession.'

'Red Dust Lane!' Chen said excitedly, copying the address in a notebook. 'By the way, anything different about him that night – during his last visit to your restaurant?'

'His last visit? No, nothing I can think of. He seemed to be satisfied as always. Been here more than fifteen times, I'd say. But why that question?'

'For the article, I want it to be as objective as possible. It's good to know that he's not complaining or anything like that,' Chen said, rising. 'I'll probably come back. Thank you so much, Aixin.'

Then he noticed on a shelf a stainless-steel basin of fried fish chunks immersed in special brown sauce.

'House specials. Made of live carp,' Aixin said, with unmistakable pride. 'Big wok, big fire, then immediately immersed in the special soy sauce with sugar and other secret spices for hours.'

'That looks so delicious. I'll have a few pieces for my mother.'

Chen had the chef put two pieces in a plastic box. It was more expensive than he had imagined, but he did not have to tell her, and he was sure she would like the fish from the Imperial Recipes restaurant.

On the way back to the bureau, Chen tried to think like a real cop. More likely than not, it was a case of a botched mugging, as Detective Ding had said, a scenario Chen was also inclined to.

Still, there were things that didn't seem to add up. For one, how could an old man in ordinary clothing have made a likely target for a desperate thug at that particular locale? Not to mention the fact that there was no sign of a struggle at the scene or on the body. Just one single vicious stab.

And then something else in the crime scene report, too. With Fu's wallet missing, a diamond ring was found in his watch pocket. As a possible scenario, the murderer could have been startled away by an unexpected passerby, but Fu's body was not discovered until the next morning, at least five or six hours later.

The location too lent itself to the puzzle. It was not one of the high-end residential areas where people walked around with their bulging wallets, but it was not a slum-like neighborhood either, which would be haunted with desperadoes.

And with the identity of the dead established as an old man living in the center of the city, a new question came up. How was it possible that four or five days had passed without a missing person's report submitted to the police?

He played with the idea of making a visit to Red Dust Lane that afternoon. It was a lane not unfamiliar to him from his childhood, but with all his college years in Beijing, he had not been to the lane for a long time. He had thought of the lane as a page turned over in his life. But no, he was going there again.

Was there something providential in it?

Still, he decided to go back to the bureau first. Detective Ding seemed not to have been paying any special attention to the case.

Would that change now, with the identity of the dead being discovered?

Stepping into Detective Ding's office, Chen reminded himself again that he was hardly a cop in the eyes of his colleagues.

'It could have been nothing but coincidence, Detective Ding,' Chen started with a diffident manner.

'What do you mean, Chen?' Ding said, eyeing him up and down.

'I was having lunch with a friend – another impossible epicurean like Dr Xia. Among the cups, I mentioned what Dr Xia had told me about the body discovered on Zhejiang Road near the railway station. Particularly about the bizarre fusion of the food undissolved in the stomach of the dead. My friend said he knew which restaurant could have provided such an unbelievable meal of mixed cuisines.'

'You're kidding, Chen. He could tell the restaurant by what Dr Xia discovered on the autopsy table! What's the name of your gourmet friend?'

'Now that's a favor I have to ask of you, Detective Ding. He does not want to get implicated in a homicide investigation. So I gave him my word that I would not give his name away.'

'But how can that possibly be of any help, Chen? What's the name of the restaurant then?'

'Aixin's Imperial Recipes.'

'Aixin sounds like a Manchurian name.'

'Yes, the chef/owner claims his great-grandfather served in the royal kitchen of the Qing dynasty. And Aixin also knows the name of the dead, too. Fu Donghua, a regular customer to his restaurant.'

'Now that's something. Tell me more about it.'

'Fu was a resident of Red Dust Lane on the corner of Fujian and Jinling Roads, I've just learned.' Chen decided to be vague about his visit to the restaurant, unsure about Detective Ding's reaction regarding Chen's stepping on his turf.

'Really!' Detective Ding said, hurrying to pick up the phone before Chen even had time to say another word. 'Operator, I want the phone number of the neighborhood committee of Red Dust Lane, Huangpu District.'

Chen hesitated, lingering there for a minute or two before he backed out without waiting for the phone call to get through to the neighborhood committee.

For the following discussion, Chen's company might not be needed, even though it was Chen who had provided the clue. As he was retreating, Detective Ding made a vague gesture with his raised hand, but did not really try to stop Chen.

Back in the reading room, Chen picked up *Roseanna*, an Inspector Martin Beck mystery by Maj Sjöwall and Per Wahlöö. It was ironic that the Swedish writers had set out to write about the evils of the Swedish capitalist society, but ended up producing one bestselling detective story after another, though with a determined social focus. It did not take long for him to get lost in the laborious investigation pushed on by the stubborn Swedish inspector, following a number of false clues.

Before any decisive breakthrough came in that far-away investigation, however, the phone rang in the reading room.

'Yes, that's him, Mr Fu. Confirmed. He's been missing for days. The neighborhood committee is gathering info for us,' Detective Ding said at the other end of the line. 'It's a promising breakthrough, Chen. I'm going there first thing tomorrow morning. Let me know if there's anything new from that gourmet friend of yours.'

'It's just a random harvest,' Chen said, wondering at the plural pronoun 'us' used by Detective Ding.

Early the next morning, on the way to Red Dust Lane, Detective Ding could not help having doubts about Chen's 'random harvest'.

Cops do not believe much in coincidence. It appeared implausible for Chen's friend to turn up at this opportune juncture to establish the identity of the dead, with nothing to go on but the description of the mixed delicacies left in the stomach of the dead. Was Chen trying to do something on the sly regarding the investigation?

Detective Ding did not think he had anything personal against Chen, in spite of some stories he had heard about the bookish young man in the reading room. Some said Chen was studying for an MA test at Fudan University, and some said he was striving for a different career, writing modernist poems. It was understandable for a young man to try his hand at something different, Detective Ding reflected, when Chen had been state-assigned a job not exactly after his heart. But why the sudden interest in the murder case?

With his steps slowing down, Detective Ding stepped into a public phone booth on the corner of He'nan Road and called his assistant Liao.

'Don't worry,' Liao said with a chuckle after hearing his boss out. 'Even if Chen tries to take a look into the case, what difference can he possibly make? He has no training or experience whatsoever.'

'Chen has succeeded in identifying the dead. Any further breakthrough on his part would mean a loss of face for our squad, Liao. It would not hurt to stay on the lookout.'

Still, the head of the homicide squad had one advantage, Detective Ding believed. The case was his, officially, and he had the authority and resources to conduct the investigation.

In the neighborhood committee office tucked near the back exit of Red Dust Lane, the head of the committee, a middle-aged man named Jun, received Detective Ding with due respect and gave him a quite detailed report of three pages in a manila folder. Comrade Jun had done an effective job after the phone conversation with Ding the previous day.

'You may read it here, Detective Ding, if you like. I'll be in the back room – oh, I think I'll have to go to Fu's home first. And we can discuss afterward.'

So Comrade Jun put a 'closed' sign on the front door after him, and Detective Ding lost no time immersing himself in the basics about Fu.

Fu had lived in the lane in a wing unit of the *shikumen* house toward the mid-lane for more than forty years. In the late 1940s he started a seafood company, initially in the court-yard, but soon expanding; as a result, he was classified as a capitalist in Chair Mao's class system after 1949. In 1966, at the beginning of the Cultural Revolution, he and his wife suffered brutal humiliation and persecution at revolutionary mass criticisms, during which she abruptly dropped dead one night. Shortly afterward, his son Xiaoqiang and daughter

Hongxia moved out in a politically determined break from the family. Fu had since lived there by himself. In recent years, with his financial situation dramatically improved, he rejected his children's efforts at reconciliation, and hired a maid named Meihua for help at home. In the lane, he was known as an eccentric old man who hardly mixed with his neighbors, but it was understandable after all he had gone through.

Once Comrade Jun came back to the neighborhood committee, Detective Ding wanted Xiaoqiang and Hongxia to come to the office for interviews. The two children happened to be in the lane at that moment. They were trying to take back the wing unit from the sobbing maid.

They talked rather incoherently, perhaps anxious to defend what they had done to the old man during the Cultural Revolution. If there was anything surprising to Detective Ding, it was their complaining in chorus against the maid Meihua as an insatiable gold digger.

Around three in the afternoon, Detective Ding believed he had learned enough about the Fu family saga, but he was not that sure about its direct bearing on the murder investigation.

'Like in a proverb, their father's body is not that cold yet,' Comrade Jun said to Detective Ding with a stern frown after they were left alone in the neighborhood office, 'and they're already fighting like cats and dogs.'

'But they are his children.'

'But he practically disowned them.'

Comrade Jun then moved into an account about the bad blood between Fu and his children. There was not any legal document left by Fu, however, to cut off his son and daughter, nor any move taken by Fu known to the neighborhood committee in that direction. Detective Ding listened patiently to the end, thanked Jun, and left the office.

Detective Ding chose to walk back to the bureau, at least for part of the way, trying to sort through his entangled thoughts.

A black cat jumped out of a pebbled side street. Allegedly an ominous sign. He spat on the ground three times, superstitiously, in an effort to dispel any potential bad luck for the investigation.

For a murder case like that, a possible first step was to question who would have benefitted from the victim's death. The answer seemed to be simple: Fu's two children. No one had any knowledge as to whether Fu had intended to leave his huge fortune to anyone other than Xiaoqiang and Hongxia, but it was not likely. At least nothing had been done about it by the time of his death.

According to Xiaoqiang and Hongxia, there was one suspect with a plausible motive: the gold-digging maid, but as it was, Meihua gained nothing from the old man's sudden death. No arrangement had been made – according to Jun – in her benefit. So their focus on her could only have been something like a preemptive strike.

Detective Ding then thought about that mysterious friend of Chen's, who might be able to provide some additional background information. He decided, instead of walking on, to get a bus back to the police bureau.

The light was fading in the late afternoon. Chen was still reading *Roseanna* when Detective Ding barged in without bothering to knock at the door.

'Oh, it's a Swedish mystery. I'm trying to learn some investigation techniques from it,' Chen said, showing the cover of the book that represented a drowned female body.

'Just back from Red Dust Lane,' Ding said, pulling a chair over. 'According to Comrade Jun, the head of the Red Dust neighborhood committee, Fu had told his maid Meihua – the day before he got killed – that he might go to Suzhou for the seasonable food by taking the night train after the "imperial recipes" dinner. That's why nobody reported him missing even after he was not seen for a few days.'

'Yes, that makes sense,' Chen said. 'And the restaurant in question is close to the railway station.'

Detective Ding produced two cassette tapes without waiting for Chen to go on.

'Here are the tapes of the interview with Fu's children, Xiaoqiang and Hongxia. There may be something in them. The old man refused to see them because of what they had done to him during the Cultural Revolution.'

'So you think the two of them could have some unrevealed motive?'

Chen noticed a frown flashing across the detective's forehead. Possibly because of the assertive way he talked, having forgotten himself in the suspense of the mystery novel.

'About their family matters, that's just like in a proverb: it's difficult even for an incorruptible and capable judger to tell what's what, but you are interested in the investigation, aren't you?'

'It's the first time for me, and it'll be so exciting to listen to a real police interview tape. Thank you so much for giving me the opportunity, Detective Ding.'

'Party Secretary Li has just called me. People in the city government are talking about it too. There may be something special in the case.' Detective Ding added as if in afterthought, 'Let me know if you have anything new from that foodie friend of yours, anything and everything he can think of. He must have been really well informed.'

Afterward, Chen wondered whether the tapes left by Detective Ding were meant merely as an acknowledgment of his help. He could not shake the feeling that the detective did not like his meddling in the investigation. Still, Detective Ding's request for information could come close to a green light for him to go on.

Before Detective Ding's visit that afternoon, Chen had actually considered his job on the Fu case finished, which didn't seem too bad for a first attempt on his part. Besides, it was not a good idea for him to appear too pushy among other real cops.

But his interests were roused by his initial success, he admitted to himself. He put the son's tape into an old recorder. Before pressing the start button, he dug out a packet of instant coffee and made a cup with the lukewarm water from a bamboo-shelled thermos bottle.

> Yes, what we did during the Cultural Revolution hurt the old man. But who was not hurt at the time? Because of the black shadow cast by his capitalist class status, I got nowhere for all my hard work at the company. No

promotion. Nor bonus. Not to mention all the horrible discrimination I suffered because of the black family background.

Now think about it, even Liu Shaoqi's daughter denounced her father in public. Indeed, none other than the daughter of the Chairman of The People's Republic of China, second only to Mao, the Chairman of the Chinese Communist Party. What choice did I have? You surely know better, Detective Ding. And what did I do? I only wrote a half-hearted statement against him, which was far from a public denunciation. And it was only for the sake of my baby son that I moved out of the lane, so that he would have an unshadowed life, different from mine. It was a move totally understandable under the circumstances.

After the ending of the Cultural Revolution, I would have liked to come back to take care of him in the lane here. He was old. It was up to us to help. It had nothing to do with his unexpected fortune. As an engineer in a joint venture company, I've been doing fine, so I'm not after his money, not at all.

Having said that, I want to add that Hongxia is a far less lucky one. In reality, no less a victim of the Cultural Revolution than our father. She married the first time in a hurry like some damaged goods. Just for the sake of obtaining the working-class status through her husband. But what then? He started to abuse her like a dirty mop even on the honeymoon, taking her family background as the ready excuse. They got divorced in less than three years. And what about her second husband? Worse than the first. An ex-Red Guard who lost all his money in cricket fighting and ran into a high debt. For a woman of her age, however, it's difficult for her to think of getting rid of him and marrying for a third time . . .

Some of the contents seemed to be neither here nor there, Chen observed. Unlike Detective Ding, Chen had no overall background information from the neighborhood committee. But he found some details in the tape helped, though they were at the same time vaguely disturbing. Not so much in terms of possible clues for the investigation, but more like a reminder of what he himself had felt toward his father during the Cultural Revolution.

Next Chen put in the daughter's tape, which, not rewound properly, started somewhere in the middle.

Father did not forgive us, I know, for what we did such a long time ago. But did we have any choice? A schoolmate of mine was beaten into a cripple for life because of her refusal to denounce her black family at the time. We too have suffered an unimaginable lot during the Cultural Revolution because of him, he knew better than anybody else.

Now, it's just proper and right for him to leave all his things to us. It's nothing but the Chinese way. As you may not know, I actually contributed to the existence of the list of the things taken away by the Red Guards that night – the very list that survived the "Sweeping away Four Olds Campaign" at the beginning of the Cultural Revolution. That night, I was shivering beside our poor mother in the midst of those Red Guards. I still remember vividly as she showed us the jewelry box, saying in tears, "I have never shown the jewelries to you, but after today, you may never be able to see any of them again. Look at this diamond ring. When your father bought it for me, I swore I would never part with it. So I'm wearing it for the last time." A young Red Guard snapped there and then as he overheard her words. He accused her of urging us to remember the decadent luxuries in the old society. As a result, she was dragged out as a target of the revolutionary mass criticism. With the chaos following her sudden death, the Red Guards forgot to take back the very list of the things seized as "Four Olds" from our home, and it's the list which later made possible the compensation, and then the reunion with his old buddy from abroad, and the stock shares too. The long, long chain of cause and effect indeed, you may say. The old man was simply befuddled by the bewitching maid . . .

Chen pressed the stop button. All in all, not too much for the investigation. If there was anything that sounded like a possible lead, it was their insistence on making the maid into a gold digger, and consequently a suspect. But that seemed understandable, nothing too suspicious in it.

Was it possible that he had missed something on the tape? Or perhaps there was not a lot in the interview to begin with.

He thought about discussing the tapes with Detective Ding, but thought better of it. The detective seemed to have not budged from his initial position. There was nothing new Chen could tell him after listening through the tapes.

And then he found himself drawn toward the sociopolitical background of the family drama.

For years during the course of the Cultural Revolution, Chen too could not help holding a secret resentment against his father for being a 'black monster', which practically meant the end of the world in a young boy's imagination. Years later, he bitterly regretted having felt like that toward his father, but it was too late. So the murder investigation could turn out, hopefully, to be something he had not been able to do for his own father. A sort of personal redemption, at least symbolically, he thought somberly.

Then he was determined to go for a couple of extra miles. It could serve as a sign – if nothing came out of it – that he was not meant to be a cop. But for the moment, he wanted to try, and in a different way from Detective Ding's methods.

For Detective Ding, the investigation had turned in an unexpected direction once the victim's identity was established.

Party Secretary Li had called him immediately, and then several times more, saying repeatedly that with Fu's connections abroad, including a super-rich businessman surnamed Cai in the States, the case was now the top political priority for the bureau, which had to push the investigation to a conclusion in a quick and satisfactory way.

The scenario of a botched mugging was practically brushed aside. In the view of the office of the United Front Work of the city government, it would have appeared too unconvincing to Fu's overseas friend Cai and others like him, who were debating about the prospect of investing in Shanghai.

So Detective Ding hurried over to Red Dust Lane again. With the help of Comrade Jun, a list of possible beneficiaries from Fu's death was hammered out.

The list, inevitably, had his two children at the top. When Detective Ding called back to the bureau, however, Party Secretary Li lost no time ruling out that possibility. Xiaoqiang and Hongxia might have panicked about the maid manipulating the old man, but they could have tried – even in desperation – to get rid of the maid instead of their father. It was improbable, with no convincing motive on the part of Xiaoqiang and Hongxia, and also politically unacceptable to the Party authorities, since the 'family skeleton' would have been dragged out of the closet of the Cultural Revolution.

So Detective Ding started working on a different list of people with a possible grudge against Fu. Comrade Jun once again proved to be more than competent. In little more than an hour, a number of names were put together on a large piece of paper, along with some basic information about them.

Old Hunchback Fang was a retired neighborhood security activist who had shouted revolutionary slogans at Fu during the Cultural Revolution, and after the Cultural Revolution complained and cursed about Fu's dramatic financial improvement. He was recently heard saying in indignation: 'Chairman Mao's equalitarian society is really gone to the dogs. The capitalists are staging a comeback. Imagine that old bastard Fu having a young maid – young enough to be his granddaughter – to wait on him head and foot, and behind the closed door, too! He should have dropped dead with his equally black-hearted wife that long-ago night.' Hence there was a convincing motive in terms of class hatred on the part of Old Hunchback Fang.

Second on the list was none other than an ex-Red Guard surnamed Zhu, who had been sentenced to two years for dragging Fu's wife out to the mass criticism and then removing the diamond ring from her not-yet-cold finger when she dropped dead in the courtyard. To ex-Red Guards like Zhu, the sentence appeared to be too severe a punishment, and he was released after less than a year. So he could have had a motive for taking revenge against Fu.

Ironically, another suspect on the list was the other ex-Red Guard, surnamed Pei, who had given Fu the list of things taken away from his home. Years later, when the news of Fu's stock fortune came out, Pei was heard arguing with him about his entitlement to a portion of it, which he believed he deserved. And about a month or so before Fu's death, Pei was again seen in the lane, intercepting the old man, begging. Fu would not have been able to get away but for the maid coming to his rescue, pushing Pei away like a fury. According to the neighbors at the scene, Pei was shouting, 'You cannot bring any money into the coffin, can you?'

Detective Ding started making enquiries about their alibis. For Old Hunchback Fang, he maintained he had had a meeting with other Maoist activists that evening, and afterward played mahjong late into the night. It should not be difficult to have his alibi confirmed. From Zhu's neighborhood committee, it was learned that Zhu had been doing business far away in Shenzhen for the last few months. But Pei's neighborhood committee mentioned something suspicious, though perhaps not that uncommon for people like Pei, who had been seen coming back after twelve that night with unsteady steps.

Immediately, Detective Ding got in touch with Ouyang, the cop in charge of Pei's neighborhood. It took less than fifteen minutes for Ouyang to drag Pei into the office to talk with Detective Ding on the phone. Still out of breath, Pei stammered on the other end of the line as Detective Ding started questioning him about his whereabouts the night Fu was murdered.

'Well, let me think. I was seeing . . . seeing a late-night movie.'

'With whom?'

'Alone.'

'Really! What's the name of the movie?'

'It's . . . *Little Flower*.'

'Which movie theater?'

'The Peace Cinema, you know, on Hankou Road.'

After he was through with Pei, Detective Ding dialed his assistant Liao, who promised to check into it and call back the moment he got anything and to give a detailed report the next morning at the latest.

'That will be fine, Liao. But call me any time you have anything new.'

It was quite late, but more background information started to roll in. Several people confirmed Old Hunchback Fang's presence at the mahjong table, losing and cursing all the time. One was positive that Fang stayed there until after midnight as he left at the same time, looking at his watch once outside. As for Zhu, his neighbors in the apartment building also confirmed that he had not been home for months, with the door locked and mail uncollected.

It took quite a long time for Detective Ding to talk to the people through the public phone service. Then he realized that he had missed the last bus back home.

That evening witnessed Chen walking toward Red Dust Lane, as if moving back into an evening of his childhood. There was something still vivid in his memory – the 'Red Dust evening talk', as it was called, in front of that lane, where the neighborhood residents sat out in the open, especially in warm weather, telling stories, exchanging gossip and cracking jokes. As early as his elementary school days, he had heard of the evening talk, and he had since been there quite a number of times, spellbound by those unconventional stories.

Just like in his memory, a group of people were gathered on small bamboo chairs or wooden stools, a scene seemingly unchanged after all these years. But he must have changed a lot. No one there seemed to recognize him.

There's no stepping twice into the same river, Chen thought as he approached the audience of the evening talk, greeting those gathered with a smile.

'I came years ago for all the wonderful stories here in the company of my friend, who was then a resident of the lane. This evening I have just run some errands not far from the neighborhood, so I came over here just like in the good old days.'

No one seemed to be wary of his self-introduction, which

happened to be true – at least the part about his visits to the lane in the past.

A young man pushed over a bamboo stool to Chen while eyeing an elderly man sitting in the middle.

'Old Root, how about a new, exciting story tonight?'

'There's nothing new or exciting under the sun,' Old Root responded, waving a paper fan like a Suzhou opera singer about to perform on stage. 'Things are new or exciting only in people's talk.'

'Or in the newspaper,' Chen said, seizing the opportunity to take out a copy of *Legal Daily*, in which the Fu case was briefly mentioned. 'There's a story about Mr Fu from the lane here.'

'Exactly, the murder story is known all over the city. I read about it in the *Xinming Evening*,' another middle-aged man with a week's growth of beard joined in the chorus. 'If there's anybody Fu befriended in this lane, it's none other than you, Old Root.'

Old Root lit a cigarette, shaking his head and then nodding slightly, as if debating with himself about whether to start telling the story about Fu.

'Well, a disclaimer first. I cannot really claim Fu as my friend. Yes, he talked to me now and then, but it's just because no one else cared to talk to him in the lane during those years of the Cultural Revolution. If I know something about his life, it does not mean I have a right to tell tall tales about him in front of the lane. But with his death, people are coming up with all sorts of irresponsible speculations, so I think I may as well tell you some of the things I knew first-hand.

'"*In misfortune, there is a fortune; in fortune, there is a misfortune.*" That's from *Tao Te Ching* thousands of years ago. And it's still so true about the beginning and the ending of Fu's dramatic vicissitude in the mundane world of Red Dust.

'In the mid-1940s, Fu got an accountant job for a seafood company, and he managed to save enough money for a first-floor wing unit for his family in the lane. An easily contented man, he indulged himself only in the occasional experiment with the not-too-fresh fish and shrimp bought with the employee discount from the company. In the days when refrigerators were seen only in foreign movies, he "invented" recipes for fish and shrimp balls, capable of keeping them for days without going bad. Whenever successful with his gastronomical experiments, Fu would step out into the lane, treating the neighbors to the tiny yet tasty samples. Neighbors could never forget the first bite into his special eel ball. Such an unbelievable texture!

'One year after his son Xiaoqiang was born, his company boss lost huge in the market and fled away in the dark night. Unable to find a new job, Fu resorted to making fish and shrimp balls in the courtyard and selling them like the peddlers in the street food market behind the lane. But unlike them, what with his experience as an ex-accountant, and with his connections in the business circle, he was able to expand his product line into a small yet successful seafood company out of the lane.

'So Fu "established himself" before he reached his thirties – earlier than in the Confucian formula. At the end of that year, he bought a diamond ring for his hard-working wife, who had been busy peeling shrimp and deboning fish, first in the courtyard of the *shikumen* house, and then at the workshop, her fingers swollen with too much immersion in the water, yet never complaining about it.

'It's an incredible stroke of luck for us,' she said with grateful tears in her eyes, putting the ring on her finger with difficulty.

'It did not take too long for them to doubt, however, whether it really was such "an incredible stroke of luck".

'With the Communists taking over Shanghai in 1949, Fu was labeled a "capitalist" because of his seafood company – even with the company having gone through the nationwide campaign of socialist, state-transformation of private enterprise. Black in his class status, he no longer mixed with neighbors like before. People called him Mr Fu. Not so much out of respect as out of the difference in the class system. "Comrade" was politically popular, but only for some of us, the working-class people, which he was not. Considering the circumstances, I don't think he had too much of a choice at the time he started that company in the courtyard of the *shikumen* house.

'In 1966, in the campaign of "Sweeping Away the Four Olds" at the beginning of the Cultural Revolution, Red Guards raided his home for whatever "olds" they could lay their hands on – jewelry, foreign currency, gold, mahogany furniture – as the criminal evidence of his exploiting the working-class people in the pre-1949 era. In order for him to write a detailed guilt-pleading statement, a Red Guard gave him a list of the "Four Olds" stuff seized at the *shikumen* house. But before he was through with the first paragraph, another Red Guard overheard his wife telling her children to take a last look at the jewelry.

"'I've not shown any of them to you before. So just take a look and you may never see them again."

"'What, you evil, black-hearted capitalist wife!" the Red Guard snapped. "You want your children to remember and to seek revenge?"

'As a result, she had to stand out in the lane, holding overhead a blackboard with her name written and crossed out, plus a line beneath: "For my resistance against the Cultural Revolution, I deserve to die thousands and thousands of times." Later that same night, she collapsed while still holding the blackboard, and hit her head against the common concrete sink in the lane. She never regained consciousness. The Red Guards did not even raise a finger to help. Believe it or not, the one who had snapped at her earlier bent to wrench the diamond ring from her cold and stiff finger before her body was sent to the funeral home.

'And it turned out to be the bleakest funeral in the history of our lane, with no one except Fu himself standing at the funeral parlor. Neither of her children chose to attend, unwilling to be seen close to her, and complaining about the horrible humiliation and discrimination she had brought upon them. In short, people in the neighborhood avoided Fu like the black plague. I was the only one that sent a wreath to the funeral as a neighbor, but to tell the truth, I wasn't brave enough to go there myself.

'Shortly afterward, Xiaoqiang moved out. Hongxia

denounced Fu in another mass criticism before she married a worker, claiming that it was for the sake of obtaining the working-class status through marriage.

'So Fu was left all alone here, with nothing else to do except go on pleading guilty, hanging his head low under Mao's portrait on the lane wall every morning, sweeping the neighborhood on the weekend, too benumbed to care about what was happening around him, and increasingly withdrawn like a hermit crab forever shut up in its broken shell.

'After Nixon's visit to China in 1971, things began to improve a bit for people like Fu. A new government policy came into effect regarding so-called compensation for the loss they had suffered during the campaign of "Sweeping Away the Four Olds". But it was easier said than done. At the time, the Red Guards had been so anxious to seize the "Four Olds" in response to Chairman Mao's call, but with no idea about what to do with the seized stuff. Most of the things had been chaotically disposed of, and hence were unrecoverable. Fu was considered as extraordinarily lucky because he had been handed a list of seized "Four Olds" with which to write the guilt-pleading statement, and then the list was forgotten and left with Fu because of Mrs Fu's sudden death. In contrast, most of the affected families did not have such a list.

'To the surprise of the lane, Fu stubbornly declined the compensation offered by Xiahou, the new director of the state-run company. Even after 1976, with the Cultural Revolution ending in a whimper, Fu did not budge from his position. So Xiaoqiang wanted me to accompany Director Xiahou to Fu for a discussion about the large sum of compensation in accordance with the list.

'"The Cultural Revolution's over," Director Xiahou argued. "It's a national disaster. So many suffered or died, including Comrade Liu Shaoqi, Chairman of the People's Republic of China. Still, our Party proves to be a great one, capable of turning over a new page for our socialist country. We all have to take a correct attitude toward it and accept the compensation in accordance with the Party policy."

'"What's the correct attitude?" Fu retorted defiantly. "Not

everything can be compensated in terms of money. What about my wife's death?"

"'I understand, Mr Fu. But you have to think about your children, especially your daughter. She divorced for 'irreconcilable differences' the first time, and her second marriage seems not to be going well, either. Her husband has been losing steadily in cricket gambling. Enough punishment for her, I have to say. If you don't need the money, it may greatly help her.'"

"'No. They did not even come to their mother's funeral. That nailed it. Like in an old proverb: no wealth can last for three generations. Compensation or not, that's not the end of the world for them.'"

"'It's the government policy that all the affected families should take the compensation, or the authorities would blame me for not doing a good job. And that's so unfair for me. I was not one of the Red Guards that came to your home that night, you know that.'"

"'Well, what was seized that night had all come from the capitalistic exploitation in the old society, according to the editorial of the *People's Daily* at the time. Why should I take it back today? I'm now retired with a pension, thanks to the Party and the government. What more do I need?'" Fu said in a satirical yet adamant manner. "If you really want to do something about it, just give me back the diamond ring taken from her finger by one of the Red Guards as she lay cold, dead in the courtyard."

'The diamond ring turned out to be unrecoverable, unfortunately. The Red Guard denied taking it, and as a result, Director Xiahou's responsibility remained unfulfilled.

'But the amount of compensation appeared to be incredibly large, much more than an ordinary worker could have made during their whole life. Fu must have been pushing for more, as was commonly believed in the lane. With most of the black families in the city having accepted the compensation, Fu still held out. Anxious to wrap up the issue, Director Xiahou approached the Shanghai office of the United Front Work for help. As it happened, the official there had recently come across Fu's name in a letter from overseas. An American billionaire businessman named Cai had contacted the office about Fu. According to Cai, with his father being classified as a landlord in the countryside in the early days of 1949, he managed to flee to the United States, but he would not have made it there without the help of his "sworn brother" Fu, who gave Cai the money he had saved for a new apartment on Huaihai Road. In the subsequent years, for fear of causing trouble to Fu on the mainland, Cai made only indirect enquiries about his friend, with no success due to the continuous political movements in China. It was not until after the end of the Cultural Revolution that he made renewed enquiries, and this time, directly to the city government. And Cai also stressed his intention to invest in China's economic reform, so his request was taken seriously.

'At Director Xiahou's suggestion, I double-checked with those neighbors acquainted with the Fus in the late forties. The part about Fu's help to his friend proved to be true. At the time, Mrs Fu had talked to them about a plan to move out to a new apartment complex on Huaihai Road. While Red Dust Lane was not without its status, it was not considered a high-end area, so it was a matter of course for the prosperous to move up from here. Then all of a sudden, she dropped the subject, without explaining to the neighbors about the abrupt change of plan. When pressed, she simply said that Mr Fu was allowed to spend the money whatever way he liked. So he must have spent it to help Cai out.

'Now the city government saw it as a political task to reassure Cai of Fu's wellbeing in Shanghai, and a dramatic difference was immediately made.

'Because of Fu's demand for the return of the diamond ring as the precondition for acceptance of the compensation, the police arrested the Red Guard surnamed Zhu who had been seen snatching the ring from Mrs Fu's finger, and discovered it at his home along with the other jewelry seized from Fu's home that long-ago night. As a result of governmental insistence, the compensation turned out to be extraordinary, with all the bank savings returned carrying the highest interest rate at the time. Because of the recovered ring, Fu could not fail to accept the compensation.

'But what's more, a notarized certificate of stock shares was then officially delivered to Fu through the city government. Cai declared that Fu's loan so many years earlier had been in reality an investment in his companies in the United States. The message from such a move was unmistakable. Fu was not just a "capitalist" here, but a Big Buck partner in American companies.

'For the long and the short of it, Fu proved to be so well off on the interest from the compensation alone, that he did not have to touch the shares at all. Unsurprisingly, speculation about the incredible fortune pulled his children back to the lane, again and again, but there was no bringing Fu around. One evening, Xiaoqiang left curses under the Red Dust blackboard newsletter: "The old man's brains must have been damaged by the blackboard hung around his neck." And the next day, Hongxia reacted more theatrically, storming out and screaming over the trash bin near the lane exit, "The old man died in 1966."

'They kept coming back, nevertheless. So Fu went to the neighborhood committee to make a formal statement to the effect that he wanted nothing to do with them – in a deliberate move to forestall their continuing attempts to return – but it did not seem to work out.

'In addition to the reconciliation efforts on the part of his children, there also came long-out-of-contact or out-of-the-blue visitors. For instance, the head of the Huangpu District Education Committee, who approached him with a proposal for a neighborhood kindergarten pending donations from "generous people like Mr Fu". Then the ex-Red Guard surnamed Pei, who had forgotten to take back the list of the seized stuff that long-ago tragic night during the Cultural Revolution, also came to claim that his negligence had actually made the subsequent compensation possible, and then everything else as well. As the first link in a long chain, at least so it appeared in Pei's logic, he maintained that Fu should reward him with a small part of the stock shares—'

'Oh what a penniless, pathetic alcoholic that ex-Red Guard named Pei is. I happen to know him, a frequent visitor to the cheapest eatery on Yunnan Road,' a red-nosed man named

Zhang in the audience cut in. 'Like in an old saying, "He who tries to drown the sorrow in the liquor inevitably drowns himself in it." Pei tells his story in the eatery too, saying it's so unfair to him. More than fifteen Red Guards went to Fu's *shikumen* house that night, all of them wholeheartedly following Chairman Mao's call to take revolutionary action against the class enemies with "Four Olds" at home. Pei just happened to be the one who ordered Fu to write the guilty plea with the list. Years later, however, Pei was singled out for punishment and then dumped by his wife. Nothing but a scapegoat for the Cultural Revolution, period. Now down and out, he cannot afford even the cheapest booze on Yunnan Road but for the pity a waitress there takes on him, saving leftover liquor from the bottle bottoms at other tables, and occasionally bits and pieces of food possibly untouched from the leftover dishes. As the waitress works nights, he comes there close to midnight—'

'Don't interrupt, Red-nosed Zhang!' A young man called Little Huang cut him short. 'Let Old Root go on with the story.'

'Anyway, none of these visitors, Pei or others, left the lane with any success, though all of them vowed to return. Fu had to avoid them by dining out, one day for fried milk at Xingya, the next day for salted duck tongues at North Cloud Pavilion, and the third day for spicy fish head pot at Old Sichuan – like waging a guerrilla war, except that he was too rich, too old to be a guerrilla soldier. Besides, it was no fun to eat out the whole time. At least that's what Fu told me.

'As you see, good or bad luck, no one can really tell, so it's just like in *Tao Te Ching*,' Old Root concluded, taking a long, deliberate sip of his tea, as if inspired by the green tender leaves unfolding in leisure like a dream in the cup.

'But what's the point from *Tao Te Ching*?' Little Huang said, adding more water to the narrator's dented cup.

'Wasn't his life stocked with ironies? The loss of his job in the forties actually worked in his favor – the start of his company of shrimp and fish balls. Only not for too long – he turned into a capitalist because of it in the light of Chairman Mao's class system. Then the misfortune reached its peak during the Cultural Revolution, but that list of the things seized by the Red Guards actually brought about the reunion of two old friends, not to mention the stock fortune from overseas.'

'Indeed there's no telling or foretelling the causality of misplaced yin and yang,' a serious-looking man in his mid-forties observed, adjusting the black-rimmed glasses along the edge of his nose. 'Who could say that his death was not related to his incredible wealth?'

'Exactly,' Old Root said, picking at a green tea leaf stuck between his tea-stained teeth, looking at the bespectacled observer. 'He was killed after a visit to an expensive restaurant, according to Comrade Jun. So the way things work out in this world of red dust is way beyond us. But now it's your turn to continue, Four-eyed Liu, with all the details observable in the same *shikumen* house you have lived in with Fu during the last years of his life. More than fifteen years, I think.'

It was already quite a long story, and Chen wondered at its relevancy to the investigation. But back in the police bureau, there was nobody waiting for him to make a report, and back at home, it could be unbearably hot and humid in the attic, especially when he knew he would not be able to fall asleep there any time soon. Earlier, he had left a message for his mother through the public phone service, saying that he would work late on the translation at the bureau, and that she would not have to stay up waiting for him.

So why not stay on for Liu's part in front of Red Dust Lane? Liu had lived in the *shikumen* house with Fu – possibly with more immediate and up-to-date information. If nothing else, at least it could be an intriguing way to spend a summer evening. A different perspective could dramatically change the meaning of a story.

'You're the one on speaking terms with Fu, Old Root,' Liu said, seemingly reluctant to start the part two, 'not me.'

'Hot stinking tofu. So hot, so stinking, so delicious, you'll bite off your tongue . . .'

A peddler came over to them unexpectedly. Stinking tofu was a popular snack among Shanghainese. Smelling so pungent even from a distance, but once in the mouth, the special taste and texture could turn out to be addictive. The peddler was pushing a wooden cart with a small coal briquette stove, and on top of it, a large wok of sizzling oil. Upon getting an order from a customer, he would put into the oil a bamboo stick with four pieces of tofu, and in a minute or two, the fried tofu would be pulled out hot, shining, crisp and stinking. Perhaps the peddler too was familiar with the evening talk in front of the lane.

'I'm a visitor this evening,' Chen said, taking in the smell with a deep breath. 'The stories here are absolutely wonderful. So one round of stinking tofu for each of us here – on me.'

It was inexpensive, ten cents for four pieces per stick. With about ten people in front of the lane, it was a treat Chen thought he could afford. And he himself liked it too. As a child, his father had once treated him to the special snack, he recalled, while listening spellbound to the Suzhou opera performance in the Old City theater.

The peddler, apparently overjoyed with the 'big order', was quick to produce the sticks of tofu generously strewn with red pepper sauce.

Chen's might have been a gesture not that common for the evening talk. Old Root took a stick, looked up at him, and then sideways at Liu, who was busy smacking his lips over the hot spicy tofu. 'It really tastes like nothing else. You have to tell your story now, Four-eyed Liu. Such a rare treat is surely not for nothing.'

Liu turned to Old Root with a sudden challenge in his tone. 'From your perspective, Fu's impeccable. Nothing wrong with your loyalty to a late friend, Old Root. But being his neighbor in the same *shikumen* house for years, I could not but have seen things from a closer distance.'

'Isn't that what makes our evening talk unique? Multiple perspectives, I mean. That surely contributes to the depth of a story. What Doctor Watson sees must be so different from Sherlock Holmes,' Old Root said with a throaty chuckle. 'You know Fu's children pretty well too, I've heard.'

'Yes, I met them before the Cultural Revolution, but they moved out shortly afterward, as you have described in that story of yours,' Liu said, nibbling at the tofu. 'So I'll start from where you left off. With the compensation, the pension and the stock shares, Fu became so incredibly rich. But he just wanted to be left alone – an old man in an old lane. If there was any change about him, he was seen dining out much more than before, being capable of indulging in any of his gastronomical fantasies. His frequent visits to those expensive restaurants made no dent to his bank account. Only it's not that fun to eat out for three meals a day, seven days a week.

'After a couple of months, he could not help coming back to the common kitchen in the *shikumen* house, but preparing meals turned out to be too much work for the old man. Besides, he still appeared uncomfortable talking to his "proletarian neighbors". Somebody suggested he hire a maid for help, which became politically OK in the new reform age for socialist China. And it was not difficult for him to make the arrangement. In the wing unit, he needed for himself just the front room looking out to the courtyard, while the maid could take the back room with the living room and dining room in the middle.

'About a year and a half ago, Fu hired a young woman named Meihua as a live-in maid, and Xiaoqiang and Hongxia asked me to look out for anything between Fu and her. Meihua took good care of him, but it would not have been fair to his children, I agreed with them, if the old man had chosen to leave everything to that young maid.

'Meihua's in her late twenties, coming from a small village in Jiangxi Province. Fu was the first person or family she had served in the city of Shanghai. At first, none of the neighbors believed that a "provincial sister" like her was capable of satisfying a sophisticated gourmet like Fu.

'But to our surprise, he turned out to be very patient teaching her in the kitchen, and she appeared more than willing to learn, absorbing his instructions like a sponge. One of the first specials she made in the *shikumen* house was a platter of steamed live perch. The Jiangxi village being close to a river, she was quite knowledgable about preparing fish, and she also showed a natural preference for the taste of the fresh food itself instead of bothering with MSG or other fancy sauces of dubious natures. The only suggestion from him was

about how to pour the boiling oil over the fish strewn with
chopped scallion and ginger. It turned out to be a huge success.
That evening, he insisted on her sitting out and sharing the
fish with him in the courtyard, their chopsticks crossing each
other's over a folding table in the gathering dusk.

'It surely was a good job for her, as was the consensus of
the residents of the *shikumen* house. Board and food free, she
could save all the money paid by him. And for a relatively
healthy old man like Fu, there was not that much for her to
do. After about a month, he let her do all the shopping without
checking her list of expenses, and soon afterward he simply
gave her a monthly amount for the household in advance.

'So it was more than natural for her to try to prove herself
as a capable, conscientious maid. Also, she could have been
touched by all his suffering during the Cultural Revolution.
At least that's what she said in the common kitchen of the
shikumen house, killing a turtle trodden under her blood-
speckled bare foot.

'"After the national disaster of those ten years, that's the
only thing Mr Fu enjoys. And that's all I can do for him."

'The street food market being located just behind the lane,
she would jump out of bed in the early morning and trot over
there in two or three minutes, carrying the bamboo basket.
But not just in the morning, she made a point of going there
two or three times a day. What remained unsold from the
morning would be sold at a discount in the late afternoon,
though she did not have to worry about the expense. She
appeared to be just naturally practical, like other housewives
in the neighborhood. If there was anything still not Red-Dust-
like about her, she talked little to her neighbors, perhaps too
self-conscious of her Jiangxi accent.

'As Fu came to enjoy the home-cooked meals more and
more, she spared no time or energy in developing the homely
menu, such as tofu mixed with green onion and sesame oil,
plain egg soup steamed with clam, pork slices wok-fried with
red fermented wine dredge, and so on and so forth. Those
simple dishes seemed to delight him. And she put her youthful
imagination further to work. With big croakers extremely rare
in today's market, for instance, she used instead the tiny

croakers by carefully deboning them, and then made the fish soup with pickled cabbage over a small fire for hours until the soup turned deliciously milky with a fragrance that permeated the whole *shikumen* house.

'It's just like in an old saying: "The best way to a man's heart is through his stomach."

'And she cared about more than just the need of his stomach. I'm not talking about all the washing, cleaning, mending there, such as would have been expected of a well-paid maid. She went so far as to remodel the old wing unit, bustling around in a *dudou*-like top and shorts, bare arms and feet covered with water and concrete, together with a couple of handymen in the courtyard.

'Now, you're all familiar with the layout of Fu's unit – except for our visitors tonight. Enter through the living room door, you turn right into the front room, also Fu's bedroom, and across the living room to the left is the all-purpose room with a retrofitted attic and partitioned-out notch for the chamber pot, and further to the left, the back room. Not too long after her arrival, dramatic changes appeared in the unit. An electronic toilet and a shower head with a water heater were installed in the all-purpose room, and then an air conditioning unit on the window of Fu's front room. These modern conveniences proved terribly satisfying for the old man, who had the money but neither the energy nor the mood for the remodeling. In recognition of her extraordinary job, he purchased a large color TV for her in the back room. That's something unusual between an old man and his maid.

'Naturally, like other neighbors, I wanted to find out more about her. Indeed, she turned out to be much more than an ordinary provincial sister. Mind you, it was not just because of the request made by Xiaoqiang and Hongxia. It was more like an intriguing drama unfolding in the *shikumen* house around us.

'What I managed to gather about her background was rather sketchy, though. She came from Jiangxi Province, where she lost her husband in a tractor accident less than one year after their marriage. His family blamed her for the rotten luck she brought on him, calling her a "white tiger". It was a poor, backward village, where people had a lot of superstitious beliefs and practices, so she left for Shanghai. After working in temporary jobs here and there, she landed herself in Red Dust Lane.

'Then came the questions. With all those things she did for him, we began to notice her staying in his front room a lot. Particularly in the evenings. For summer, it might be understandable with the air conditioning installed at his bedroom window, but what about those days and evenings when it was not so hot?

'In the cover of the night, she had frequently been seen throwing the water out of a wooden basin into the courtyard. Why? The shower head with the water heater had been installed for the unit. Soon, as one of the neighbors discovered, she made a point of washing his feet in the evening, claiming that he could enjoy better sleep afterward. In a way, it was not too surprising. Quite a number of provincial girls started as foot-washing girls in the city of Shanghai. It was more than possible that she had served in one of those dubious salons before coming to serve Fu in Red Dust Lane.

'But behind the closed door, was she doing nothing but washing his feet?

'Sitting out in the courtyard with him, fanning him intimately with a round paper fan, she appeared to be quite a presentable companion. And she was fast losing the provincial about her, wearing a white tank top and short jeans like a Shanghai woman. If you saw the two of them for the first time without knowing her as a maid in his household, you could have taken them as a couple in spite of the huge age difference. Gold digger or not, she was doing an exceptional job for him.

'According to Hongxia, it was just too obvious that Meihua was trying so desperately to win his affection – and then, of course, his money. If she had not yet achieved the goal, it was because of his loyalty to the memory of his late wife. But how long could a lonely old man hold out to a cute, cunning, calculating young woman? The way things were going, it would only have been a matter of time for him to eventually succumb to her.

'Well, talk of the devil,' Four-eyed Liu suddenly said in a

subdued voice, adjusting the glasses on the ridge of his nose, 'and here she comes.'

'What do you mean?' Chen said.

'Meihua, the devil that bewitched the old man.'

Chen saw a young woman moving out of the lane. She was wearing a white T-shirt with a black crepe fastened on the short sleeve, white pajama pants, barefoot in wooden sandals with canvas stripes. From a distance, she looked the picture of a Shanghai widow in mourning. True, she was not exactly a beauty, but with fine features and a youthful figure.

'No one can really tell what she's up to – going out alone at this hour.'

Chen made no comment, but he did not agree with Liu's implication. Dressed like that, she would not be planning to go too far.

In less than five minutes, she was seen hurrying back to the lane, her wooden sandals clinking; they looked almost antique, but possibly fashionable in the city, which was busy rediscovering itself through the memories of the old glories. She was carrying a pack of bulbs in her hand. The light in her room must have suddenly gone out.

'What's her reaction to Fu's death?' Chen raised a question instead.

'She cried like a heartbroken widow. Little wonder about it.'

'Is she leaving?'

'No, she's staying. Fu did something for her. Something truly uncommon, unimaginable. He managed to obtain her city residence permit in the family register of Fus.'

'How could that have been possible?' Old Root too seemed astonished. 'It may take years to do so, even for a real family member. And she's not a member of his family – not yet.'

'No one knows. That's why I'm saying there was much more going on behind the closed door. Yesterday morning, Xiaoqiang and Hongxia tried to evict her, but she took out the family register. So there's nothing they can possibly do about it.'

'Now I see why they failed to drive her out. But what does that mean?' another one in the audience asked.

'I don't know what it means. Legally, she'll be able to have the apartment to herself now. In a way, she may be seen as the only legal resident of the wing. At least she can stay there as long as she likes.'

'Come on, Four-eyed Liu,' Little Huang said incredulously. 'Why should Fu have done that?'

'Likely as a first step for her to live with him,' Four-eyed Liu said. 'A sort of private arrangement between the two.'

'Is there anything particular she is doing for the moment?' Chen cut in again.

'That I cannot tell. She shuts herself up in the room most of the time. She's heard crying at night. She still goes to the food market, but only for the sake of the "seven seven sacrifice" – at least that's what she told us while preparing all the dishes for the first seven sacrifice in the common kitchen of the *shikumen* house.'

'Wow! Seven seven sacrifice!' It referred to a Buddhist ritual lasting seven weeks after one's death, according to which, on every seventh day the family members would prepare a good meal, with candles and incense burning on the table, and with the netherworld money burning in front of the table, so that the spirit of the deceased would get the signal in the wind and come back for the meal and the money.

'She said to the neighbors, "He likes what I cook for him, so he is bound to come back on every seventh. I could truly feel his presence at the table. The moment I served his favorite dishes, the candle started flickering without any draft coming through the closed window." So she went to the food market so early this morning – the first seventh day – carrying back a full basket, and spending at least half a day preparing for the banquet. She plans to observe the seven seven sacrifice to the last day.'

'But where does she get the money?'

'According to her, he had given her the household expenses for a month, and she vowed to use every penny on him. But that's no more than a make-believe pretense, you know, since the spirit would not touch the food. Afterward, it's for her to enjoy all the untouched specials alone for the whole week.'

'For the whole week, how?' Old Root asked out of nowhere.

'Fu has bought a small refrigerator for her. That will not be a problem. To be fair to her, it does seem she seriously plans to live on the leftovers for days. Before the first seventh day, she only went out for some vegetables at a discount in the late afternoon. Of course, that could have been just a part of the cover for her.'

'The cover for what, Four-eyed Liu?' Little Huang asked sharply.

'She wants people to believe that she's devoted to him – to him alone.'

'And do you have any reason to believe otherwise?'

'For one, there's the handyman who installed the air conditioning. He seemed to know her quite well, speaking with a Jiangxi accent, as the neighbors noticed at the time. It's most likely that he's from the same countryside. Now for a provincial sister like Meihua, how could she have known so much about those modern facilities in the city of Shanghai?'

'Supposing she had learned all that from Fu, so what?'

'No, Fu's so old-fashioned. In fact, months after the job was done, the handyman came back to the lane, where she had a long talk with him just outside the *shikumen* – quite a long, heated talk.' Liu added deliberately, 'And then about a week later, Fu was killed.'

'That's your theory about the murder case?'

'You can never tell the thing between the two, can you? She could have known the handyman back in the countryside. A man about her age, maybe just a few years older – tall, strong, virile. Just like Ximen Qing in *Plum in the Golden Vase!*'

'That's absurd! She's no beauty, but possibly not without youthful attraction for an old man like Fu,' Old Root said, shaking his head like a rattle drum. 'But for someone from the same countryside, she's but an ill-starred widow. If there's anything attractive about her, it's the possibility of her getting the money from Fu. So why now – before the old man left everything to her?'

'Well, that handyman could have believed she had already got everything from Fu. Alternatively, he could have been helplessly smitten, unable to bear the thought of her dumping him for the old man—'

'Come on,' Little Huang jumped up from his bamboo chair. 'They might have been arguing about the payment for the service he had done. I happened to overhear two or three fragmented sentences. She called him a greedy nuisance with an unmistakable expression of disgust on her face.'

'Whatever,' Liu said, suddenly losing steam and shifting the subject. 'Whatever it could be, it's none of our business. No point us getting too excited in the evening talk here.'

'Indeed the world is but a stage,' Little Huang too said in reconciliatory tone, 'with some people playing, and some people watching. It's just good or bad luck for the men on the stage, as Old Root has summed up well. After all, if Fu had not been that rich, he would not have gone to the restaurant that night and got killed afterward. Up above, there must have been something way beyond us.'

'If it was a chance street mugging gone wrong, how could the murderer have known that Fu was such a rich man?' Chen added in haste, 'And that he was going there that night?'

The moment he blurted out the questions, he became aware of Old Root eyeing him with a focused sharpness before making a response, and waving the fan slowly like a Suzhou opera singer.

'There are more things in heaven and earth, young man, than are dreamed of in our evening talks. Thanks again for your tasty treat. It's quite late now. And it's the time for an old man like me to go to bed.'

Chen rose, bowing, and saying in earnest, 'Thank you all so much. I've had a wonderful evening here. Trust me, I'll come back.'

But Chen was in no mood to go back home right now. Like after a full meal, he wanted to walk for a short while to digest what he had just taken in.

He had learned nothing too substantial from the evening talk, though intriguing details here and there contributed to a more comprehensive background picture.

As for the thing between Fu and Meihua, that might have been tantalizing fodder for the spicy gossip in front of the lane – but not for the investigation.

Besides, both Old Root and Four-eyed Liu fell into the category of 'unreliable narrators', in that their personal interests were involved in the narration, though understandably so. For Old Root, the loyalty to his late friend; and for Four-eyed Liu, the need to top Old Root with salacious details, like those about her washing Fu's feet at night and her arguing with the Jiangxi handyman about a week before the murder.

It was quite late. Chen kept strolling on, far from being tired. Nanjing Road came into view, striking him as unexpectedly deserted, with the well-known restaurant named Shen Dachen on the intersection of Zhejiang Road standing closed, lost in the surrounding darkness. There was only a lonely, shabby-looking man smoking, leaning against the restaurant window with one foot raised backward against the wall, and connecting one half-burned cigarette to another, which seemed to tremble like a long, sleepless antenna probing into the eerie darkness.

Soon, he found himself moving across Beijing Road, drawing close to the bridge over the Suzhou Creek, breathing in the familiar tang given off by the darksome, polluted water. Once a familiar route to him during his days studying English at Bund Park, a lot of water had gone under the bridge since then. There seemed to be something elusive, inexplicable in the somber recesses of his mind as he walked on, making a couple of turns absentmindedly.

Again, he thought of the investigation in the Inspector Martin Beck mystery, with the hard-working Swedish inspector pursuing a lot of interviews, all of which proved irrelevant, though perhaps not unhelpful for a panoramic picture, in which some of the details then took on new, unexpected meanings.

A sudden train whistle pierced the night from a close distance. He must have moved near to the railway station, and to the restaurant of Aixin's Imperial Recipes again, as if he had been pulled by an invisible hand in the dark.

He took out the crime scene report from his shoulder bag. Following its description, he arrived at the street corner, presumably on the route for Fu to go back home, or to the railway station. It did not appear to be such a likely area for a mugging, with lots of people coming and going, he contemplated, because of its closeness to the railway station.

In the case of its not being a botched mugging, however, the killer could have waited there and jumped out when Fu came into sight later that night – with no people moving around at the time.

Chen started examining the scene more closely. Five or six steps away, there was a lone toppled wall – less than half of it – still standing in the debris. It was an area designated for new construction, with most of the old houses already razed down, only a couple of them still recognizable in the dark like gigantic 'nails', which were so-called because of their inevitable removal by force. He bent to pick up two cigarette butts from the littered ground. It had not rained for days so they had not yet been destroyed. He put them into a small plastic bag.

It was hard for him to conceive of someone standing or squatting under the crumbling wall in that spot, smoking for a long while without a secret, murderous mission in mind. He rechecked the report, in which Detective Ding mentioned some cigarette butts, even the brand, *Double Happiness*, so Detective Ding might have been thinking along the same lines, though without going into details. Chen wondered whether anything had been done about the fingerprints. But then, in the case of someone without a history, not much could have been expected from them.

Who would have chosen to ambush Fu at this locale?

Someone who knew he was going to the restaurant that night. According to Liu, Meihua could have known about it, but why would she have done that?

For an alternative scenario, someone who had followed Fu all the way to the area.

There came a night bird, flying around a broken pillar and eventually perching on it and flapping its wings furiously against the surrounding gloom.

Detective Ding woke up in the office, stretching his stiff neck, letting the fragmented dream images about the crime scene fade in the light.

It had been such a hectic day, and then a half-night too, until he had dozed off over the desk.

Now still a bit disoriented from the dream, he lit a cigarette, the bitter taste getting worse in his mouth in the morning.

He wanted to go over several confusing and contradicting aspects of the investigation one more time. Sipping a second or third cup of strong black tea, he fought off another wave of sleepiness and checked his watch in the morning light. Almost eight thirty. As he was about to make himself another cup of tea, he was surprised to see Chen stepping into his office.

'Morning, Chen. What wind has brought you in so early this morning? Oh, the tapes. I remember, you must have listened to them, and . . .' Detective Ding said, accepting a cigarette from Chen instead of finishing the sentence.

'Yes, I've listened to the tapes from beginning to the end. With the information from them, I've also tried to check further – like an apprentice doing the homework in accordance with your instruction.'

To his surprise, Chen moved on to brief him about the contents of the evening talk in front of Red Dust Lane.

But that all sounded too coincidental, Detective Ding observed at the end of Chen's fairly detailed account. Just like the anonymous friend who had helped to establish Fu's identity, now another childhood friend of Chen's just happened to have lived in that lane and was familiar with the evening talk. While some of the information appeared interesting, Detective Ding did not see the possibility of it leading somewhere any time soon. Like others, neither the Jiangxi handyman nor Meihua had a convincing motive, about which he agreed with Chen.

But Chen was trying to put his finger into this pie, Detective Ding was convinced.

'It's done for the sake of money, no question about it,' Chen went on. 'But it does not add up for the Jiangxi handyman to make a move at the present stage. He should have waited until after Meihua had got hold of everything. As for the unlikely scenario of a love triangle, the murder of Fu would not guarantee her returning his passion—'

'You are talking like a real cop, Chen.'

'I've been translating the procedure booklet, you know. Some terms may have come up conveniently—'

The phone rang, interrupting their talk. It was his assistant Liao.

'Where were you last night, Ding? I called your home several times. Nobody answered.'

'I stayed here in the office. Too late to catch the last bus home.'

'Some real progress, Ding. Pei's in custody this morning. It's just a matter of time for him to confess. We don't have to worry now.'

'What? Hold on – Chen is here with me in the office. I'll put him on the speakerphone. He is eager to learn how to investigate like a real cop.'

'That's good,' Liao said with a chuckle. 'Last night, after calling your home without success, I dialed Party Secretary Li. Pei lied about his alibi. The movie theater did not show *Little Flower* that night.'

'He stammered when trying to answer my question about the name of the movie,' Ding said. 'I immediately sensed something suspicious. How could he have forgotten about a movie seen just over a week ago?'

'I called Ouyang too. After your phone call, the neighborhood cop gathered more information about Pei. Pei has been going downhill really fast for several years. What he did during the Cultural Revolution became an unwashable political stain. Despondent after his divorce, he abandoned himself to cups, taking sick leave with his pay badly cut, complaining about his being as poor as a rat, and blaming Fu and others for all his troubles.'

'He's desperate.'

'And for once, our Party Secretary Li moved so quickly. After listening to my report and talking to some city office officials, he had Pei put into custody earlier this morning, saying that a speedy conclusion to the investigation is in the interest of the Party authorities.'

'Yes, Party Secretary Li's under pressure from above. With Fu's connections overseas, the news about his murder has been spreading internationally,' Ding said slowly, looking sideways at Chen. 'With Pei's motive found, and his alibi gone, we'll move ahead at full speed.'

Putting down the phone, Detective Ding turned to Chen. 'That's a breakthrough. We made a couple of lists yesterday. One of the possible beneficiaries of Fu's death. The other of those with a grudge or hatred against Fu. Of the second list, we came to focus on Pei, the ex-Red Guard. You may not think that his motive is such a convincing one, but at this moment, we cannot afford the time to check into those not-that-possible leads. Because of the city government pressure and all that, you know. We'll focus on Pei first for the moment. A speedy solution, as you have just heard, serves the political need of the Party authorities.'

'Political need, I totally understand. So you have moved really fast.'

Chen was not convinced.

There was a certain measure of justice in having an ex-Red Guard like Pei punished. The fact that Pei had had the nerve to demand part of Fu's fortune spoke volumes about his twisted, unremorseful mind. But that did not necessarily cast him as a murderer.

But what could Chen do? Detective Ding – or rather the city government – seemed to have said the last word. As Liao had put it, 'it's just a matter of time for him to confess'. The bureau had ways and means to make sure of it. He could try to point out some inconsistencies in the scenario, but he was in no position to turn the table. Not unless he could succeed in pointing his finger at the real murderer.

At noon, Chen went down to the crowded canteen, where he failed to see Detective Ding nor his assistant Liao. Dr Xia walked over to his table for a few polite words, having just finished his portion of wok-fried pork liver, and Chen stuffed down his portion of Yangzhou-style fried rice without finding a single shrimp in it.

After spending another two unproductive hours on the trans-lation in the reading room, Chen took out the copy of *The Unbearable Lightness of Being*. It was truly a masterpiece, with some metaphysically disturbing questions scattered throughout the book, but he found himself incapable of concentrating on that book, either.

It was not his case. No heaviness of responsibility as far as he was concerned. In fact, he had already done more than was expected of him. In accordance with a Chinese proverb, 'Only without a real official position, does one enjoy the whole lightness of being.' In the bureau, he was literally marginal, but he felt so depressed instead of light-hearted.

He decided to leave the bureau for another visit to the lane.

In the audience in front of the lane the night before, a middle-aged man nicknamed 'Red-nosed Zhang' seemed to know Pei well, Chen recalled. Zhang might be able to provide more information about the suspect in custody.

But when Chen got there, it was hardly four thirty. It started drizzling. People would not come out that early for the evening talk in weather like that. He did not know Zhang's full name, or his address. Unlike Detective Ding, Chen could not contact the neighborhood committee for help in any official capacity. Nor did he want to appear suspicious to people like Old Root by snooping around the neighborhood.

He walked around the lane aimlessly, hoping to run into someone he had seen the previous evening, but he was disappointed to not recognize anyone.

Near the mid-entrance of the lane, however, he caught sight of an elderly hunchbacked man hurrying out with a bright red armband. He was struck with a feeling of déjà vu, yet without any exact clues.

As he circled the lane for the second time, drawing close to the back entrance, he saw two elderly men playing a game of Chinese chess in an unoccupied booth in the street food market. The booth was a well-chosen one with a bamboo awning overhead, so the two players did not have to worry about the drizzle. They were absorbed in the battle on the chessboard marked with the border of Kingdom Han and the river of Kingdom Chu, as if having won and lost the ancient world in their present games. From a distance,

however, there was something comic about the two players
– one stripped to the waist, with his bony chest grooved like
a worn-out washing board; the other in a motley pajama top
with unmatching pants, one slipper missing. Moving over,
Chen joined several onlookers around the booth.

As the two players prepared to start a new game, Chen
looked up across the street to note the saleswomen of the
market beginning to display on their counters the unsold food
from the morning. He was reminded of something else he had
learned last night: Meihua's occasional visit to the market for
the discounted food in the late afternoon. So he might well
stay on beside the booth, like one of the onlookers. If nothing
happened, he would move back to the front entrance of the
lane around seven.

After one and a half chess games, and three cigarettes, Chen
heard a flurry of chinking steps from the lane. Meihua was
walking out in the wooden sandals of hers, carrying an empty
bamboo basket.

He followed her footsteps down to the street food market,
not too sure about what he was going to say or do. But he
had to try, sorting through a confusion of thoughts swirling
in his head. He kept himself at a fairly close distance behind.
Apparently, she was unaware of anybody following her.

Across Fujian Road, she put a bunch of not-so-fresh green
vegetables into her basket. Half a block further on, she picked
up a five-cent bunch of scallions from a peddler on a stool,
bargaining for a small piece of ginger thrown in for free. She
appeared to be really practical; Chen could not help thinking
of the description of her in the evening talk. At the corner of
Zhejiang Road, she came to a stop, looking around before she
turned back.

Chen walked up to her.

'You're Meihua?'

She nodded in surprise.

He took out his police ID – the first time he had done so
since his entrance into the force. She studied it, even more
surprised.

'I do not want to approach you as a cop in that *shikumen*
house, and I think you can guess the reason. You too may

have heard of the gossip and speculation among the neighbors in the lane.'

'Thank you, Comrade Chen, for your understanding.'

'How about having a talk with me here?' He pointed at a shabby snack eatery on the street corner.

It was the time of day when few Shanghainese would care to spend money on snacks. Chen and Meihua stepped in, found themselves the only customers there, and chose a slightly shaky corner table.

The old waiter put down on the table a platter of fried mini buns, lukewarm yet with the bottom crust still crispy, and two bowls of spicy beef soup. She took a bite of the bun. He observed without immediately starting to question. A speck of white sesame stuck to her upper lip, she was not without charm, possibly more than enough for an old man to feel helplessly drawn toward her. But what about her own feelings – a young woman in her mid-to-late twenties – sitting beside an old man in his seventies?

He helped himself to a spoonful of the oily soup, and added a pinch of chopped green onion to it.

'What do you want me to tell you?' she started, putting down the chopsticks.

'Tell me the story between you and Fu.'

'What do you mean?'

'Don't get me wrong. The Fu case is under police investigation. We have a list of suspects, but it's far from conclusive. You were the one with Fu in the last years of his life. Whatever you tell me may greatly help.'

'There's no story between me and Mr Fu. Who am I? A poor, ill-starred woman from a poor, backward Jiangxi village. After bumping around in the city for months like a headless fly, I was lucky enough to meet with Mr Fu, who kindly gave me a job, and shelter too. His neighbors, and particularly his children, may have wild speculations about me. What could I have done about it? I'm nothing but a maid in his household, a "provincial sister" to the people in the lane.'

'Let me rephrase it, Meihua. Tell me about your experience working for Mr Fu. From the very beginning, please.'

'From the very beginning, I knew my job was mostly about

cooking. He was so well informed about it. It could be a really useful skill, I soon realized. So I learned a lot from him. A kind, patient, instructive employer he was, and he paid me good money too. In five or six years, I thought I might be able to save enough to try my hand at something different in the city—'

'In five or six years, you thought—'

'No, that's something he mentioned, saying his days were numbered, and that it would not be a life job for me to help in his household. He suggested that I might try to work as a chef or start a small eatery for myself "in five or six years". He also said he knew a number of people in the circle, and that I did not have to worry about it.'

'But Fu needed you, and he was only in his seventies. People live longer nowadays. What about himself by that time?'

'Possibly in a nursing home, when he could no longer take care of himself, at least that's what he said to me. He did not want to be too much of a burden to . . .' she broke down with a sob.

'You had been doing an extraordinary job for him, I've heard.'

'For the money he paid me, I had to do my best.'

'But his children have made things difficult for you?'

'I knew why they were so worried, but they worried for nothing.' She added reflectively, 'The son is not too unreasonable, but the daughter can be hysterical. During one of her visits, when Mr Fu was not at home, she made a terrible scene, screaming and scratching at my face. Afterward, her husband Song came over to apologize to me in person. If I had told Fu about it, it could have led to another big family fight; Song was worried about that. But Song's a strange man too, asking me a lot of irrelevant questions about Mr Fu.'

She might not be telling him everything, Chen reflected. Why should she? He was not even a cop assigned to the case, and holding few cards in his hand. Nevertheless, he had to go on, trying to do his utmost, improvising as he proceeded.

'Fu put you into the city residence register like a family member of his, I've also heard.'

'It was just accidental. According to the city regulation, for someone like me to stay here, Mr Fu had to report my temporary residence once a month. Several months ago, somebody from one of those government offices paid him a courtesy visit—'

'The office of the United Front Work?'

'Yes, that's it. Mr Fu told me that he complained to the visitor about the inconvenience of filing for me every month, and about a month later, the neighborhood cop had my name added to the Fus' residence register. It's beyond me how his complaining could have made such a difference.'

'Well, nothing but politics. I happen to have a friend working in that office. According to him, in China's effort to attract foreign investment, Fu could have played a symbolic role. The official actually made a hard bargain with him. Fu had to agree to a newspaper interview, stating that the city government had been taking good care of a retired entrepreneur like him, in exchange for the city government to grant your residence permit.'

'He never told me anything about it,' she said, another catch in her voice. 'He said that it was just for the sake of his convenience, but it was more than that, I know, it was for me to stay in the city as long as I like.'

He could see an emotional change flashing across her face.

'He thought so highly of you that he was willing to do that. As you may not know, the government office had been pushing him hard for months, but he did not agree until that day.' Chen went on, taking out a cigarette without lighting it, 'Yesterday I was at the evening talk in front of the lane, you know. It's such a sad story, that life story of Fu's. In fact, Red Guards also came to my family at the beginning of the Cultural Revolution, subjecting my parents to horrible suffering and humiliation. So I want to bring justice for him. That's also what you want, I believe.'

'Yes, you have to do something for a good man like him.'

'According to some of your neighbors, he looked like a changed man after your arrival at the *shikumen*. You've done an incredible job, taking good care of him head and foot.'

'I think I can guess what they have been telling you. Among

other things, foot-washing for him, right? But it's nothing. Back in the village, people make a point of washing their feet in hot water before going to bed for better sleep. When I first arrived in Shanghai, I worked at a foot salon for weeks. So I know a thing or two about the practice. I quit because most of the foot salon clients never sat still, pawing and touching me all the time, and talking dirty too. But if I had done that for others, why not for him? And it was so different with him, a decent, old-fashioned gentleman. Not for once did he say or do anything indecent to me. And he took good care of me too. One evening, I had a bad attack of diarrhea with high fever, and he sat by my bed for half of the night, feeding me the porridge he himself made with Chinese herbs, and washing me – head and foot too.'

'It's not easy for an old rich man like Fu to do so.'

'People may talk about the age difference, but in today's society, a man with his wealth could have had much younger women, and prettier too. I'm but an ill-starred provincial "white tiger", but in his company I felt like an equal human being. If anything, it's me who was so unworthy of him. I was willing to do anything for him. One evening after my recovery, I believe I made myself clear, washing his feet, murmuring that in the village it's what a woman does for her man. He sat up and said to me in earnest,

'My wife passed away at the beginning of the Cultural Revolution, you know, taking away the better part of me with her. Years later, when I got the diamond ring back, I made a pledge to her memory: I would never give it to another woman. She died wearing the ring because of me. Now I'm an old man. Not many years left for me in this world of red dust, but you're young, with your life unfolding in front of you. It would not be fair for you. Having said that, I appreciate your taking care of me like that. And I'll do whatever possible to have you properly taken care of.'

'Believe me. We never crossed the line. Because of his suffering from gout attacks, I slept on the couch in his room from time to time – for help at night, but never on the bed.'

The story seemed to be taking her breath away. She paused to drink the soup directly from the bowl, like from a cup. Still

a provincial sister in her way, but Chen did the same, as if
making a subconscious gesture of solidarity.

'I understand,' he said. 'But not some other people. What
they're talking about is just like throwing dirty water on his
memory. Worse than you could have imagined. That's why
we have to do our best to solve the case.'

'What dirty water are you talking about?'

'In front of the lane, someone yarned at length about a
Jiangxi handyman who installed the air conditioning for Fu.
About the possible relationship between you two, with real or
imagined details. And about Fu's singular acquiescence, too.
And even about that Jiangxi handyman as a suspect involved
in the murder case because of his clandestine affair with you—'

'Say no more, Comrade Chen. For an ill-starred woman like
me, they may say whatever they like. But not about Mr Fu.
Absolutely not,' she said, turning pale. 'You have to catch the
murderer, or the evil-tongued gossips will never stop. I know
why you told me all this. Yes, I'll answer whatever questions
you want to ask, if you think that may help the investigation.'

'Yes, I have several specific questions, some of which may
be personal, and I hope you will take no offence. It's all for
the sake of the investigation. Since we're on the subject, please
tell me something first about the talk – they said it was a long,
heated talk you had with that handyman outside the *shikumen*
house about a week before Fu's death. Mind you, that does
not mean I give any credit to those wild stories circulating
among your neighbors.'

'His name is Dabao, that handyman. He comes from the
same county in Jiangxi Province. Believe it or not, we never
met there, but in the city of Shanghai it's natural for people
from the same countryside to get introduced and acquainted.
It's like a small community, in which people are supposed to
help each other. When I tried to remodel the wing unit for Mr
Fu, Dabao gave me a couple of useful suggestions. So I
suggested to Mr Fu that he hire Dabao for the job, and Mr
Fu paid him fairly. That's all there is to it. About two or three
weeks ago, the air conditioning seemed not to be working
properly, so I had him come over to do the maintenance job.
To my chagrin, Dabao maintained I should have paid him

more since it was Mr Fu's money anyway. I was so upset with his greediness. That's why we argued.'

That matched with what Chen had learned from Little Huang in the evening talk, who happened to have overheard fragments of the argument between the handyman and Meihua. So it ruled out the line of Liu's speculation.

'Thank you. Once the investigation is successfully concluded, those busybodies in the lane will shut up. You can count on that. Now for another question, did you notice anything unusual or suspicious during the last days of his life?'

'No, I did not. He said or did nothing unusual, at least so it appeared to me. He liked my cooking, but he still dined out, once or twice a week. But those restaurants can be ridiculously expensive, yet with the food not clean or healthy. So I suggested that he eat more at home, and he said he would do that when it was too hard for him to walk out. He seemed to be in a reasonably good mood.'

'Did he tell you about his plan to visit the restaurant that evening?'

'Yes, he told me about it, saying I did not have to cook for him that night. He also mentioned a possible trip afterward to Suzhou for special noodles. He said he could take a nap for three or four hours on the night train, and get out just in time for the first pot noodles in Suzhou. People like him believe that the noodles from the first pot early in the morning – with no flour residue in the water – taste the best.'

'He's a knowledgable gourmet.'

'That he was. Particularly about the Suzhou specials. According to him, the local foodies there make a point of enjoying the seasonal specials. In summer, they must have the noodles with three shrimp toppings – shrimp brain scarlet, shrimp roe rounded, promenade-like, and peeled shrimp transparently white, and that with the fresh fragrant lotus leaves in the soup too.'

'I've heard of the three shrimp noodles,' Chen said, gazing at the cold soup in front of him and shaking his head in spite of himself.

'But not just the noodles, he would stay there for a day or two tasting other specials. Like the soft shell-shedding baby crabs, the goose immersed in yellow wine, and the yang berry too. He liked talking about them, and it was a great opportunity for me to learn. After all, what else enjoyable was there for a lonely old man like him? The trip would bring back the memories of those years he had spent with his wife, who had accompanied him for such whimsical trips to Suzhou.'

All of a sudden, she stretched out her feet, sighing, and gazing down at the worn-out wooden sandals, which could once have been brightly painted, but were now discolored and worn-out, with the straps simply made of faded canvas. He wondered why she chose to gaze at her sandaled feet at the moment, though the wooden sandals had the effect of accentuating her shapely bare feet.

'His wife wore the sandals. That's why he kept them in the attic,' she said in a low voice, as if reading his mind. 'I came upon the dust-covered sandals without knowing anything about them. I did not want to throw things away, so I thought it might be a good idea for me to wear them. That morning, he turned ghastly pale at the sight of my walking to him in the sandals. He told me they reminded him of his late wife, who too was very economical, wearing the sandals for years with the straps replaced a couple of times. Nevertheless, he wanted me to go on wearing them. It was a very special permission he gave me. And truth be told, he sort of insisted on it afterward.'

Xiaoqiang and Hongxia might have had reason to be worried. The old man had shared a lot with Meihua, and perhaps more than that, Chen thought, helping himself to another spoonful of the cold soup, which tasted greasy.

'You may look down on me,' she went on, almost inaudibly, 'but when I'm wearing them, I feel as if . . .'

There was something infinitely touching about the way she uttered the unfinished sentence, and there was nothing contemptible in it whatsoever.

'A different question, Meihua,' he said, changing the subject abruptly. 'According to the neighborhood committee, an ex-Red Guard surnamed Pei approached Fu in the lane not too long ago. But for your help, Fu would not have been able to get away from him that easily. Can you tell me a bit more about that?'

'I had a hard time trying to separate the two in the lane. And I remember Pei kept on saying he needed the money, that he deserved the money because of some precious list a long time ago. I had no idea what Pei was talking about. Later on, Mr Fu told me that Pei begged for a loan for his sick son, but Mr Fu did not believe him.'

'I would not have believed him either,' Chen said. 'Another specific question: did Fu ever talk to you about the future arrangement of his wealth?'

'No, not exactly. He cared little about money. That's no secret to people. He once mentioned to me that he might donate the money to some charity fund in his wife's name, but I don't think he had made up his mind about it yet.'

'What about you?'

'What about me? I have no objection whatsoever to his arrangement – whether it would go to his children or to the charity. It has nothing to do with me.'

'But what about your future plans, I mean, now with the city residence permit for you? As we all know, he wanted you taken good care of.'

'I think I will stay in Red Dust Lane for a while. That's what he wanted me to do, I believe. But I'm going to find a job, and then I'll move out. He wanted me to have a place to stay in the city, but not necessarily here when I can take care of myself.'

'That's up to you to decide, but legally speaking, you may be able to stay on in the *shikumen* house as long as you like. If you need any legal advice in that aspect, I can ask people in the bureau for help,' Chen said, finishing the last fried bun with the soup inside cold and dried up. 'Now there's something else I have just thought of this afternoon. Of late, to be exact, perhaps just one or two weeks before Fu's death, did you notice any suspicious stranger lurking, prowling around the lane?'

'That I cannot say for sure. I did not go out a lot. Once in the morning, once or twice in the afternoon, mostly to the street food market and back. And a few other shopping errands. But now you mention it—'

'Yes?'

'About a week or so before his death, I walked out of the

shikumen house and happened to catch a glimpse of someone. Perhaps there was something about him that struck me as vaguely familiar, but he vanished out of sight before I could take another look.'

'Hold on, Meihua. Can you tell me more – exactly where and when?'

'I was going out for the late afternoon shopping in the food market. About five o'clock, I would say. The man was just outside the mid-entrance of the lane, on Fujian Road. Now Mr Fu's *shikumen* house is located in the sub-lane around the mid-section of the lane, you know. As soon as you step out of the *shikumen* house, you're able to see the mid-entrance of the lane.'

'In other words, the one staking himself there can also see people coming out of the *shikumen* house.'

'Yes, you can certainly say that. But why?'

'Any unusual experience afterward?'

'No, things like that may happen from time to time. Someone familiar-looking can turn out to be a total stranger. I'm mentioning it because I believe I saw him again, just one or two days before Fu's death. Like the first time, he instantly ducked his head out of view, as if he was afraid of being seen or recognized by me. At least, that's the feeling I had at the time, but I was not one hundred percent sure about it.'

'That may really be something, Meihua. How about the distance – from where he stood to the *shikumen* house?'

'About fifteen feet, give or take a little.'

'Can you give me a description of the man?'

'Middle-aged. Of medium height. Hair gray-streaked,' she said, with evident uncertainty. 'But as I've said, it was just a fleeting impression. I can be wrong. There's a tiny convenience store near the mid-entrance. Some people in the neighborhood hang out there too.'

'But he's not someone in the lane?'

'No, I don't think so.'

'And you can tell it is not Pei, the ex-Red Guard.'

'No, not Pei, who's taller.'

'I see,' he said. 'A final question. Do you know Red-nosed Zhang's address in the lane?'

'He's also in the mid-section of the lane. In the *shikumen* opposite to Fu's. Second floor.'

'Thank you so much, Meihua. What you have told me surely helps a lot. Here is a business card of mine, with the phone number on it. You can call me any time. Now give me the number of the public phone service here and I'll also call you with any progress.'

'Here it is,' she said, putting down the number on a paper napkin.

'I think I've kept you long enough. It's six forty now. You may leave first. I'll come to the front of the lane in a short while, to see if there's still an evening talk today.'

As Meihua stepped out with the bamboo basket, he rose to watch her moving away, her bare heels flashing above the clinking wooden sandals in the gathering dusk.

He paid for the snack. It was not expensive, but together with the stinking tofu treat the previous evening, he had to be more careful with his monthly budget.

First, he walked around to the mid-entrance of the lane, where he did see a tiny convenience store on Fujian Road. An elderly man, possibly the owner of the store, was idly stroking a white cat on the counter. No real customers there at the moment, except for several youngsters hanging around nearby, standing or squatting, yet all of them at a distance from the mid-entrance – much more than fifteen feet. They were busy smoking energetically, like there was nothing else left for them to do in the world.

As he headed back to the front of the lane, the drizzle was still going. Not too surprisingly, no one sat out for the evening talk.

He turned, whistling to himself, as if entering into the depths of the darksome woods, before he knocked on the door of the old *shikumen* house opposite to Fu's.

Back home, it was past ten thirty.

His mother had gone to bed. Chen saw on the table under-neath the attic a bowl of Shanghai-style cold noodles prepared with vegetable oil. Beside the bowl stood bottles of soy sauce and vinegar and sesame butter, in addition to a small dish of sliced cucumber for the topping. There was a small note on the table saying, 'That's for you. Just add whatever seasoning you like, stir the noodles with them. You know how to do that.'

He climbed up to the attic, which was partitioned with a wall-like book shelf. He tiptoed to the other side, bowl in hand, and finished the noodles in silence, though he was not really hungry.

Then he slumped down on the bed, leaning against the headboard. The excitement experienced during the talk with Meihua, and then with Red-nosed Zhang in the *shikumen* house, was receding. Zhang too had provided some interesting information, especially with his theory about Pei's alibi. More importantly, the presence of the suspicious man seen around the mid-section of the lane was confirmed. Like Meihua, Zhang could not tell who it really was, though he had a vague feeling that he had seen the man there before. But it was not Pei. Not a lane resident, either, Zhang was positive.

Nevertheless, it could turn out to be just a red herring.

Chen massaged his temples, feeling the onset of a dull headache. Sleepiness appeared to be the farthest thing from his mind. He took out *The Unbearable Lightness of Being* again. Reading a book in English often helped, paradoxically, with his falling asleep. Perhaps it was because of the nature of the second language, which more easily tired him out after a short while.

He was more than halfway through the novel, and that night, in Part 5 of the book, he unexpectedly came across a German phrase: *Es muss sein.*

From the little German he had studied as the second foreign language at college, he knew it meant 'it must be'. According to Kundera, the phrase develops from a joke among friends into a motif for one of Beethoven's songs, which acquires a solemn ring, as if issued directly from the lips of Fate, and then, in turn, into a crucial concept for the novel. When Tomas is debating whether or not to return to Prague after Tereza has left him in Zurich, he tells himself '*Es muss sein*'. In other words, he has to follow her all the way back, whatever the cost. Even though it's a decision hardly understandable to others under the circumstances, it makes perfect sense to Tomas, changing his otherwise unbearable lightness of being.

Chen put down the novel, feeling tired. It was brilliant, that metaphysical digression made by Kundera in those paragraphs. People tell themselves '*Es muss sein*' when making a difficult decision just like that, yet with the real reason unknown to others, and sometimes not even to themselves.

He jumped up as the book fell to the attic floor with a thump, which could have woken up his mother sleeping below.

Then things suddenly started falling into perspective . . .

The next morning, Chen stepped into Detective Ding's office again. It was about eleven fifteen. The detective had on the desk a paper cup of beef instant noodles, with the lid half torn away from the cup. A hot water bottle stood ready at his feet.

Chen could read the surprise on Ding's face. Perhaps more than surprise. A visible trace of annoyance in spite of his effort to conceal it.

'Another report from an apprentice under your guidance,' Ding said with a disarming smile, half-jokingly. 'So you are continuing the investigation on your own?'

'No, not exactly, it's just that your discussion about the action taken against Pei put things into perspective for me, so I want to make another report to you.'

'How?' Ding said curtly, without so much as pulling out a chair for the unwelcome intruder.

'In our last discussion, you pointed out to me that Pei's motive may not necessarily be a strong one, but with the pressures from the city government, you had to work on the only workable scenario for the moment. You've been so busy, I know. But for someone like me, not a real cop with any workload, I can well afford the time to check and explore in the direction you have carved out. Remember I told you about someone nicknamed Red-nosed Zhang in the evening talk?'

'So you went to the evening talk again?'

'No. But Zhang had mentioned that he knew Pei well. So I went to have a talk with him at his home. From what he told me, several things seemed to not add up. For one, he ran into Pei in that eatery on Yunnan Road shortly after Pei was seen arguing with Fu in the lane. Curious, Zhang bought a cup of beer for Pei, who immediately started talking with a loose tongue. As it turned out, Pei's son had a bad flu, but nothing serious. Pei simply used that as a pretense to get money from Fu. As it seemed to the ex-Red Guard Pei, he could have succeeded but for the intervention of the maid. So he would try again. For a soft-hearted old man like Fu, Pei believed it was just a matter of time to bring him around.'

'According to you, Pei does not sound like he bore any real hatred against Fu?'

'According to Zhang, when Pei was drunk like a skunk, which was quite common, he would curse Mao and the Cultural Revolution, but not Fu. Deep down, the ex-Red Guard knew better. So not too much of a murder motive for Pei, you're absolutely right about it.'

'I've thought about it too. But drunk or not drunk, he might have chosen not to tell everyone about his grudge against Fu,' Ding said, rising to pull out a chair for Chen.

'Thanks, Detective Ding. Supposing Pei had the motive, how would he have come to kill Fu at that particular locale?'

'He could have ambushed him there. The area is largely in ruins, with few people moving around late at night.'

'But he knew nothing about Fu's plan for that night. Meihua alone knew something about it, but she had no idea of the exact location of the restaurant, nor the route Fu was going to take. So we can rule out the possibility of her having told Pei anything about it. For another more likely scenario, the murderer could have followed Fu from Red Dust Lane, all the way to the neighborhood of that restaurant of imperial recipes, where he waited for Fu to come out after dinner and deliver the fatal stab with no one visible around at night, as you recounted the scene to me.'

'That's a possible hypothesis, Chen. Go on.'

'With that in mind, I asked Zhang whether he had seen some suspicious people lurking around the neighborhood in the days before Fu's murder.'

'Come on, Chen. There're several entrances to the lane. I too walked around there a couple of times. How could anyone have managed to keep an effective stakeout for that purpose?'

'Zhang lives in a *shikumen* opposite to Fu's, in the mid-section of Red Dust Lane. If someone had positioned himself near the mid-entrance, he could have easily kept in sight of the people moving in and out of the *shikumen* houses in that section.'

'Did Zhang see someone suspicious?'

'Yes. Just one or two days before Fu's death, as Zhang was walking out, he saw a stranger prowling there, and when Zhang came back about an hour later, the man was still there, stealing furtive glances toward the direction of Fu's house. Zhang remembered it because he had a feeling he looked like someone he had seen before, though Zhang failed to recognize him. Definitely not Pei, Zhang was positive about that. And I raised the same question to the maid named Meihua, whose response was similar. Someone was lurking around the mid-entrance and looking at the *shikumen* houses there in a stealthy way. It was not Pei, she was adamant about that too, and it was possibly the same person that she had noted on two different occasions. She too thought that it could have been someone nervous about being recognized; both times, he hurried away at the sight of her.'

'So you interviewed the maid too, *Inspector* Chen.'

'I was coming out with Zhang, and she happened to be walking out of the opposite *shikumen*,' Chen said, taking note of Detective Ding's sarcasm in calling him an inspector, which he was not. He was determined, however, not to mention the talk with her in the eatery. For some reason not exactly understandable to himself, he wanted to keep Meihua out of the investigation as much as possible. 'So Zhang introduced me to her. We said just a few words in the lane. But what she told me made sense. Whoever the mysterious man was, with no knowledge about Fu's movements that night, he had to have waited around the mid-lane entrance for days, or even weeks, before he succeeded in following Fu all the way to the murder scene.'

'This could be a wild, wild goose chase, you know, the more so as we're short of men and time. Besides, your scenario is at best supported by circumstantial evidence.'

'Now let me bring up something else in the crime scene

report you've made,' Chen said, taking it from the folder. 'It's so detailed, that report of yours. It's an area designated for housing reconstruction, as you noted, but it's not far from the restaurant in question, nor from the railway station. And your report also touched on, among other things, some cigarette butts scattered near a toppled wall. You would not have included those details, evidently, if they were totally irrelevant. So you must have thought about the possibility of someone hiding himself behind the wrecked wall, smoking in the dark, waiting for Fu to come out, and to deliver the blow.'

'About the cigarette butts – they're just evidence we had to collect, but that detail supports your scenario, I have to say. You have your point, but . . .' Detective Ding pulled open a drawer and produced another cup of instant noodles. 'But we must have something to eat first, Chen.'

'That's fantastic. I've seen such an instant cup only once before. Wow, made in Japan too.'

'My wife works in a joint venture instant noodle company. So that's a benefit for me.' Ding rose to pour hot water into the two cups, and find a plastic spoon. 'Now go on, Chen.'

'To my surprise, Zhang also told me something that may account for why Pei made up the alibi for that night.'

'That can be important. Pei has denied any criminal activity, but he has failed to explain why he made up the alibi.'

'In the evening talk, Zhang mentioned something about a waitress taking pity on Pei at the eatery, and saving the leftover liquor from other tables for a penniless alcoholic like him, so I asked Zhang more pointedly about that at his home. The waitress turned out to be Pei's girlfriend. She's married, but with her husband working on an ocean liner, coming back home only once a year – for no more than two or three weeks – it's Pei who warmed her otherwise cold bed the rest of the time. She usually worked the night shift, and he went there after ten or eleven, enjoying whatever she had gathered for him from other tables. And then he left about the same time with her, more often than not to her home not too far away. Supposing that's the case, he could have tried to keep her out of trouble by making up the movie story for that night. After all, when you first questioned him on the phone, he might not have known anything about Fu's death, nor about himself being a possible suspect.'

'We can certainly check with the waitress. But if Pei—'

But if Pei was not the one, Detective Ding would be back to square one. And the pressure from the city government all over again. It was an idea not that pleasant for Detective Ding.

'What's more, you have inspired me in another aspect, Detective Ding. It's in the lists you have made.'

'The lists of possible suspects?'

'Exactly, Detective Ding. To paraphrase an old proverb: Studying your list for one night is more beneficial than studying textbooks for ten years.'

It was another bogus, disarming statement Chen thought he had to make, though Detective Ding no longer looked that displeased, sitting opposite, sipping at the noodle soup contemplatively.

'The list of those who may benefit from Fu's death, Detective Ding. It comes down to Fu's two children at the top, and some others related to them in the list. Regarding Xiaoqiang and Hongxia, you did not push too far after them, as you said to me, because they just needed to wait for a few more years. At the old man's demise, the huge fortune would inevitably go to them. It's true they might have been worried about the maid taking their place in the line of inheritance, but they were not aware of anything like that really happening. In fact, they looked totally flabbergasted when Meihua showed them her name in the family residence register – thanks to the city residence permit obtained by him for her. That's serious, but even that did not make a genuine threat to their status as the legitimate successors to Fu.'

'No, they did not have to be that desperate, not unless they became aware of some possible status change in terms of inheritance.'

'That really puzzled me. Last night, unable to sleep, I was rereading your list for the sixth or seventh time, still with no clue, and then moving on to read a novel. A leitmotif of the book – *Es muss sein* – galvanized me. And that's a point exactly the same as you have made to me.'

'A leitmotif of a novel?'

'It suddenly enabled me to see the light in the direction you have shown me,' Chen said, hastening to check himself from going too far. 'The heart of the matter is, as we have discussed, Fu's immense fortune. If someone became aware of the possibility of his inheritance being jeopardized, that could be a genuine motive for the murder.'

'What are you talking about, Chen?'

'To put it another way, the murderer believed he had no choice but to commit the crime at the present point in time. Any delay could possibly mean the disappearance of his claim to Fu's money.'

'That's a novel way to work for a police investigation.'

'But it's a possible scenario, isn't it?' Chen paused for another sip of the spicy noodle soup before going on. 'With Xiaoqiang and Hongxia ruled out, who else could benefit from Fu's death at this moment?'

'You mean someone else on the list?'

'Yes, someone else on the list. And there's something else I've learned from the evening talk, and from your interview tapes, too. Hongxia's miserable marriage with her second husband, Song.'

'Song is a good-for-nothing guy. I took a look into his file. Their marriage has been bad for years, but it's not that uncommon for some Shanghai couples to muddle along like that to the bitter end.'

'Well, I invited Hongxia out this morning. To a breakfast in a traditional eatery in the City God's Temple Market, where she told me a lot about Song.'

'You have dined out well for the investigation, Chen, with your gourmet friend, and now with Hongxia as well.'

'According to her, Song gambles not only on cricket fighting, but on practically everything. As a result of the heavy debt incurred, there're debt-collectors frequently knocking on their door—'

'The gambling debt,' Detective Ding cut in with a frown. 'I should have looked into that.'

'But it's more than that. A couple of months ago, she came back home earlier than usual and overheard the talk between Song and a triad-connected collector. As it turned out, Song had borrowed using his taken-for-granted prospect of inheritance as a sort of mortgage. The lender was getting impatient, so Song had to make up a story of Fu being terminally ill with his days numbered. That became the last straw for her. Things have long been rotten between the two, but she'd still wanted to keep up the appearance for the family. Though continuously gambling and losing money, Song managed to provide for the family in his way, even buying some small gifts for her, occasionally, to show his affection. The overheard speech proved, however, that he had her living in a deliberate lie all these years. From the very beginning, Song had married her with his eye on Fu's money. So devastated, she declared to him that night that she was going to file for divorce, and that he'd better not dream of getting a single penny from Fu's huge fortune.'

'Yes, that could be a real motive. It may take some time for the divorce to go through, but it's just a matter of time if she's determined.'

'*Es muss sein*, right? Then I asked Hongxia about Song's whereabouts that night. She remembered he did not come back until long after midnight, telling her that he'd played mahjong with his usual buddies in the Zijin Building, and winning a lot at the table. I asked her for the names and addresses of his mahjong associates, which she gave to me, all of them in the same building.'

'I know where the Zijin Building is. An old, ugly concrete one near the Renming Road,' Detective Ding said, taking from Chen a piece of paper with the names written on it. 'By the way, you must have bought her a huge breakfast for her to tell you such a lot.'

'Not that huge. A bamboo steamer of soup buns, two bowls of shrimp dumpling soup and a portion of spring rolls.'

'Wow, I hope she has not bankrupted you.'

'No, but I have to be really careful with my budget for the next two months. From what Red-nosed Zhang told me, she has inherited, if nothing else, the epicurean genes from Fu, except she's more of a gourmand than a gourmet. That's why she accepted my invitation without any hesitation,' Chen said, picking up the last piece of the dried cabbage stuck at the bottom of the noodle cup.

'Oh, something else, Detective Ding. Whether Pei smokes or not, I don't know, but I know if he has any money it immediately goes into his cup. In contrast, Song's a heavy smoker, and a swaggering one too. He could have been losing a huge amount of money while still chain-smoking those brand cigarettes, *Double Happiness.* I think you mentioned that particular brand in the crime scene report. Hongxia confirmed that it's his favorite. The cigarette butts must be kept here as evidence. So we may be able to check the fingerprints or DNA. But I'm not so sure about the proper procedure. I'm just beginning to translate the booklet, you know.'

'I know what we're going to do, Chen. With his gambling history, we can easily put him into custody first. In the meantime, I'll check with the waitress about Pei's alibi, and with Song's mahjong buddies too,' Detective Ding said, rising and glancing at his watch. 'The canteen must be closed. But I owe you a lunch, Chen. The instant noodle cup does not count.'

It never rains but it pours.

Chen was stepping into the reading room the next morning when Detective Ding came to him.

'Song has made a full confession, Chen. At first he tried to keep up the same old mahjong story, but as soon as I showed him the testimony of his mahjong mates in the Zijin Building and the fingerprint report, he knew he was finished. He spilled out. According to him, his relationship with Hongxia has been on the rocks for years, but he made do with it because he needed his chance at the inheritance. Up to his neck in gambling debt, he managed only with the pledge to lenders that he would pay back upon Fu's death. A couple of months ago, to his consternation, Hongxia suddenly turned serious about filing for divorce, which drove him up the wall. And like in a proverb, when really desperate, a dog will jump over the wall. In his calculation, only with Fu dead before the divorce went through could he keep his claim to Fu's money. With no children from their marriage, as Hongxia's spouse he should be able to have half of her share, an incredibly huge sum, more than enough to cover all his debts. He knew for a fact that Fu dined out from time to time. And he also knew better than to strike somewhere close to Red Dust Lane, where he could have been seen and recognized. So he waited for an opportunity to follow Fu to a locale at quite a distance, deep in the night. The rest of the story, I think you know only too well for me to tell,' Detective Ding said, taking out a pack of cigarettes. '*Phoenix*, a more expensive brand than *Double Happiness*. That's for celebration, Chen.'

'Thank you, Detective Ding. It's really worth celebrating.'

'I've tried to tell Party Secretary Li about your help with the investigation. He may have been too busy in discussions with the city government to pay much attention to it. But let me say something to you, Chen, you have the making of a cop despite your English major at college. No question about it.'

For such a political case, Detective Ding might not have been too eager to share the credit with a young novice, which Chen understood. Whether it had caught Party Secretary Li's attention or not, such a speedy conclusion appeared to be enough of a reward in itself.

'Thank you, Detective Ding. I have truly learned a lot from you during the course of the investigation.'

'For your help, you have made quite a number of trips, and paid for breakfast and stinking tofu and what not. At least you should have your expenses covered. Here is three hundred yuan from our squad's special fund.'

'Wow, that's about three months' salary for me!'

Whatever it could have possibly meant, it was not a small sum. That was something worth celebrating too.

After the conversation with Detective Ding, Chen found in the mail a letter from Lijiang Publishing House. It contained an offer of quite a generous advance for his translation of *Roseanna*. That was another piece of good news.

In a moment of impulse, he dialed the Red Dust Public Phone Service, waiting, pacing about the room with the phone clutched in his hand, till Meihua's voice came over the line, almost breathless. She must have run over in her wooden sandals.

'Any news, Comrade Chen?'

'Good news. The criminal was caught. He confessed.'

'Who?'

'There're some details we're still working on. I'll tell you all about it this evening. Now I've to ask a favor of you. Please prepare a good meal in the *shikumen* house tonight. I'll come over with two other people who have helped a lot with the investigation.'

It could come close to an imitation of the dramatic ending of a classic detective story: with the people gathered together, the brilliant detective reveals how he managed, step by step, to solve the case, pointing his finger at the real criminal in conclusion. The only difference would be that Song would not be present at the climactic scene. In real life, however, such a coup might have appeared to be too melodramatic.

There was no immediate response from Meihua, who was probably too confounded for the moment.

'It will also be a dinner in Fu's memory, Meihua. As I've mentioned, his suffering during the Cultural Revolution reminded me of what my father went through during those years. It's proper and right for me to burn a bunch of incense for him.'

'Yes, a bunch of tall incense, and I'll tell the news to him over the dinner with all his favorite dishes. In the Jiangxi village, we also do that. He then can really rest with his eyes closed. Thank you so much, Comrade Chen. You're such a capable police officer. In the snack eatery, I immediately knew you were different from other cops.'

'Well, it's the first case I've helped to solve since I started working in the bureau. It too is worth celebrating. Spare no cost. How about three hundred yuan? It's on the bureau. The special investigation allowance. Oh, please invite Old Root, too. He's Mr Fu's friend.'

'Old Root's a good man, the only one that spoke to Mr Fu in the lane during those horrible years, he told me about it.'

But there was another reason Chen chose not to discuss with her. With those gossips speculating about the relationship between Fu and Meihua, Old Root's first-hand account of the apprehension of the murderer should settle the dust.

'I'm going to the food market right now. I know a seafood peddler with the freshest supply from Zhoushan. Mr Fu left

some money behind, you know. I don't think you should
spend yours for the dinner. He would be so pleased with your
presence at the dining table.'

Then he called Dr Xia and Overseas Chinese Lu,
asking them to meet him at Red Dust Lane that evening.
He told them that it was an investigation-related occasion
without going into detail, and that for their help, they would
enjoy a private-kitchen dinner with him in a *shikumen*
house there. The two foodies promptly agreed, with their
curiosity roused and their expectations raised.

And he himself also had great expectations for the dinner,
considering the fact that even a sophisticated epicurean
like Fu had been pleased with her culinary skills, her serving
around the dishes steaming hot from the wok, and her
wooden sandals clinking pleasantly on the flagstones of the
courtyard.

What else could he bring to the dinner party? For gourmets
like Lu and Xia, something from a delicatessen on Jinling
Road might not really work. Then he hit on a cool idea. Ice
cream. It took only five minutes for him to bike from the First
Food Department on East Nanjing Road to Red Dust Lane.
With the rare luxury of the refrigerator in Fu's wing unit, they
could have the ice cream as dessert.

Before he could leave his spot in the reading room for the
day, the phone started ringing. It was Party Secretary Li.

'Detective Ding has told me about your great passion for
police work. You talked to him about the case, even with some
original ideas from a novel.'

So Detective Ding had talked to Party Secretary Li about
him. Ding might have merely touched on 'some original ideas
from a novel', without mentioning in detail about the real
difference his work had made to the investigation or about
any credit due to him. But Chen was not surprised.

'To be more exact, some original ideas come from books,
particularly the police procedure booklet I've been translating in the reading room, a project you assigned me, Party
Secretary Li,' Chen said respectfully, thinking that it was
not entirely untrue.

'That's fantastic. The translation of the booklet truly helped, right? Indeed, as Comrade Deng Xiaoping has pointed out, we need to further open up to the world. You're young, and you'll have a great future as a police officer with higher education in the unprecedented transformation of our country. I told you so the first day you came to report yourself to the bureau. You must have heard of our Party's new policy regarding the promotion of young cadres with college degrees. Indeed, a long way for you to go.'

That came as a surprise to him, but he said simply, 'Thank you so much, Party Secretary Li.'

'Oh, one more thing. It's such a high-profile case at the moment. With Fu's connections abroad, we'll have to give an official version of the investigation. Detective Ding will tell you more about it. Revelation of some politically sensitive details in the case won't serve the interests of the Party.'

'I understand, Party Secretary Li,' Chen said, though he failed to see any politically sensitive details relating to the case.

Putting down the phone, he found himself much less excited at the prospect of the dinner, particularly about the dramatic revelation in the midst of the narration about suspenseful twists and turns after the fashion of the incredible Poirot. Chen now had to modify his theatrical account in accordance with Detective Ding's official version, about which he hardly knew any details yet.

Perhaps he was required to say that he had merely discussed the case with the experienced detective, without bringing up any exciting details about his part in the investigation. It was not that the true story of the investigation would mean a terrible 'loss of face' to his senior colleague, but perhaps to the Party authorities, he guessed.

Chen felt he had no choice. Again, *Es muss sein*, that is, if he wanted to become a real cop.

He did not know whether he really wanted it or not.

There was something satisfying in solving the case, though. It was the first time that he found himself, to his surprise, looking forward to the possible career with some genuine interest.

But there were so many things for him to think about. He

decided not to worry any more – at least, only about things just now, such as the ice cream, as he was somehow reminded of an absurd cartoon he had seen in his childhood: a man staring at a cup of ice cream with a green-headed fly in it.

Instead, he picked up the copy of *The Unbearable Lightness of Being* and started reading again. He was going to say no to his friend who wanted to join him in the translation job. It was a great book, definitely worth translating, but the job should be up to someone with a good command of the French language, he told himself again. Nor would he have the time. Nevertheless, he had to read through Kundera's novel one more time. '*Es muss sein.*'

He liked the book and lit a cigarette for himself. It was a short break he thought he deserved.

In spite of the philosophical digressions by the author, Chen came to the realization, turning over pages, that he had just gained another inspiration from Kundera's discussion about Sabina's bowler hat, which unexpectedly shed light on Meihua's wooden sandals. Only the symbolism in Red Dust Lane was not that complicated. When she wore the wooden sandals, Meihua felt as if she was in the other woman's shoes. And she would have felt like that toward Fu, too. At least, she could have imagined that 'It was a very special permission he gave me'.

Chen wondered whether the old man had really given permission in that sense – to her, and to himself.

Perhaps that could be said to be another disadvantage of doing a cop's job. Sometimes it's better to leave things unsaid, unexplained, uninvestigated. Like in one of Li Shangyin's poems, so elusive from the echo of a Tang dynasty zither with half of its strings broken, simply titled as 'Untitled'.

> *A pearl holds its tears*
> *against the bright moon on the blue ocean;*
> *a jade-induced mist arises*
> *under the warm sun over Lantian field . . .*
> *Oh, this feeling, to be recollected later*
> *in memories, is getting confused . . .*

The phone rang again. This time it was Meihua, seemingly through some mysterious correspondence.

As it turned out, she wanted to make a report of the dinner menu to him. Chen listened with some interest. It was not a dinner for him alone. Xia, Lu, Old Root and Meihua, all of them deserved a good night. As she moved on to the description of small croaker soup, he made a suggestion.

'Add tofu to the soup. And a lot of minced scallions and gingers. I've had it before. It tastes delicious.'

'Oh yes, tofu. A dinner in his memory should definitely have tofu. Tofu dinner, that's a conventional must for the deceased. How could I have forgotten about it for his memorial meal?' she said, sobbing, suddenly breaking down again.

It was so unexpected. He'd mentioned it simply from a gourmet's perspective. Then he heard her in the midst of weeping, 'He's the only one that really took care of me. Now I'm left all alone in this world of red dust. Who's there to help? Old Root told me that he would not come to the dinner this evening. Probably because of Mr Fu's children. Xiaoqiang has contacted the neighborhood police for Red Dust Lane through his connections. So he's planning to move back in, whether I continue to stay in the *shikumen* house or not. And Hongxia too may come back as early as tonight – to get hold of the things allegedly left by her mother.'

So what if Hongxia came barging right into their dinner party tonight?

Already, there were things so unpredictable, troublesome, helpless in being a cop. And he could hardly claim to be the one in charge of the investigation.

He whistled, putting down the phone, and thinking of an ancient saying, 'Eight or nine times out of ten, things in this world do not go the way one really wants to go.'

Or to paraphrase it, he murmured to himself, thinking he still needed to buy some fruit for the dinner in Red Dust Lane, 'Eight or nine times out of ten, people in this world do not become the ones they really want to be.'

SEVEN

*H*e keeps on wading precariously across the treacherous *river, stepping on one stone after another, most of them jutting barely out of the water's surface, when he looks up, panic-stricken at the sight of a face-masked girl stumbling in the distance, shouting for help, struggling in vain toward the other bank, and drowning against the horizon shrouded in the impenetrable smog except for a yellow butterfly winging its way to him—*

And he is transported with the butterfly, fluttering, flying so high suddenly, it seems to be bringing the distant horizon beyond the unknown land, the mysterious ocean, all the way into the dark eye of the sun, with the immense landscape changing dramatically under its flapping wings, before it abruptly starts failing, falling with a thud to the ground, turning into a round black pebble sticking out of the food market's pebble street covered in white snow, but trembling almost imperceptibly, like a blackened human toe—

Startled out of the dream, he thought that the sound had come from his mother knocking into a chair under the attic. She got up so early, preparing for him the breakfast of white rice soup with small dishes of pickled cucumber and ferment tofu, and getting ready for her routine shopping trip for fresh vegetables in the morning, even though the Ninghai Street Food Market had long disappeared, along with the original pebble street which had been repaved in gray concrete.

It had been a night full of eerie dreams, with the background scenes continuously shifting back to those he must have seen twenty or even thirty years earlier. And it was not just because of his sleeping in the old attic, he was pretty sure of that now.

His mother was tiptoeing around with only a tiny nightlight flickering downstairs, believing he was still asleep overhead. She slept less because of her age. He could hardly see the first ray of gray light peeping in through the attic window.

He lay quietly in bed, trying not to disappoint her, thinking in the dark that still surrounded him.

In the dream, he had seen a face-masked girl drowning in the river. It vaguely disturbed him, though he failed to recognize her face behind the mask. Then the no less perplexing scene of a colorful butterfly soaring out of nowhere, flapping its wings, and bringing an unbelievable metamorphosis across the vision of the land. Cudgeling his brains out, he managed to recall something he had read in his college days, but he could not help wondering at its relevancy to the present moment.

The butterfly effect, that was the term in the book. With a butterfly flapping its wings in Chicago, a tornado occurs in Tokyo thousands and thousands of miles away, as the analogy describes in a poetic hyperbole. But to him, it seemed not to be just about something insignificant happening here which was capable of leading to another significant thing happening far, far away, or vice versa. It was also about the seemingly unrelated proving to be related through the complicated interactions among people known or unknown to each other, through which one's identity was constructed or deconstructed. In other words, something unnoticeable happening to him at one point in time – or for that matter, happening to somebody else – could have an unbelievable impact on the people directly or indirectly concerned at a much later point in time.

Occasionally, he had thought about it during some of the complicated investigations. A criminal or a cop could have been made through those interactions – with or without his or her own knowledge – which turned out to be more challenging for him to sort through.

Then another thought jumped out to him. Was it possible that the Webcops and Internal Security had taken him as the one writing and posting the poem *Reading Animal Farm*? It was preposterous, but it might not have appeared to be totally unthinkable from their perspectives. Known as a published poet, Chen had undertaken investigations into those tricky moves and maneuvers in cyberspace, and now as one not 'politically correct', he had both the expertise and motive to deliver an anti-Party attack online like that – or to be more exact, an attack against the supreme Party leader, which was one and the same thing to Internal Security.

Also, the way the poem had spread so quickly among the netizens, without giving away the identity of the poet, suggested something of a well-executed scheme. As a matter of fact, in a case the chief inspector named for himself 'Shanghai Redemption', his secret investigation actually contributed to the downfall of a mighty politburo member. What he had done on the sly might never have come out in its entirety, but Internal Security could not help but have suspected.

What's more, the chief inspector had connections higher up in Beijing. For one, Comrade Zhao, the ex-First Secretary of the Central Party Discipline Committee. Zhao had been seen as a patron of Chen, choosing to back him up in several high-stake political cases. Though not as powerful after retirement, Zhao's name was still mentioned in connection with the power struggle at the top. So it was not unimaginable for Chen to write and post the poem as a part of Zhao's charge against the Pig Head.

It was absurd, but given the opaqueness of China's politics, anything seemed to be possible. And the trap set up – as a preemptive strike – by the paranoid Internal Security was far from insane . . .

The train of his thought was intercepted by a cock crowing in the neighborhood. Was it the same cock that crowed those long-ago mornings when he went to his English studies at Bund Park? At the time, he'd talked with his friend about a young hero in ancient China, who made a point of practicing the sword the moment a cock started crowing at dawn.

Time really flies. Decades had elapsed in a finger-snap. But he had truly heard the cock-crowing in those days, he was positive about that, in the neighborhood of Red Dust Lane, the back exit of which joined the street food market.

And the black pebble throbbing in the dream could have come, he realized, from the pebble street of Ninghai Street Food Market . . .

Long Chain of Karma

For the evening talk at the entrance of Red Dust Lane, the participants were not necessarily all residents of the lane. For instance, this story came from an unexpected visitor from the Shanghai Police Bureau, who looked more like an intellectual than a police officer. Needless to say, people were initially worried about the possible purpose of his visit.

'Don't be alarmed, folks. My name is Chen, and I'm here this evening not as a cop, but as a participant of the evening talk. I've been to the lane quite a few times. It was years ago, and I enjoyed the incredible stories in the audience.' Chen smiled an apologetic smile before perching himself on a shaky bamboo stool offered to him. 'So it's my turn to tell a story, which happens to be one connected to this neighborhood – to be more exact, to the Ninghai Street Food Market at the back of the lane. That's why I want to share it with you here.'

To the confusion of the audience, he then launched into a rambling account of the demolished food market, as if having a sudden second thought about what he was going to say. The well-known street market of open booths, stalls and counters, once a huge convenience to the neighborhood, had become an unbearable eyesore for the increasingly metropolitan city of Shanghai, hence the eventual removal of the market into a building at the intersection of Ninghai and Zhejiang Road. Much smaller, but with a clean-looking appearance. The metamorphosis of the market was not something new or intriguing to the people sitting in front of the lane, but they all waited with patience. It was not common for a cop to come to tell a story there.

'It's a story about a colleague of mine. Let's just name him C . . .' Chen seemed to be finally coming to the point. 'In the late sixties, people had to come to the food market early in the morning, as you know, a couple of hours or even earlier before its opening bell, stepping into long queues, waiting, because of the food supply shortages under Chairman Mao's command economy at the time.

'For his family, it was his mother's job to make the daily visit to the food market, but that year she came down with hepatitis. The doctor emphasized the importance of the necessary nutrition as well as proper rest for her recovery. So C offered to go to the food market instead. There, by sneaking up to one of those kind-looking, middle-aged women in a position near the counter, murmuring something like, "Auntie, my mom is sick," which happened to be true, he was capable of jumping the long queue. Naturally, some people turned out to be hardhearted, cursing and chasing him out of the line. For a skinny kid with little face to lose, however, he would instantly approach another line, applying the same thick-skinned technique, smooth-and-sweet tongued. More often than not, he would have pulled off the trick in less than fifteen minutes, and brought back home a full basket.

'Soon he became known for his expertise among his mother's friends, some of whom appeared to be quite envious. Those days, it was one of the few things his mother chose to pride herself on.

'Then a special challenge presented itself with the coming Chinese New Year. Usually, the holiday celebration would last from the first till the fifteenth day of the first month in the lunar calendar, during which people's relatives and friends would come visiting, greeting, gift-giving and dining at each other's homes. In accordance with the time-honored tradition, "big fish, big meat" and other presentable dishes had to appear on the dining table, or the host would lose face big-time – the Chinese New Year time. And the guests would be so understanding, for instance, as to not touch the fish in the platter; and if they did, their chopsticks would touch just one side of the fish without ever turning it over, claiming a superstitious taboo that it could symbolize something unlucky like an overturned boat in the new year's fortune. In reality, it was done so that the other side of the fish might still be served on another occasion. That might have illustrated what a matter of importance it was for people to stock up as much as possible before the market closed for the holiday.

'Consequently, that meant a tough job for him. With all the families of the neighborhoods seized with the holiday anxiety at the food market, those thick-skinned approaches of his might not work out like before. What made it even tougher was an unexpected request from Auntie Qing of Red Dust Lane, a friend of his mom's, who wanted C to take her daughter, nicknamed "Little Phoenix", along with him for the holiday shopping. He was panic-stricken with the responsibility for a slip of a girl like Little Phoenix, several years younger, who knew nothing about the jungle of the street food market.

'But there was no choice for them, Little Phoenix and C, saddled with the joined blessings and urgings of the two families. He racked his brains for possible tricks. Among them, one was to put baskets, ropes, bricks or whatever into those lines in the street food market, as early as eight or nine o'clock the previous evening. It was like sticking flags into the soil to indicate sovereignty, so they could come to claim their recognized positions before the market opening bell. For the long shopping list for the Chinese New Year, they had to secure positions in at least seven or eight lines. But these "flags" might not prove to be that reliable. Others could kick them away – if unprotected – in the middle of the night. Consequently, after placing them, he made a detailed plan to patrol around their "flags" throughout the night. He insisted on his coming to the street market earlier, like a protective elder brother, but Little Phoenix too made it there shortly after midnight, unwilling to stay at home any longer.

'It had snowed earlier that night. A good sign for the coming year, but not for the two kids shivering out there. Her nose red, her hands chapped, she followed him around in high spirits like a little phoenix tail with admiration shining in her large eyes. A naughty little girl, she traced her fingers on the snow-covered back of his cotton-padded coat. When he discovered what she had written was "elder brother", she giggled like crazy. "So I won't lose sight of you, my elder brother."

'Near five o'clock, he had her stand in the line with a sign for "pig trotter", a must for the Shanghai families during the holiday season. And he himself kept shuttling back and forth among the other lines. When one of those lines began edging close to the counter, either she or he could run over to jump in.

'About fifteen minutes before the opening bell, however, a commotion broke out about the unexpected shifts of the produce signs over the concrete counters. The moment people discovered themselves lining up to the wrong counters, they rushed around helter-skelter, pushing, shoving, crashing and elbowing their way in the market. Most of their "flags" got lost in the chaos. He managed to secure only two previous positions – for pork steaks and a frozen goose – before he turned to look toward her line, which appeared to be much shorter than before, leading to the counter under a new sign of "green cabbage".

'As it turned out, the original sign had inexplicably shifted to another counter near Fujian Road, so the line formed over-night for "pig trotter" had moved too. But he failed to spot her there. Alarmed, he searched back and forth until a wailing sound was heard over the chilly wind, like that of a lost kitten, wafting from behind the once pig trotter counter. He hurried over to the bizarre sight of something like black dates twitching under a stack of overturned wire boxes. In the earlier stampede, she had stumbled and fallen under the empty boxes which cushioned her like a shield. She was not too badly hurt, except for her shoes being trodden off and her toes crushed black – like broken dates, frozen in the snow.

'After the fiasco that morning, his confidence in his "market touch" vanished. The snow-covered memory of his kneeling helplessly beside her haunted him. He could not bring himself to see her again. And he avoided the sight of her in the lane. Things were said to be much worse for her there. Because of her failure to bring back anything good that morning, not to mention the loss of a new bamboo basket and valuable ration coupons in the pandemonium, her family lost face during that holiday season, with nothing presentable on the dining table. Her father slapped her in a fit . . .'

Chen paused, accepting a cup of Dragon Well tea handed

over from a younger man in the audience, and having a *China* cigarette lit respectfully by another of his own age.

'Perhaps that was one of the reasons that he continued his path to becoming a cop after his initial positioning. The realization did not hit home until after he started taking a psychology course as part of his career training. Childhood trauma and subsequent compensation. The subconscious urge for him to be able to protect the helpless ones like Little Phoenix.'

A spell of silence ensued. In the socialism of China's characteristics, a cop could more or less throw his weight around, maneuvering in the midst of corruptions and connections under the one-Party system, which leaned heavily on the police force. So C was no longer helpless, to say the least, not like on that long-ago snow-buried morning in the street market. But a question then quivered around the narrator's cigarette in the deepening dusk. After all, that incident had happened years earlier. What was the point of recapturing it this evening? Little Phoenix must have moved away long ago. No one in the audience knew or remembered anything about her.

'Sometimes C could not help wondering at the long chain of causality in terms of misplaced yin and yang. With all these links inexplicably connected came the unexpected, unimagined result. Had he not succeeded earlier in the street food market, he would not have brought her into trouble on New Year's Eve.' Chen seemed to have lost himself in the philosophical diversion, taking another deep draw at the cigarette.

That did not sound like the end of a story. The audience waited. The chain of misplaced yin-and-yang causality had to be longer. Or the narrator would not have chosen to tell the story in front of Red Dust Lane.

The cigarette burned Chen's fingers before he resumed. 'Not too long ago, the narcotics squad of the city police bureau talked to C about a junkie captured behind the Great World on Ninghai Road. With the street food market long gone, that section of the street remained squalid, with cheap and shabby eateries, and with suspicious characters hanging around. She was not just one of them, but connected with drug dealers in that shady corner, and possibly with one of the Big Brothers too. She refused to say anything in custody. It was a no-brainer to figure out why. With her lips sealed, she would be punished on account of drug possession. But it could turn into something far more serious if she spilled.

'After the successful conclusion of the old gourmet murder case, Party Secretary Li, the number one boss of the police bureau, had hinted about the possibility of C's promotion as a young intellectual Party cadre in accordance with the new Party policy, even though C had received no training in the field of police work. Li wanted him to take a look into the case.

'"It's not just because of the connections you have made with Red Dust Lane, but also because of the course you have taken in psychology," Party Secretary Li said in earnest. "In the event of the successful conclusion of another case, I would talk to people in the city government about your extraordinary work. Indeed, a couple of politically important cases in a row, and none of your colleagues will ever complain again about your lacking experience in the line of our work. In the last analysis, it's a matter of following the Party's policy of having more young intellectual cadres in the Party system."

'It was an unmistakable signal. But unlike the first case, C had no idea about the new one, except that the suspect in custody had been an erstwhile resident of the lane.

'Besides, C was not sure that was the only reason for the assignment from Party Secretary Li. While a good change from the police procedure translation he had been doing in the bureau reading room because of his college major in English literature, he had heard that the new assignment could have been designed for him to lose face. Some of his "real cop" colleagues were not so pleased with his "nosiness" around their investigations. So they pushed the difficult, impossible mission to him, and the failure expected of him would serve as further proof of his incompetence in the field.

'Nevertheless, C headed to the interrogation room, thinking of the clichés about "treating a dead horse in whatever way possible, as if it were still kicking and alive".

'The junkie in question sat alone in the room, emaciated, disheveled, probably in her late twenties or early thirties, looking haggard yet still defiant. A hard nut to crack, he knew for sure. Like in another old saying, "a dead pig worries not about the scalding water". She was done in, she knew, so why should she worry any more?

'He started routinely, sitting opposite her across the desk, pressing the start button of the recorder, and quoting Chairman Mao for the first sentence. *"Confess, you'll have leniency; resist, you'll take punishment.* This is our Party's policy, you surely know that. So now start to talk."

'"Talk and I'm dead, that I know only too well," she said, flicking cigarette ashes to the floor, setting one bare foot on the edge of the chair. "Do you really think I'm so stupid as to do that for your credit?"

'He had no answer to that. But he went on mechanically. He did not really care about promotion in the police bureau, as Party Secretary Li had discussed with him. It was not exactly a job he had dreamed about. At the end of half an hour, having exhausted the standard questions reservoir, he rose with something like a touch of relief, ready to give up. Still, he handed her a business card.

'"Here is my card. If there's anything you think of later and want to talk, just let me know."

'"No. There's nothing whatsoever, I've already told you," she said, scratching her ankle, with blue veins standing out like mutilated earthworms, before she cast a glance at the card.

'To his confusion, she suddenly looked up with a visible change of expression, turning to stare hard at him like a demented addict caught red-handed with a hidden package. Uneasy with her focused gaze, he lowered his head, dropping his glance to the floor, to a discolored toe with the nail not painted, but possibly damaged in a recent scuffle, looking like a black date.

'"Elder Brother – C!" she blurted out.

'"What?"

'"That night before New Year's Eve – in the street food market near Red Dust Lane, you still remember?"

'"Little—"

'"Yes, you still recognize me!"

'Then, all of a sudden, she started talking, gushing out non-stop as if from a crumbled dam, oblivious of the recorder blinking with a faint red light like a monster's eye in the haunted night woods.

'Not long after that street market fiasco, as it turned out, her family moved across the river to Pudong. C had not seen Little Phoenix again, nor heard anything about her move, nor had he asked about her, for he remembered her only by the nickname.

'It was a page he thought he had turned over, and he was in no mood to read it again.

'Like in an old saying, a lot of water had gone by, first in the gutter of the street food market, and then with the street market itself also gone, so when he got the case file from the bureau Party boss, he did not know anything about her identity. Nor about what had happened to her through all these years.

'But there might have been nothing too surprising about that journey of hers – from that broken line in the street market to the shady corner near the Big World. In terms of physical distance, it was less than half a mile. And still on the same Ninghai Road.

'Actually, it turned out to be just like one of the often-heard stories about an unlucky girl in present-day China. After her failure to enter high school, and to find a job because of her family lacking any connections, she helplessly turned into a loser in the eyes of the increasingly materialistic society. And it was only a matter of time for her to fall into bad company, and then as prey to drugs.

'What she said in the interrogation room regarding her involvement in drug trafficking incriminated her beyond any hope of redemption. It was all recorded. Unerasable.

'But why had she suddenly chosen to spill out like that? Perhaps the shock of the recognition broke through her psychological defense. It was not until toward the end of her narration that she spoke in a subdued voice, clearing her throat, gazing up at him in afterthought.

'"You still remember that night, Elder Brother? What a pathetic loser I was, and I still am, incapable of doing anything good. Believe it or not, the realization hit home for the first time with all the wire boxes collapsing and burying me in the street market on that morning. Now I'm totally finished, I know. You don't have to worry about me. I'm glad that I've talked to you today—"

"'No, you don't have to talk like that! I'm so sorry about what happened—"

"'You put the steak and goose into my crushed bamboo basket, I still remember, and you went back home almost empty-handed that morning. Of all the people, you were the only one being really nice to me, helping me at your own expense. But I'm worse than nothing – nothing but trouble."

'She simply believed he had gone out of the way for her, but it was just because he'd felt so guilty at the sight of her crushed toes under the stack of wire boxes that snow-covered morning in the street market. Still, people choose to see what they want to see, from a perspective preferable or acceptable to themselves.

'But the question remains, why should she have chosen to speak out at such calamitous expense for herself?'

No one chose to make a comment as Chen came to an unexpected stop in his narrative. There was no missing the question he did not raise in so many words. Could it have been a favor to C – if *favor* was the word for it – that she did for him in the interrogation room of the police bureau?

'As a cop, your friend had to do his job,' someone nicknamed 'Amateur PI Huang' said in the audience, rubbing his hands as if they, too, had got frost-bitten that cold morning, years earlier, 'particularly at this important juncture of his police career.'

'Anyway, he succeeded where other cops had failed to make her talk,' Chen resumed, with a sarcastic edge to his voice. 'Some of his colleagues were not pleased with the unexpected outcome on his part, but Party Secretary Li seemed very much satisfied with his work, raving about it in a bureau meeting and recommending that C start working as an inspector in charge of the special case squad. After all, several notorious dealers were apprehended as a result. It was a huge breakthrough for the city police.

'After the meeting, C tried to say something on her behalf to the Party secretary. He maintained that it was in line with the Party's policy that those who confess should be dealt with leniently. But those years, narcotic arrests were few, and the unwritten regulation was very strict. Those caught had to be most severely punished. Period.

"'A really harsh blow to the dealers," Party Secretary Li declared. "It's a credit to our bureau. You were the only one who succeeded in making her talk. Indeed, a fantastic job you have done. Who says that college education is not helpful to our line of work?"

'It would not have made any difference, C realized, to tell the truth about why she had spilled out. The always politically correct Party Secretary Li was capable only of seeing things from a higher political level, "The good job you've done speaks volumes for our Party's new policy regarding young intellectual cadres. They are playing an important role in the unprecedented reform of our socialist country, and in our police force too."

'So his effort to introduce the narrative of the long-ago street food market experience to Party Secretary Li for her benefit – though how it could have worked out, he had not thought – was brushed aside even before he had started.'

'Nothing would have mattered any more for her,' another one in the audience said. 'There was no way for her to climb out of the fathomless abyss. Confess or not, she was beyond help, she knew that better than anybody else.'

That sounded like a plausible interpretation. None in the audience supposed, however, that the cop had come to the evening talk to hear it.

Perhaps there was another question not raised, and not answered, either. What exactly had happened to Little Phoenix in the end? But then the words 'most severely punished' seemed to have covered all.

What cannot be said has to pass over in silence.

Chen passed a pack of cigarettes around, and lit one respectfully for an elderly man nicknamed Old Root, an authoritative figure in the evening talk, before he took his leave.

Presently, Old Root said, 'Did you notice his fingers trembling while trying to light the cigarette for me?'

'Yes, but what about it?'

'Like a guilty man burning a candle for forgiveness. Hold

on – I have a vague feeling that I may have seen him here years ago – at the evening talk. Possibly still a kid at the time. Anyway, guess who Inspector C could possibly be?'

'None other than Chen himself?'

'Exactly, he feels so guilty, he has to come and tell the story here.' Like Chen, Old Root took a long pull at the cigarette before resuming, 'It's like people burning netherworld money at a spot particularly meaningful to the deceased. If that's the case, he may turn out to be a conscientious cop.'

EIGHT

He comes to a standstill, so horrified at the sight of a blindfolded man riding desperately along a treacherous mountain trail, whipping at a blind horse like crazy, as if being chased by invisible soldiers in the depth of the night. The darkness lies motionless, like a patient etherized on a white-sheet-covered table. Under the crumbling cliff, along the narrow trail stretching on like an extra-long footnote to a foregone conclusion, the horse is tearing headlong to the brink of a fathomless lake—

And he is galvanized by the realization that the rider is none other than himself, cursing, pushing on to the dark shore, and at the same time watching the horrendous scene helplessly from a distance. To his confusion, there seems to be another voice saying to him in persuasion, 'You have to keep going, going in the dark—'

It's then that the horse stumbles toward the water's edge—

The dream had probably come, he supposed, from a couplet in an ancient collection of absurd anecdotes titled *New Tales of the World*, in which a Chinese scholar tried to excel in representing the most horrible scene imaginable in a poem: 'A blind man is riding a blind horse / to the lake shore deep at night.'

Chen must have been thinking too much about the hazardous approach to the netizen named Huyan in Red Dust Lane the next morning, so the dream arose as a vivid projection from his subconscious. As in an old Chinese saying: 'What comes into one's dream at night comes from what he worries about during the day.'

And the next morning – to be more exact, this morning – he would be the blind rider racing toward Red Dust Lane, with no idea about what disaster he was heading towards, and with nothing visible around in the pitch blackness for him to make any possible judgment.

A text message came in from Detective Yu.

'You have to be there, keep going all the time, even when you are going nowhere, and with luck, you may be able to have a breakthrough.'

And just one or two minutes later, another message from Peiqin came vibrating into his phone. She, too, must have gotten up early.

'Huyan appears to be a professional photographer, with his photos frequently posted online, and occasionally in the company of others' poems or stories. It is said that those pictures actually bring in a sizable income. His works have been displayed in exhibitions. Huyan's a rare family name, but I'm not one hundred percent sure about his being the very one in Red Dust Lane.'

Another crucial clue. So Huyan could have been connected with Dragon Brother because of the juxtaposition of poetry with photography. It was not an uncommon practice for netizens, as their posts would attract more readers that way – in imitation of a popular practice of combining poems with paintings in classical Chinese literature and art. It was conceivable that Huyan liked the poem, added a photo relevant to the contents, and a repost with the two together was seen by Webcops. While it did not necessarily mean Huyan knew Dragon Brother personally, it surely narrowed the range of door-knocking and question-raising for Chen. Like doing an Internet search, the combination of two key words could help to produce a faster and more reliable result.

But once again, searching his memory down Red Dust Lane's history did not yield anything new. He was unsure if he remembered any photographers in the lane, and definitely not one – or any lane resident – surnamed Huyan. It was perhaps no surprise. For the last ten years or so, he had been too busy to step into Red Dust Lane again, and to learn things that had happened there. So how could he find out?

Some people he knew long ago in the lane, but they did not necessarily know him – especially not now. Like Mr Ma in the tiny bookstore before the Cultural Revolution, and then in a herbal medicine store afterward, but he was not even sure if Mr Ma was still there. There was an elderly man nicknamed Old Root, a prominent figure in the evening talk of the lane, who might remember him. But Old Root must be really old – too old to come out like before. Only once had Chen disclosed his police identity through a story told in front of the lane. Now no one knew or remembered him, so how could he presume—

But wait. There was one in the lane who might remember him, and that with the knowledge of his being a cop. He jumped up, almost hitting his head against the attic beam. A teacher in his middle school during the years of the Cultural Revolution. He had visited her in the days just before his promotion to the chief inspectorship in the police bureau. She'd talked to him about things happening to some lane residents she knew, including one that got into trouble because of his picture development in the attic. But his name was not Huyan, Chen felt pretty sure. Afterward, she wrote Chen a thank-you card for his help, which was nothing, and respectfully called him 'Chief Inspector Chen'.

It was not that likely that there were two photographers in the lane. Still, he might be able to locate Huyan through the one his middle school teacher had told him about. If Huyan was there, truly connected with the poet, he might be able to ferret out more about Dragon Brother; if not, it would not hurt for Chen to talk to him and give some advice about what to say to Internal Security . . .

Then he heard his mother moving light-footedly, stepping out and closing the door quietly after her. She was going shopping, even though the street food market had long disappeared.

It was time for him to get up too. The 'case' was waiting for him in Red Dust Lane. His effort might be just like the scary dream scene, but failing to make the attempt meant he was beyond any hope of redemption.

In China, people might have one scenario after another about a political case, but more often than not, the true one would turn out to be much wilder and stranger than imaginable in a fiction book. It was useless to work on those theories in the attic, just as Detective Yu had said in the message.

After a long night of dreaming and looking back at how far

he had come, he finally found himself ready to confront the possible end of his police career . . . or a new beginning.

'Even if you know it's something impossible for you to do, you have to try your best as long as it's the right thing to do.' That was another Confucius maxim his father had taught him so many years earlier. Whether or not he could achieve a breakthrough, or continue to be a chief inspector, he had to go to Red Dust Lane.

Because of Doctor Zhivago II

M r Ma of Red Dust Lane was released one day in 1987, several years ahead of time. He had been wronged, it was said, when thrown into jail as a 'current counter-revolutionary' at the beginning of the Cultural Revolution.

It came as a huge surprise to Red Dust Lane.

Even more so to Comrade Jun, the head of the neighborhood committee. Usually, the higher authorities would have contacted the neighborhood cadres first about such an unexpected development.

Things were changing, of course, after the end of the Cultural Revolution. A number of 'wrong cases' had been rectified. For instance, Chairman Liu Shaoqi, the Chairman of the People's Republic of China, had been wrongly accused by Chairman Mao Zedong, the Chairman of the Communist Party of China, and brutally killed like a naked rat in prison. Liu's pictures now reappeared in the *People's Daily*, though Mao's portrait still hung high on Tiananmen Square.

Mr Ma was a nobody in comparison. Still, people were truly happy for Mrs Ma in Red Dust Lane. Like in a Beijing opera about Wang Baochuan, a virtuous wife in the seventh century who waited for eighteen long years in an impoverished earthen cave for her husband's return in triumph as a general, Mrs Ma, too, finally had her man back, even though Mr Ma was by no means like a great general returning home in the Tang dynasty.

All those years, Mrs Ma had fared far worse than the heroine in the classical Beijing opera, sweeping the fallen leaves all alone in the lane, day after day in rain or shine. She'd turned into a taken-for-granted scene of Red Dust Lane – a fragile woman dragging a long bamboo stick broom taller than herself, invariably carrying a humble smile on her face and a plastic waste basket on her back. Ironically, her health appeared to have somewhat improved because of the physical labor. At least red spots were seen in her cheeks, though some people argued it was because of her constant exposure to the sunlight. During the Cultural Revolution, it was a matter of course that she suffered humiliations and persecutions as a black family member, but probably not much worse than other 'birds of the same black feathers'. And all those years she made her monthly visit to him in the prison. Eventually, the lane came to respect the woman for her unwavering dedication to her husband.

'The man may not be too bad after all. No, not with a good wife remaining so loyal to him these years,' Old Root commented at the news of Mr Ma's release.

So a group of the neighborhood residents poured out to the entrance of the lane that morning, waiting to pay a sort of respect to the Mas. For a wronged man, but also for a virtuous woman who believed in the innocence of her man.

But it was a totally changed Mr Ma they witnessed – silver-haired and silver-browed, like a white owl in the mountains. He dragged his unsteady steps into Red Dust Lane, leaning heavily on the shoulder of his frail wife, wearing a pair of glasses as thick as the bottoms of beer bottles, his eyes blinking incessantly in the sunlight. He was said to have damaged his vision reading too much in the black prison cell. Nevertheless, the couple presented a touching sight: a white-haired man in the company of a rosy-cheeked woman, hand in hand, as if walking out of an ancient Chinese love story, though their age difference was not large in reality.

Afterward, Comrade Jun delivered a well-prepared speech at a special neighborhood meeting. 'It was politically necessary – politically correct – for the Party authorities to maintain high alert against any possible sabotage attempts made by the class enemies during the Cultural Revolution. All in the interests of socialist China, as we understand. You, too, have to take a positive attitude toward that part of the history, Mr Ma. And it is now correct, politically correct, of course, to redress those wronged cases. Look forward, not backward. That is our

Party's new slogan. If there's anything the neighborhood committee can possibly do for you, please let us know.'

'There's one thing the neighborhood committee can do,' Mr Ma said slowly. 'My wife does not mind going on with the lane-sweeping job, but I, too, have to do something for my living.'

That came as a legitimate request. At his age, it was impossible for Mr Ma to find a new job for himself. If he had worked at a state-owned company before, he might be able to go back there in accordance with the new Party policy. But he had not. No one claimed responsibility for that.

Comrade Jun suggested that the Mas resume their book business. It was providential that Mrs Ma had kept those books, dust-covered, yet otherwise intact, in the back room all these years. In the mid-eighties, private bookstores or book booths had started to reappear in the city. It should not be too difficult for them to have their license renewed, for which Comrade Jun offered to apply on their behalf. In addition, he returned to the old couple the front room which had been used for the storage of the neighborhood propaganda material. It was another surprising move, but no one said anything about it. After all, the Mas had suffered so much.

'No, a bookstore will serve only as a daily reminder of my prison years,' Mr Ma said, his eyes blinking like an owl. Instead, he wanted to open a Chinese herbal medicine store in the front room.

The next week, Mr Ma submitted the license application. Comrade Jun took it upon himself to smooth the process. At the evening talk, Old Root asked the audience to help in whatever way possible. Weeks passed with the application traveling from one bureaucratic desk to another, without having made any progress. Mr Ma looked more and more like a withered white owl, sighing in a hollow voice, which sounded like eerie hooting in the night woods.

Then, all of a sudden, a business license was express-delivered to Mr Ma. Comrade Jun and other neighborhood committee members appeared to be totally in the dark about the unexpected development.

As it turned out, somebody in the city police bureau had put in a word for the old man. Again, it confounded the lane. People had never heard of Mr Ma's connections there. Comrade Tang, the head of the neighborhood police office, shook his head without saying anything. It was said that he had recently got into some trouble, and would soon be transferred to a smaller neighborhood office in the far-away Jinshan district.

Whatever interpretations and speculations there may have been in the lane, a new signboard was soon made with the eye-catching name: Old Ma's Herbal Medicine Store.

'Congratulations, Mr Ma! The Wheel of Fortune is finally turning in your favor.' Comrade Jun added in an official tone, 'The Party authorities are now encouraging private business in our socialist country.'

'Thank you, Comrade Jun. We owe everything to the Party's new policy,' Mrs Ma said, clasping her fingers in a sincere gesture of appreciation.

Amidst the people gathering in front of the herbal medicine store on its opening, Old Root struck a match to a long chain of firecrackers dangling from the tip of a bamboo pole. It was a celebration practice that was no longer encouraged in the city for safety concerns, but for once it was allowed in the lane because of its supposed potency in scaring away the evil spirits associated with a place and ushering in the good Fortune.

'You surely know your way around, Mr Ma!' Old Root said in the chorus of the firecrackers. 'Your business will gallop for thousands of miles, like a horse after a break!'

The comments referred to a clever combination of Mr Ma's surname and old Chinese sayings. The character *ma*, a Chinese family name, can also mean a horse. So old sayings came in handy, such as 'An old horse knows its way around' and 'Though taking a break in the stable, the old horse still wants to run for thousands of miles'. To all appearances, Old Ma's Herbal Medicine Store seemed to be a well-chosen name for the business.

An old horse could also turn out to be a dark horse, and the lane prayed for his successful venture into the new, un-familiar line of business.

For all the blessing and firecrackers, concerns lingered in

the lane. Those days, the majority of people working for state-owned companies still enjoyed the state medical insurance, and it did not appear likely that they would come to a small, privately-run herbal drug store at their own expense, not to mention the fact that it took time to build up a customer base. For an old man like Mr Ma, newly released from prison, how could he become known to people out of Red Dust Lane?

But the lane was proved wrong. It hardly took any time at all for his business to begin galloping ahead. Soon, visitors were lining up outside the herbal store, and Mrs Ma had to move out two wooden benches for the customers waiting in the lane.

Was it because of his expertise as a self-made doctor? An old horse, Mr Ma might know his way around the herbs, but such popularity could not have materialized overnight. The people in the lane could not help wondering and speculating again.

Then foreigners, too, came to the herbal store – almost like in the good old days of the bookstore. Perhaps there had been something truly inexplicably suspicious going on in the small front room, one of his old neighbors declared, to make the Party government put him behind bars in the sixties.

Finally, Old Root decided to take a closer look into the matter. Comrade Jun more than approved, though it was no longer the age of the class struggle.

Old Root went to the store with the excuse of sending the Mas an urn of Shaoxin sticky rice wine. The wine was supposed to serve as a token of his gratitude for those books he had read for free in the bookstore years earlier.

That morning he stepped in and found Mr Ma's front room furnished like a combination of a doctor's office and a herbal medicine store. Its white walls were lined with oak cabinets sporting numerous tiny drawers, each of them bearing a label for a particular herb, and in the midst of it all, Mr Ma sat at a mahogany desk, a white-haired, white-bearded man wearing silver-rimmed spectacles and a long string of carved beads. An immaculate image of a Taoist recluse enjoying longevity in harmony with nature. Beside the desk, a glass counter exhibited an impressive array of herb samples, along with unfolded books, magazines and pictures, all illustrating the beneficial effects of the Oriental herbs.

But there was a 'foreign devil' in the room, too. A young girl, her long blonde hair falling over her bare shoulders, was sitting in a chair opposite Mr Ma, her wrist like white jade shining on the mahogany desk.

'Let me take a look at your tongue,' Mr Ma said in a serious voice.

He examined her tongue, nodded, and then pressed her wrist for the pulse with his eyes closed.

'Nothing seriously wrong. The yang appears slightly high at the expense of the yin. So the energy does not flow in perfect harmony within your body's system. Perhaps too much on your mind, young girl. I'm writing you a prescription, with some herbs for the yin-yang balance, and some for the blood circulation to the benefit of the whole system. It's a holistic approach. And all fresh herbs here, I guarantee you.'

'That's fantastic,' the girl said in Chinese. 'No way to get these fresh herbs in the United States.'

Mr Ma flourished a skunk-tail-blush pen over a piece of bamboo paper and handed the prescription to Mrs Ma. 'You choose the freshest herbs for her.'

The business practice appeared truly impressive. The consolidation of handing out the prescription and herbs in one visit proved so convenient to the customers.

But how could an American girl have learned of the herbal medicine store hidden away in a lane, which had been in business for only two or three weeks?

'You're busy with your customers, Mr Ma,' Old Root said. 'So I'm leaving the wine here. It's nothing, free from my nephew who now operates a wholesale chain supplying Shaoxin sticky rice wine to hotels and restaurants. I'll come back when you are not busy.'

But he waited outside the store. About five minutes later, the young American girl walked out with a large package in her hand, and he approached her with the question.

'How have I learned of his business?' she said, giggling. 'Because of *Doctor Zhivago*!'

'What?' He was totally lost.

'You have read *Wenhui Daily*, haven't you? The thirtieth, last month.'

Shortly afterward, a copy of the *Wenhui Daily* came up on the desk of the neighborhood committee office. Sure enough, the third page of it showed a special report entitled:

Because of *Doctor Zhivago*

Mr Ma, an ordinary bookseller in Red Dust Lane, had been thrown into prison at the beginning of the Cultural Revolution – for the crime of having stored a copy of *Doctor Zhivago* in English years earlier. It was then regarded as a counter-revolutionary book.

Who the devil was Dr Zhivago? A decadent bourgeois intellectual who tried to go against the red tide of the Russian revolution. As Chairman Mao said, 'It's a new invention to write a novel in conspiracy against the Party.' It certainly applied to Mr Ma's shelving *Doctor Zhivago*, too. The existence of the novel in the bookstore was reported to the Shanghai Police Bureau – along with the information that some bourgeois intellectuals had regularly visited the bookstore, including a rightist writer who had come back from the United States. So the charge was made, the bookstore was closed, and Mr Ma was sentenced to thirty years in jail. He was allowed to carry inside with him only a Chinese medical dictionary. It was because Chairman Mao had declared that Chinese medicine is an invaluable treasure.

Fortunately, it did not take thirty years for the Chinese translation of *Doctor Zhivago* to appear in our state-run bookstores. What the novel really is about, readers may certainly have different opinions. But no one nowadays would take it as criminal evidence against a harmless bookseller.

It took almost twenty years for Mr Ma to get released. Still, nearly ten years less than his punishment, thanks to our Party's new policy. Released and rehabilitated, Mr Ma did not have the heart to reopen the bookstore. Instead, he opened a herbal medicine store with the knowledge acquired through self-education from the one and only book available to him in the prison cell. Presumably, he did not want that part of his life to be a total waste.

As an English proverb says, every black cloud has a silver lining. So because of *Doctor Zhivago*, Mr Ma has become a doctor.

In the evening talk of the lane, Comrade Jun kept shaking his head over the article, unable to make a comment to the expectant audience.

'An article in *Wenhui Daily*!' Long-legged Pang said in the audience. 'Old Ma surely has his connections. The publicity is worth a fortune.'

'But how could the *Wenhui* reporter have learned of his story in our lane?' Four-eyed Liu asked.

It was a question none of them could answer. What kind of a man was Doctor Zhivago? Possibly a good doctor like Mr Ma, who had now started giving free herbs to his neighbors.

Not until about a month later did the lane come to hear another story from Four-eyed Liu, who had learned it from an old acquaintance connected with the *Wenhui Daily*.

A rising Party-member police officer surnamed Chen, in charge of 'rectification of wronged cases' during the Cultural Revolution and who would soon be promoted to chief inspector in the Shanghai Police Bureau, was said to have visited Mr Ma's bookstore years ago. Possibly a teenager at the time, standing and reading there for free just like others. Anyway, the moment he heard of the story of Mr Ma, he contacted the district official in charge of 'rectification of wronged cases' and managed to have the old man released ahead of time. The would-be chief inspector continued to look further into Mr Ma's interests, going so far as to make sure that a special license was granted for the herbal medicine store. He too must have been a reader of *Doctor Zhivago*, so he told Mr Ma's story to his girlfriend, a young journalist on the *Wenhui Daily*. To humor him, she had the story published in the newspaper.

'It reminds me of another old Chinese story about horses,' Long-legged Pang said deliberately, in imitation of Old Root. 'When the old man of Sai lost his horse, it was not necessarily a bad thing, because the lost horse brought another horse home in its company. There is no telling the causality of things in this world. Indeed, all because of *Doctor Zhivago*.'

'So he became Inspector Chen,' Old Root blurted out of nowhere, nodding his head.

'You mean it's because of Inspector Chen?'

It could have been somebody Old Root had known before, but the old man declined to elaborate, grinding out the cigarette end on the street curb.

Merry Go Round

Jiang Xi was one of the ordinary residents in Red Dust Lane, a high school teacher, with her husband Yiqiang, a technician at a state-run factory, and their only son Kaikai, a middle school student. For so many years, the three of them had been squeezed together in a sixteen-square-foot eastern wing room, which was partitioned by a makeshift bookshelf after Kaikai entered a neighborhood middle school, but they were hardly heard complaining about anything.

In the eyes of her neighbors, however, the late eighties witnessed unexpected improvements for the family. With the job market getting more and more competitive in China, a good college education would make a huge difference for the young people, and their parents came to spend generously on college preparation classes for them. In a *tingzijian* room subrented from her neighbor in the same *shikumen* house, Jiang found herself busy tutoring private students for a second income, which was estimated as incredibly sizable in the collective calculation of the lane.

For some other people, private tutoring was still considered a gray area, politically speaking. At least, 'a second job' was a subject not yet officially encouraged in the Party's newspapers. 'Private' remained a word with so-called negative energy in socialist China. With so many new things happening and changing in Deng Xiaoping's reform, people had a hard time adjusting, having to tread a fine line in the constantly shifting political background. Not to mention those neighborhood activists like Old Hunchback Fang, who remained on high alert, ready to deal a crushing blow to anything officially declared as capitalistic practices, which could have included Jiang's private tutoring in Red Dust Lane.

To the consternation of the lane, however, Comrade Tang

Changguo, head of the neighborhood police station, was seen one June evening taking his son Xiaojun into the *tingzijian* room where Jiang was tutoring her students. That served as an unquestionable political endorsement. Those neighborhood activists then saw no point in pointing their critical fingers at her any more. And more private students came pouring in to Jiang's classes.

So much so that she hardly had any time left for her son Kaikai, who remained in the ordinary middle school. For a successful college entrance test, an officially designated 'first-class' high school was considered a must. Not that Kaikai failed to be a good, hard-working student, but in a society of omnipresent materialistic connections, his parents did not have enough connections, nor 'red envelopes' fat enough, to get him into such an elite high school. In spite of Jiang's extra-curricular income, they still had to save every penny, as Yiqiang explained to the neighbors, to lubricate the cogwheels for Kaikai's school transfer.

Just a couple of weeks after Comrade Tang's visit to Jiang in the lane, Xiaojun passed a mid-term test with flying colors; a success supposedly crucial to the subsequent college-entrance test. Comrade Tang invited Jiang and several others to a celebration dinner in a private room at the Delicacy Heaven Restaurant. An excessively luxurious room it was, with a large TV set on one side, an impressive wine cabinet on the other, and a phone on the wall, too.

'It's one of the top restaurants in the city. A place new and fashionable in the eighties, with all the expensive food imaginable under the sun. Believe it or not,' Comrade Tang declared in high spirits at the banquet table, 'the finest Chinese delicacies are tasteless in themselves. Like the shark fin, sea cucumber, swallow nest, bear paw or camel dome, to name just a few of them. The taste comes from something else, like sauce or soup, which is the very essence of trad-itional Chinese cuisine. This restaurant is really celebrated for that.'

Comrade Tang appeared to be familiar with those extravagant delicacies, Jiang observed, gingerly putting a slippery chunk of sea cucumber into her mouth, and nodding her head, though tasting nothing special to her, commenting, 'Yes, it's just like in *Tao Te Ching:* "From nothing comes everything."'

'Exactly, it's just like Xiaojun has learned everything from Teacher Jiang. Cheers!'

Jiang felt both flattered and flabbergasted. Such a lavish banquet in her honor was an experience she had never had before. Even more so from someone as powerful as Comrade Tang.

'All the progress made under her guidance,' Comrade Tang repeated for emphasis. 'Let me tell all of you. She's worth every penny of the tuition.'

His recommendation sounded somewhat condescending to her, but he made it purposely, she understood, for the benefit of the other guests at the table. And for her, too. Sure enough, one of them instantly turned to her for contact information.

So Jiang started introducing her *tingzijian* room class in the midst of those exotic plates and platters arriving at the table. She could not help wondering at the extravagance, becoming more nervous as Comrade Tang respectfully placed a bowl of shark fin in front of her.

Comrade Tang had paid for Xiaojun's tuition like other students, but the truth be told, Jiang would have taught him for free, considering Comrade Tang's power in the neighborhood police office. His official rank might not be that high, but as in a popular saying, 'a mayor may not be as mighty as a manager who directly commands and controls'. As whispered in the neighborhood, 'red envelopes' were frequently pushed to Comrade Tang – on the table or under the table. Anyway, his son's excellent score in a mid-term test seemed far from enough to justify such an exorbitant banquet. The bill at the end could be more than a thousand yuan – way too much for Comrade Tang's far-from-extravagant salary.

'The shark fin is fantastic, Teacher Jiang. Add several drops of red vinegar and it will bring out the special flavor of the shark fin so fabulously,' Tang said with great gusto.

'I've never had red vinegar before,' Jiang said in bashful honesty, 'you know such a lot, Comrade Tang.'

'Well, I'm no gourmet like the would-be chief inspector Chen in the city police bureau. Still quite young, he knows so much more. Not just full of gastronomical expertise, of course. A truly versatile, talented man. He has a long way to go in the system. A most promising career in front of him, I tell you,' Comrade Tang said, turning to Jiang with a mysterious knowing smile, as if she knew exactly what he was talking about. 'A long, long way to go indeed.'

Again, she nodded mechanically, though not sure whether she had ever heard of the would-be chief inspector in question. Besides, what was the relevance to her anyway? It mattered not to her whether he would be promoted or not. And she could not help wondering how a rising Party cadre like Chen would turn out if he was capable of dining even more extravagantly than Comrade Tang – more likely than not at the socialist expense.

It was then that a young waitress in a scarlet mandarin dress brought in a large cake, the top of which proclaimed in bright colors: 'Happy Teacher's Day'.

So it was prepared specifically for her. There was no questioning Comrade Tang's sincerity. Still, it was more than two weeks past the Teacher's Day. She was getting more and more confounded.

'The would-be chief inspector Chen is a man full of respect for his teacher, isn't he?' Tang said, smiling again.

'Would-be chief inspector Chen?' She could not help repeating it, searching frantically for clues in her memory. It was surely not for nothing that Comrade Tang had brought him up again.

'He paid you a visit about a couple of months ago, I've heard. Later he called me at the office. He talked a lot about his gratitude to you as a middle school student in your class during the years of the Cultural Revolution.'

'Chen—'

'Yes, his name is Chen Cao.'

'Oh, Chen Cao. Yes, Chen was a good student at the time.'

In reality, she hardly remembered anything about him as a student during those years. Not a troublemaker, she was sure about it, but not a politically enthusiastic Little Red Guard, either. Anyway, Chen did not stand out in the class. Not as far as she could remember.

'He got the highest grade for writing in your class – about an essay on Chairman Mao's poem. You did such a wonderful job teaching and encouraging students even in those difficult, disastrous years. That's what he said to me.'

'Yes, we all had to memorize Chairman Mao's poems those days for the sake of showing our loyalty to him. That's so true. You had no choice,' one of the guests at the banquet table sort of echoed, head-shaking, mouth-watering, helping himself to a large piece of soy-sauce-braised bear paw, which looked absolutely fatty.

She was now trying desperately to recall something, but her mind remained largely blank.

'Yes, we had to teach Chairman Mao's poems in the class. No text books those days. The students had to write essays about them.' It was all she could do to come up with some vague words about it with a piece of slippery sea cucumber dropping from her chopsticks.

Fortunately, Comrade Tang got an unexpected phone call. It must have been important as Comrade Tang raised his fore-finger to his lips to the guests in the banquet room before he spoke into the receiver in an abated voice, nodding and smiling in the midst of saying yes over and over again.

She heaved a sigh of much-needed relief, grateful that she did not have to put those indescribable delicacies into her mouth for a couple of minutes.

But was her memory already failing her so much? She must have been too busy with the private tutoring classes in the *tingzijian* room.

Even Chen's visit to her, recent as it was, seemed to be so blurred, elusive in recollection. She hastened to take a large gulp of the iced water, which seemed to refresh her mind a bit.

It was nothing but an unannounced visit, as Chen had put it, she now remembered, in order to show gratitude to his middle school teacher. According to him, he had used to live quite close to the neighborhood, so he knew about her home in Red Dust Lane. Possibly in his late twenties or early thir-ties, Chen did not say anything about his being a cop, and certainly not about his being one on the rise . . .

She took another large gulp of the water. Chen might not have come over just to visit her. Placing down the water cup, she was struck with another thought. He seemed to know several others in the lane as well, though he mentioned them in a casual manner. Among them, Mr Ma, the once private bookseller jailed because of a 'black book' and nowadays a successful Chinese herbal medicine doctor thanks to the knowledge learned from a medical dictionary in prison; a woman named Minmin, who had migrated to the US by marrying someone much older, an overseas Chinese related to Chen's family; a retired neighborhood security activist nicknamed Hunchback Fang; Juqing and her son Dong, about whom Jiang knew very little, except that the family of three generations still lived together in that small room with an attic at the end of the lane. After Chen's visit, she had heard, Dong changed his surname back to a rare one, something like Huyan, and he was said to be making some money as an amateur photographer.

Jiang was beginning to feel that Chen had come to the lane not so much to pay her a visit, as to collect information about those other people on the sly. But wasn't that common for a cop? That was probably why Chen had not even disclosed his police identity during his unannounced visit to her.

Still, how could all those people have gotten involved in a criminal investigation?

'Your encouragement meant such a lot to him at the time,' Comrade Tang went on, nodding and turning to raise the glass high. 'Nowadays, it's fashionable for the French red wine to go with the Chinese cuisine. This bottle's from Bordeaux, France, obscenely expensive, but it brings out the special taste of the camel dome fabulously.'

In the sunlight streaming through the window, the wine appeared rippling blood red in the glass. She suddenly remembered one particular detail in that long-ago class.

'Yes, there was an essay in class about Mao's *ci* poem *Loushan Pass*, which ends with the majestic lines: "*Green mountains stretching / sea-like, and the sinking sun, blood-red . . .*"'

Fragmented details then came flashing back to Jiang's

memory. In the essay assigned for homework about that poem of Mao's, one student traced the possible influence to the ending of a *ci* poem by Li Bai's in the Tang dynasty: '*In the west wind, the sun sinking, / shining obliquely over the ruins / of the Han imperial cemetery.*'

The comparison appeared to be more than surprising for a middle school student at the time, but the argument proved quite convincing in its way. Mao was said to like Li Bai's poems, and it was politically correct to the student to make the comparison. So the student that she gave an A+ to was none other than Chen?

'You mean Chen's essay?' Comrade Tang inquired, a slippery piece of beef in oyster sauce dropping from his chopsticks. 'He is said to be a poet, too. Little wonder. Still quite young, he is also in charge of "rectification of wronged cases during the Cultural Revolution" right now. The appointment of his chief inspectorship will soon be announced.'

Around the table, others were staring at one another in confusion. She did not consider it a good idea for her to go into detail about that essay such a long time ago, murmuring inaudibly with increasing uneasiness, munching the abalone in her mouth as a ready excuse not to speak.

More exquisite dishes arrived at the table. Almost as anticipated, Comrade Tang brought the subject back to Chen once again, sipping at his red wine.

'The would-be chief inspector talked to me about the problems for intellectuals like you. He even quoted a new popular saying: "The one making atomic bombs in the lab earns less than the one selling tea-leaf eggs on the street." That's so unfair, he said. He maintained there's nothing wrong with giving help to young students in one's spare time, and earning a little money on the side. I could not agree more. A lot of things should start to change in China's great reform.'

Could Chen be such an important man? So much so that his visit to her had actually prompted Comrade Tang to take Xiaojun to her private tutoring class, and to have the banquet arranged in her honor. She could not help wondering about it. Luckily, she had not said she hardly remembered Chen.

But she was increasingly inclined to believe the scenario

that his visit to the lane could have been a cover for some secret mission.

In that case, it made sense for Comrade Tang to try to find out from her as much information as possible. What he was doing was not just to curry favor with Chen through her. Some of the lane residents mentioned by Chen during that visit, she began recalling, had been punished or jailed years earlier for political reasons, for which the neighborhood cops could have been held accountable. But what had happened to those people had happened long before Comrade Tang's arrival here. Nor did she remember Chen raising any specific questions about this neighborhood cop sitting beside her at the banquet table.

'Did he mention anybody else in the lane?' Comrade Tang said, raising the wine again. 'Say, somebody like old Hunchback Fang?'

She had no real grudge against Hunchback Fang, though he had made her private tutoring difficult at the beginning. But Hunchback Fang had recently got into some sort of trouble, and she was no longer worried about the neighborhood security activist.

'Yes, he mentioned Hunchback Fang in passing. He must be familiar with other people in the neighborhood—'

But another phone call came in for Comrade Tang. He was speaking into the receiver with abated voice. Such a busy police officer he was, that was perhaps another reason why he chose the banquet private room here with a phone on the wall.

Then it reminded her of a mystery connected to Huyan – and to Hunchback, too – that she had heard of years earlier in the lane. Or rather, it was more like a double mystery, so to speak, she thought in frenzied confusion.

The first part of the mystery had come up more than a decade earlier. Dong, one of the lane residents Chen mentioned during that visit, had his attic raided one early May night by the joint force of the neighborhood police and a bunch of neighborhood security activists. No one knew exactly what had happened that night except for vague gossips about 'the red-curtained window' of the attic. So it was most likely about something suspicious happening there with Dong and his then

girlfriend Lanlan. The two young people were staying alone
in the attic, still single at the time, though shortly afterward
they got married instead of being punished or reprimanded.
Nevertheless, something like a 'political stain' in terms of
bourgeois lifestyle was said to have been left in the archives
of Dong and Lanlan.

And not until more than a decade later did the second part
of the mystery come up, with some more clues leaking out
about what had happened that long-ago night. With the Chinese
society in rapid transition, the neighborhood security activist
Hunchback Fang got into trouble, to the surprise of the lane,
for his once 'politically correct' insistency on adhering to
Mao's class struggle theory, and on treating his neighbors as
potential class enemies. After all, it was no longer the age of
class struggle, not like in Mao's time. So it might not have
been totally out of the blue that following Comrade Tang's
suggestion, the neighborhood committee produced a long list
of his wrongdoings throughout those years of 'relentless class
struggle'.

Among them was one about that nocturnal raid led by
Hunchback Fang and the then neighborhood cop Peng into
that attic of 'red-curtained window'. As it turned out,
Hunchback Fang had long targeted Dong because of his prob-
lematic family background. According to some unverifiable
source, Dong's father would have been officially announced
as a 'rightist' but for his untimely death in the suspicious
incident, and Juqing changed his surname to Dong – her
maiden name – as a gesture of complete cutting off from his
father. As a result, Hunchback Fang had long kept Dong under
a close watch in secret, what with the mysterious black bag
always slung across his shoulder, with the occasional red light
flickering through the attic window, and more than anything
else, with the phone message shouted out loud and clear by
the neighborhood phone service people under Dong's window
one afternoon – 'Red curtain as usual.' It immediately raised
the class struggle alert level for Hunchback Fang. Having seen
a movie of a KMT secret agent sending signals in the depth
of night, he suspected Dong of sabotaging the socialist revolution in a similar manner, with the red signal blinking through

the window to some other secret agent lurking elsewhere. So he reported this to the neighborhood cop, with all the imagined details added into it. That night, the raid turned out to be much ado about nothing – not even a red curtain for the attic window, but a red bulb for the picture development there.

More than ten years later, Comrade Tang's sudden announcement about removing Hunchback from his post-retirement position in the neighborhood security sounded so harsh, like a nail being hammered into the coffin for the old activist. So why?

After all, so many people had acted like him at the time, following Mao's class struggle theory wholeheartedly. And the night raid had caused no irrecoverable damage. The two young people got married, ironically, because of the raid. The neighbors were confounded with the belated severe punishment.

Could it have been because Dong – now Huyan again – had gained some fame as an amateur photographer? It was said that one of his pictures had won an international prize. But it was not likely. He still worked at the tavern as a salesman. In spite of his mother's talking about moving to a larger new apartment somewhere else, they remained in the room at the end of the lane.

It then hit on Jiang that the emerging police officer surnamed Chen could have been the one behind all this. As a rising Party cadre in charge of 'rectification of wronged cases during the Cultural Revolution', he must have heard about the story of the 'evidence of youth', and talked to Comrade Tang about the mystery of the red curtain. Comrade Tang would have been more than eager to comply, needless to say.

And that eventually made it possible for Dong to change his name back to Huyan?

Having finished the phone call, Comrade Tang was coming back to the banquet table, grinning from ear to ear.

She sat at the table, eating mechanically, with fragmented details resurfacing in her memory, continuing to gulp iced water to keep her mind functioning, and picking her words like in the pre-Han dynasty Hongmen Banquet, which had since become synonymous with a culinary occasion full of unknown dangers.

It was a long, drawn-out dinner, with the slender waitress serving one special dish after another, flitting around like a butterfly, with the host and guests toasting each other non-stop, guffawing, and with the would-be chief inspector being mentioned a couple more times.

Finally, as the last course of sweet sticky rice pearl soup with swallow nests was served on the table, Comrade Tang cracked his fingers for the bill. His face flushing like a cock's swain, he rose and made for the phone on the wall with the bill grasped in his hand. The moment the call got through, he pressed the speaker button with a mysterious air.

'Have you caught some guys in those private rooms, Little Hui?'

'Quite a few of them in the "Red Dust Foot-Washing Paradise",' said Little Hui in a loud voice, presumably a young cop who worked under Comrade Tang.

'Great,' Comrade Tang chuckled, his finger deliberately beating on the phone. 'I'm at Delicacy Heaven right now. Send a fat one over here. A really fat one.'

Jiang had heard of the foot-washing salon, along with the special service in its so-called private rooms. In the name of socialism of China's characteristics, no prostitution was officially permitted or acknowledged, but in the names of hair salon, massage parlor, karaoke club and foot-washing paradise, in reality a sex service industry had been booming. It was an open secret. For the sake of propaganda, the police would occasionally make a show of cracking 'indecent practice'. So Comrade Tang must have been remote-commanding a police raid while feasting in the restaurant, like the general in the three-kingdom period celebrated in Su Dongpo's poem: *'In the midst of his laugh and talk, / the mighty enemy fleet is gone / in smoke and ash.'*

But what was the point of having a really fat one sent over to the restaurant?

Less than twenty minutes later, the opening of the private banquet room door presented a middle-aged man as thin as a bamboo stick, the very opposite of a 'fat one', wearing gold-rimmed glasses, a gray wool blazer, dress pants, looking like an important intellectual, but crestfallen, with one brass button missing from the blazer, a large bruise shining on his left cheek, murmuring inaudibly with his blazer collar grasped tightly by Little Hui.

The cup in his hand, Comrade Tang rose again, handed the bill to the luckless one and said with a broad grin, 'It's your lucky day, you dirty old bastard. You are carrying your credit card with you, aren't you?'

The man took over the bill, his right hand trembling, reaching into the blazer pocket, when he appeared to change his mind suddenly, and turned toward the phone on the wall, looking at Comrade Tang for his approval.

Comrade Tang nodded without saying a single word.

'It's me, Liu Bing of Gezi High School. Right now I'm with my friends at Delicacy Heaven, but I've forgotten to carry my credit card with me. Hurry over with yours and your son's school transfer is guaranteed.'

It took just a couple of seconds for the people in the private room to figure it out. The 'old dirty bastard' must have been a high school principal or something like that, capable of determining the student admission or transfer, for which the desperate parents of students would be willing to do anything.

Comrade Tang moved back to the table, raising the cup to the others with another loud burp. 'Bottoms up!'

Before a new bottle of Merlot was finished, there came a quiet knock on the door.

Looking up, Jiang was transfixed at the sight of another man stepping in timidly and pushing a bulging bag over to the 'old dirty bastard', who remained standing like a half-broken bamboo stick.

Recognition hit her like a basin of icy water. The newcomer was no other than Yiqiang, so the one taking the bag had to be the principal of that first-class high school to which her son was going to be transferred.

'Sorry, we don't have a credit card,' Yiqiang murmured nervously, without stealing a look into the splendid private banquet room. 'But here is fifteen thousand in cash. It's all we have saved so far.'

'Really, a fantastic dinner,' Comrade Tang said to the

guests, without recognizing the man handing over the bag of money in a hurry to the 'old dirty bastard' standing near the door.

'Cheers!'

NINE

C hen awoke with a touch of self-annoyance. He had actually dozed off again after his mother had stepped out to the food market in the first gray of the morning, like so many years earlier.

For once, there was only a single dream scene he recalled, blinking at the attic ceiling. *He is sitting in front of a huge computer, typing frantically, following a long list, Internet surfing and searching with bleary eyes until a bucket of cold water falls crashing on his head—*

The old Chinese saying 'A bucket of cold water falls crashing on one's head' meant a violent awakening, literally as well as figuratively, and the background of the dream scene shifted to the present day instead of those long-ago years. And just as in another old Chinese saying, 'It is a long night that there are so many dreams,' juxtaposing the past and present, the right or wrong in a chaotic jumble.

Years earlier, there was one detail, he suddenly recollected, from that visit to his middle school teacher Jiang before his becoming a chief inspector. She'd mentioned in passing the black family background of the amateur photographer in the lane. During the Cultural Revolution, Chen too had suffered a lot of discrimination because of his family background. Some of the 'black puppies' had since forgotten all about it, but some had not. In that case, the netizen in question – whether Huyan or not – could have shared or posted online something else like *Reading Animal Farm*. Chen sat up and modified the Internet search on his phone by adding several key words – 'family background', 'Cultural Revolution', 'Red Dust Lane' and 'early years' – one by one to the original 'Huyan' and 'photographer'.

It did not take him long to locate a number of related articles, though most of them appeared blocked or deleted. One of the few surviving articles mentioned that someone called

Huyan, a late *Wenhui* photographer, had been pre-labeled as a rightist for attacks against the Party government with his pictures just a couple of days before his suspicious death in an accident. Huyan was said to have left behind a wife and a young child.

So the Huyan nowadays in Red Dust Lane was no other than the late rightist's son? Like father, like son. Apparently the son could have a motive. And it's more than likely he would open up to the soon-to-be-ex-chief inspector.

He got up, feeling increasingly reassured of the necessity of his visit to Red Dust Lane.

After he finished the breakfast his mother had prepared for him, he left a note for her, saying that he had to leave for something urgent, which happened to be true.

Stepping out, he was surprised at the sight of his mother and Peiqin talking to each other close to the door. The two of them must have just met there, his mother carrying a bamboo basket of fresh vegetables, and Peiqin having with her a tote bag and a plastic bag.

'I'm delivering our special breakfast dumplings for Aunty, and here she is, just coming back from the food market,' Peiqin said, smiling, holding up the plastic bag before taking out a folder from the tote. 'Also, some printouts for you. I got them via VPN. The new governmental regulation, you know. His works were exhibited and reviewed abroad.'

Again, Peiqin proved to be so thoughtful. In accordance with a new regulation, people who tried to visit websites outside of China could be punished for thoughtcrimes, though quite a number of people were known to be using VPNs in secret.

Given the trouble Chen was already in, he had to be careful. So Peiqin had done the VPN job for him. Hence the folder with more detailed info about the netizen in question from those websites blocked on the mainland. She'd carried the folder to his mother's place because of something highly sensitive – too sensitive for her to email or hand it to him in the open with the omnipresent Webcops and surveillance cameras all around. In the meantime, she also managed to help his mother in whatever way possible.

'Peiqin has come here so many times,' his mother said, beaming, 'taking care of things for me.'

'You're going to Red Dust Lane this morning, aren't you?' Peiqin went on before he could have uttered a word in response. 'You'll have another successful job done there, I'm one hundred percent positive about it.'

Was that just another hint about Huyan being the suspect in the investigation pushed by the Webcops? He thought so, but he refrained from saying anything in his mother's presence. Perhaps there was something more about it in the folder.

'You are leaving now, Chief. It's so urgent, I know. I'll help Aunty wash the vegetables before going to my restaurant. Don't worry about it.'

So saying, Peiqin took over the bamboo basket from his mother and moved with her toward the old home.

In the early morning light, he felt bathed in an unexpected rush of gratitude.

'Even if you know it's something impossible for you to do, you have to try your best as long as it's the right thing to do.' His father's Confucianist maxim came echoing back to him. He was doing what he was supposed to do as a cop, as expected by these close to him, like Peiqin Detective Yu, Ling, Old Hunter, his mother, but also by some others like Old Root, Teacher Jiang, Little Phoenix, Mr Ma, and for that matter, quite likely Huyan as well. Chief inspector or not, it mattered not. He had no choice. *Es muss sein!*

Watching Peiqin help his mother step into the door, he turned; instead of going to Bund Park first, he was heading straight to Red Dust Lane.